Carry on the Flame:
Destiny's Call

Avalon Publishing
Hillsboro, Oregon

Library of Congress Control Number: 9781934606292

ISBN: 978-0-9970952-0-3
ISBN: 978-0-9970952-1-0 (ebook)

Carry on the Flame: Destiny's Call *Second Edition*

The poem *Avalon Priestess* by Jodine Turner first published in Sisters Singing Anthology, Wild Girl Publishing, 2008.

Carry on the Flame:
Destiny's Call

by

Jodine Turner

About the Author

Jodine Turner is an author of Visionary Fiction, fantasy, and magical realism. She is also an Adorata practitioner in the spiritual path of embodying divine love and balancing the feminine and masculine within, as well as a therapist, consecrated priestess, and deacon in the Gnostic Church of Mary Magdalene. While living in Glastonbury, England, the ancient Isle of Avalon, Jodine began writing the *Goddess of the Stars and the Sea* trilogy. The novels are an adventure filled initiation into the Mysteries of the Goddess. Jodine lives in Oregon with her husband Chris.

www.jodineturner.com

Also by Jodine Turner

The Awakening: Rebirth of Atlantis

The Keys to Remember

Carry on the Flame: Ultimate Magic

Journey Through the Mists of Avalon—a novella

Acknowledgements

Thank you to my writing critique group for listening to my story and giving invaluable, high quality feedback: Shoshana Alexander the talented and dedicated group leader, as well as my dear fellow author members Alissa Lukara, Lori Henriksen, and Maggie MacLachlan.

Thank you to Tiziana DellaRovere, for your rich suggestions. And for being the mystic who founded the body of teachings called Adorata. I always knew that one day I would find the practical means that my novel's message would align with. Adorata went beyond my deepest imaginings for the practice of embodied love.

Thank you RJ Stewart for helping me remember my priestesshood, and teaching me the Western Mystery Tradition, the rich Celtic heritage, and the sacro-magical visionary journeys of death and transition, some of which is reflected in the rituals embedded in my story.

Thank you Sheila Foster for teaching me the devotion of staying in my heart through the practice of heart-centering Samyama.

Thank you Lesley Kellas Payne for your editing expertise, you've been there for the whole trilogy.

Thank you Sophia Cochran for your inspirational sharing of your birth experience.

Thank you Dee Burks and Liz Ragland of TAG Publishing for believing in my novels!

Maggie MacLachlan, thank you for your tireless and wonderful formatting and uploading the second editions of *Carry on the Flame*, and for all the gazillion details that project involved. You're my hero, in more ways than one.

To Morgaine, beloved soul friend in a feline body—thank you for keeping me company during the long hours of write and rewrite.

And thank you to my beloved Christopher. My love and my inspiration.

*Dedicated to the Goddess of the Stars and the Sea,
the evolutionary force of embodied love.*

Celtic Origins

Some character names have Celtic origins and meanings.

Sharay – inspired from the Goddess of the Stars and the Sea

Tahnea – silver haired one

Kallah – Hebrew for bride, Messiah anointer

Guethyn Sulwyn – Guethyn, dark skinned; Sulwyn, fair sun

Dillon Emrys – Dillon, man from the sea; Emrys, immortal

Rosheen – Welsh for rose

Aneta – Celtic water goddess

Chapter 1

Across from Sharay was a closed wooden door bearing a sign that read "Dr. Philip Deluth, Court Psychiatrist" in large black letters. Whenever she glanced at it her palms began to sweat.

"Sharay, don't dawdle!" Aunt Phoebe scolded.

Sharay jerked her head up. Her aunt's voice grated against the tender parts of her heart.

"Pay attention," Aunt Phoebe said.

Behind the reception desk in the narrow waiting room sat a middle-aged matron watching a computer screen. "The doctor will be with you shortly," Mrs. Hansen said. "You can verify our records while you wait. It says here that you're seventeen. Are these your legal guardians?" she asked, pointing to Sharay's Aunt Phoebe and Uncle Larry.

Sharay nodded.

"Very well. I need you to sign some paperwork."

Sharay's Aunt Phoebe and Uncle Larry stepped over to the desk. Aunt Phoebe grabbed a pen and took over filling in the forms. Uncle Larry stood beside his wife, his shoulders rounded. He turned his head to give Sharay a weak smile of encouragement then turned back and stared silently at the yellowed floral paintings on the wall behind Mrs. Hansen.

Sharay slumped in her chair. She willed herself to look elsewhere. Anywhere but that wooden door with its brass nameplate.

The metal coat rack would do. It sat in the corner and held her only jacket. A hazy mirror hung on the wall next to the coat rack. Sharay caught a glimpse of herself. Her white-blond hair had fallen across her face, as usual. She pushed aside the stray locks before her aunt could reprimand her for being unkempt. She was pleased that she looked very much like her mother had; long, straight hair offset by pale blue eyes, eyelids darkly lashed and tilted upward at the corner, a high forehead, and gracefully pointed chin. But unlike her mother, there were no smile lines around her eyes or mouth. The one trait she'd inherited from her father was her tall, lean frame.

Aunt Phoebe sighed impatiently. "I've already given the court the information on this form."

Sharay clutched the sides of her chair and cautiously watched her aunt.

"This office requires your confirmation," Mrs. Hansen replied curtly.

"Well, I suppose one does what one must for the sake of the girl. I've done so for over seven years now, isn't that right Sharay?" Aunt Phoebe said.

"Mm-hmm," Sharay murmured. Seven years, four months, three days.

When her aunt continued filling out the registration form without addressing her further, Sharay's hands loosened their grip on the chair. Upholstered in black leather, the chair was dull with wear, its wooden arms battered. Sharay noticed scratch marks in its wooden arm, the letters H-i-l-l-a-r-y crudely etched across the surface. She had a sudden impulse to carve her name there, too. Then someday, someone would sit in this reception room and know S-h-a-r-a-y had sat here. She grabbed a pen from her purse and quickly printed her name in the soft wood, glancing up every now and then to make sure Aunt Phoebe wasn't watching.

She completed the last slant of the "y" and softly traced the letters with her fingertips. One day I won't have to listen to Aunt Phoebe any longer, she promised herself silently. I'll be eighteen soon. Her fingers lingered on the engraved letters. *I'll apply for college. I'll study art and paint whenever I want to.*

She imagined how her paintings might one day be displayed in the avant-garde art galleries on the High Street in Glastonbury where she lived, or maybe even one of the Bohemian galleries of West London.

She stared down at her name on the chair's arm and felt more daring. *Maybe I'll train to be a priestess of the Red Well like mother was. And maybe I'll even talk to the Goddess again.* She smiled wryly. *Just to piss off Aunt Phoebe.*

The buzz of a speakerphone and the sound of a chair scraping across the floor interrupted her thoughts. Mrs. Hansen walked over to the door Sharay could no longer avoid. Using her shoulder for leverage, she propped it open and motioned for Sharay. "Sharay Kallah," she called brusquely. "The doctor will see you now."

Sharay stepped through the door alone.

Dr. Deluth didn't look up when Sharay entered. He was older than her uncle, his gray hair cut short around a receding hairline, metal rimmed bifocals propped low on his nose, mouth curved into a mild frown. The broad expanse of his desk with its stacks of neatly piled papers formed a barrier that made Sharay feel safer. She inched forward and sat down in one of the three chairs facing the desk. She jumped when the door clicked shut behind her.

The doctor continued to silently read from his stack of papers. Scarcely breathing, afraid to make a sound, Sharay sat rigid, her hands now tucked beneath her thighs.

Dr. Deluth looked up from his papers and smiled, though his gray eyes remained impassive. "I'm Dr. Deluth."

"I know."

"Do you know why you're here?"

"Yes, sir."

"Tell me."

"Aunt Phoebe says if I don't do well today, you'll put me in the psychiatric hospital."

"We're trying to do what's best for you, Sharay."

Sharay remained silent.

"Let's get started. This part of your interview measures your mental faculties. I'm going to name three objects: lamp, watch, book. I want you to remember them. I'll ask you for them later."

"Okay."

"What is the date?"

"October 18th."

"Where are we?"

Sharay rolled her eyes. "Don't you know, doctor?" she asked, not bothering to hide her sarcasm.

Dr. Deluth peered above the rim of his glasses. "This isn't a joke."

"I know that. We're in Bath, England. In an office, in a building beside the courthouse. . . ."

"That's plenty." The psychiatrist made some notes on a pad of paper.

Sharay continued to answer questions though she thought them silly. When asked, she remembered the three objects without difficulty. She began to feel hopeful. If this was all she had to do to prove herself, surely she wouldn't be committed.

Dr. Deluth coughed. "Sharay, did you hear me?"

"No. What?" Sharay said.

"I said let's talk about your guardians. What's your relationship like with your Aunt Phoebe and your Uncle Larry?"

Sharay squirmed. "I live with them. They look after me."

"Do you get along?"

"Like I said. We live together."

Dr. Deluth studied her, his chin resting on his hand. "I see."

Sharay stared back at him.

"How old were you when your parents passed away?"

"Ten."

"Did you get along with them?"

"Yes."

"Did you do things together?"

"Yes." Sharay's right heel bounced up and down.

"Did you have fun with them?"

"Yes," she said quietly. "I remember what it was like before Aunt Phoebe came."

"Go on."

"My parents loved me."

"Do you have a favorite memory of them?"

Sharay smiled softly. "The time we went to the beach. I was six. They bought me a plastic shovel and I spent hours scooping sand. My father helped me build a sand castle."

Dr. Deluth waited a moment before he spoke. "You loved them very much."

Sharay swallowed thickly. "Yeah," she whispered.

"And it made you very sad when they died."

Sad? Sharay's grief was like the knotted roots of the hawthorn bush. The hawthorn's underbrush was thick and dense, and its tangled roots forced their way into the damp earth, greedy for sustenance. She knew its nature well.

Sharay lowered her eyes and quickly brushed away the tears she couldn't stop.

"Have you ever felt so sad that you thought about hurting yourself?" Dr. Deluth's voice sounded earnest to Sharay.

"I . . . I don't know. No."

"Have you ever felt so bad that you wanted to take your own life?" he asked gently.

Sharay's hands lay limp on her lap. She hesitated as the image of her mother and father emerged in her mind. Her grief seemed to rise to her throat, threatening to suffocate her. "I don't think so."

"What do you mean, you don't think so?"

"Sometimes I think I'd like to join my parents."

"Oh?"

"But I wouldn't hurt myself." Sharay wiped her tears on her sleeve and recomposed herself. "I'd never do such a thing."

Dr. Deluth scribbled more notes on his pad of paper. "Sharay, please answer honestly. Have you ever thought about hurting anyone else?"

Sharay's eyes opened wide. "No!"

"Have you thought about hurting your Aunt Phoebe or Uncle Larry?" he asked bluntly.

Sharay's mind reeled. How many times had she wished it would have been her aunt's bloodied body recovered from the car crash instead of her mother's or father's? Of course she wanted Aunt Phoebe dead. She'd often fantasized about being free from her.

Sharay hunched in the office chair. Her aunt's voice took on a life of its own in her mind. Like a broken record, stuck in a rutted groove.

Sharay, you're a stupid girl. Can't you do anything right?

Sharay, you're as useless as your mother was.

Sharay, you're bad and crazy. Just like your mother.

Sharay, Sharay, Sharay. . . .

Sharay muffled her ears with her hands.

Dr. Deluth leaned forward. "Are you all right?"

"I'm . . . I'm okay."

"Are you hearing voices?" he asked.

How did he know, Sharay thought.

"Are the voices inside your head or outside your head?" Dr. Deluth asked.

Sharay looked up. *What kind of stupid question was that?*

"Take as much time as you need, Sharay. But I need you to answer my questions."

Dr. Deluth watched her. She closed her eyes. It couldn't be true that she was insane like her Aunt Phoebe insisted. She was just . . . different.

When Sharay was much younger, her mother had told her she had the Second Sight, that she'd know things, be able to see and hear things, that others didn't. Her mother had tenderly fostered the budding signs of the talent that had run in their family for generations.

She'd told Sharay that her special abilities would help her to receive visitations from the Goddess. But the much-anticipated visions didn't begin until after her parents' death. And her mother was no longer there to guide her.

Sharay sat up straight in the high backed office chair and opened her eyes. The doctor was still watching her, waiting for her answer.

She shook her head. No, Dr. Deluth, she thought, there would be no sorrow if Aunt Phoebe were to vacate the planet this very moment. But kill her aunt or uncle with her own hands?

"No, sir. I wouldn't hurt my aunt or uncle. Absolutely not."

Dr. Deluth rifled through the folder on his desk, his brow furrowed. "Give me a moment," he said.

The longer he studied the pages in silence, the more Sharay's heart raced. She tried the deep breathing she'd learned long ago from her mother. Inhale slowly into her belly, fan the flame of her inner power, exhale. Mother had said her belly was an island of inner strength. Sharay waited for her strength to ignite. When it failed, she tried again, and yet again. But all she could feel in her belly was what felt like the tug and pull of the tangled hawthorn roots that had taken over her insides.

Dr. Deluth finally spoke. "For the second part of the interview, I need to confirm some things with your guardians, Sharay." He pressed a buzzer on the side of his telephone.

Mrs. Hansen's voice came over the speakerphone. "Yes?"

"Bring in Mr. and Mrs. Wentworth, please."

The door opened and her aunt and uncle entered. They seated themselves on each side of her. Sharay's fingers picked at the frayed knee of her blue jeans.

Aunt Phoebe's cheap perfume saturated the air of the small office. Sharay shifted away from her, and reached up to touch the star-shaped birthmark nestled at the nape of her neck. Tracing the outline of the tiny birthmark had been a habit of hers for as long as she could remember.

Dr. Deluth spoke to her aunt and uncle. "How would you describe your relationship with Sharay?"

"We've tried hard over the years to get along with the girl. But she's withdrawn, mopey. And stubborn," Aunt Phoebe said.

Uncle Larry coughed nervously and nodded agreement.

"It's not unusual in a case like this for withdrawal and sarcasm to belie underlying anger and, deeper yet, unresolved bereavement," Dr. Deluth explained.

Sharay raised her hand and waved. "Hello! I'm sitting right here, doctor."

Phoebe glowered at Sharay. "See what I mean. Disrespectful as usual." She turned to Dr. Deluth. "Like I told you. Sharay's seriously depressed. Worse than that. . . ."

"I'll be the one to make the diagnosis, Mrs. Wentworth," Dr. Deluth said.

"Of course." Aunt Phoebe leaned back in her seat and smiled sweetly.

"As you know, in order to be involuntarily committed Sharay must show she's not in touch with reality and that she'd be a danger to herself or others."

"We understand. It's all in our petition," Aunt Phoebe said, pointing to the folder on the desk.

"What did my aunt tell you?" Sharay asked, alarmed.

"The commitment petition claims you're not competent to safely take care of yourself, Sharay," Dr. Deluth said.

"I told you I wouldn't hurt myself."

". . . and it goes on to claim you've repeatedly threatened your guardians."

"I've never threatened them," Sharay cried.

Aunt Phoebe folded her hands on her lap and sighed. "Of course she won't admit to it. The truth is she told me she would beat me if I grounded her again. She swore she would murder me if I as much as came into her bedroom."

Sharay jumped up. "That's a lie."

"Sharay, please sit down," Dr. Deluth ordered.

"No," Sharay said, her panic growing.

"Sharay, sit down," Aunt Phoebe demanded.

"Mrs. Wentworth, I must ask you not to interfere." Dr. Deluth turned to Sharay and repeated his request firmly and quietly. "Sit down, please."

Sharay reluctantly sat. Phoebe's mouth tightened in restraint.

Dr. Deluth waited a moment. "What do you have to say, Mr. Wentworth? Has Sharay ever threatened you or your wife?"

"I heard the very words my wife told you come out of the girl's mouth." He glanced hastily at Phoebe.

Sharay stared at her uncle in pleading disbelief.

Aunt Phoebe broke the silence. "There's something else. Sharay told me God talks directly to her. And I don't mean prayers. She says she's been told she has a special task."

"What does God say to you, Sharay?" Dr. Deluth asked.

Sharay twisted in her seat and faced her aunt. "That's not true. I said the Goddess came to me, not God. . . ." Her hand flew to her mouth, the words out before she could censor them.

"I warned you about it, Sharay—warned you it was all your imagination," Aunt Phoebe said.

"What kinds of things did you hear, Sharay?" Dr. Deluth asked.

"I didn't hear anything," Sharay said vehemently.

Sharay cocked her head to the side, suddenly distracted. The sound of a thousand bells, silver song of the stars, chimed softly. Herald of the Goddess of the Stars and the Sea.

She clasped her hands tightly together. *Not now! Not here!* She pleaded silently, and tried to shut out the sound, as she'd done for many years now.

She saw a blue and silver mist swirling through the room, concentrating around her, enveloping her in an opalescent cloud.

The hazy cloud filled her, the melodious jingling grew insistent. And hovering in the air before her was the translucent outline of the mysterious icon that frequented her dreams—two interlocking circles with a straight line down their center.

Sharay glanced up at the doctor, over to her aunt and uncle. They were conversing as if nothing at all was happening around them.

"Mr. and Mrs. Wentworth, it's common in someone afflicted with a thought disorder like schizophrenia, as Sharay may be, to think they get messages from God, or even from someone famous." Dr. Deluth said.

Goddess, please, go away, Sharay silently demanded.

She couldn't allow herself to sink into this vision. Not now. Not here. Her mother had warned her that most people wouldn't understand the visions that came to her. Aunt Phoebe condemned her for them. Certainly Dr. Deluth would misinterpret them.

Still, her soul felt a quickening. A rush of gale-force wind. A lightning flash of golden luminescence. A torrent of sea foam surf. Her body grew warm and she trembled.

Dr. Deluth's voice droned on. "Even the most traumatized child finds inner resources. Sharay is a young woman now, nearly eighteen, and hers are well ingrained. This is a common age for psychiatric illness to emerge."

Her aunt's reply faded underneath the melodic, resonant voice of the Goddess. "I am with you always."

Fine. But why do you come to me now? Here? Sharay silently implored.

The reply was strong, commanding. "It is time, Sharay. Trust Me. It must happen this way."

Sharay looked around again. No one was paying attention to her. Why could no one feel the powerful Presence in the room? Why couldn't anyone else hear the Goddess?

Go away. Sharay fought with all of her will to stifle the vision.

The Goddess whispered in tender resolve. "It is the time of your calling. Of your destiny."

Sharay's spine tingled, and she felt pressure rise through the soles of her feet, up her legs, and into her belly. She fought the sensations. But something magnificent arose from within her. She couldn't ignore its strength, and couldn't help but respond.

Her reply came in words that were foreign to her, the dialect soft and lilting. While she had never heard the language before, it was somehow familiar, struck an ancient chord within her, and fanned the embers of the power deep in her belly.

"Lamou dei tu wantna desare se de tu," she said aloud.

Everyone turned their heads to stare at her.

The Goddess answered in the same lilting language. Through the silver crested chimes, and gentle tones, Sharay clearly deciphered the exotic words.

"I am that which is at the end of all longing.

The love you desire is within."

"Sharay?" Dr. Deluth's voice came from far away, his face vague and distorted.

Sharay struggled against her longing for the Goddess, and wrenched herself back to the reality of the doctor's office. She covered her face with her hands, fervently shook her head, argued silently with herself.

Aunt Phoebe was right. It's dangerous to commune with the Goddess.

The Goddess still beckoned.

Leave me alone. They'll lock me away. Maybe I am crazy.

Aunt Phoebe's triumphant stare and the doctor's intense appraisal, judge and jury of her eminent fate, broke through her internal battle, terrifying her. Panicked, her breath came in quick rasps. Dr. Deluth mustn't see her like this.

"Why did you come here now?" she cried aloud to the Goddess. Her words echoed around the room.

Aunt Phoebe's shrill words were the last thing that penetrated Sharay's cloud of awareness.

"See doctor? She hallucinates. She talks to thin air."

Chapter 2

A deep moan issued from the back of Sharay's throat. It quickly turned into a piercing scream that filled the hospital room. It breached the hum of activity in the hallway outside the locked door. Sharay woke with a jolt, her body and bed sheets damp with perspiration.

The nightmare was the same. Vivid images reverberated through her mind. Screeching tires. Her mother's shriek. Her father shouting, "Oh, God, Blanche, are you all right?"

Though she'd been safe at home when her parent's car crashed, her nightmare images always reconstructed the accident in agonizing detail. Brakes failing, tires skidding, shattered glass cutting through fragile skin. Chocolate ice cream in a paper bag, melting in a burst of flames, syrupy sweetness trickling down the car seat, mingling with crimson blood. It was the dark crimson that terrified Sharay the most.

She fought to stay awake. Lifting her head, she looked about.

This wasn't her bed. This tiny room wasn't her bedroom. Here, the walls were stark white, not the pale yellow she was used to. There were no windows save a small one in the door, no furniture but the hospital stretcher she lay on. Her heart pounded even faster.

Sharay tried to sit up but couldn't. Her arms and legs were strapped inside thick leather restraints fastened with metal buckles and tied to the side rails of the gurney. She tugged at the leather straps but was unable to free herself. She frantically tried to convince herself she was dreaming in her bedroom back home.

Squeezing her eyes shut, she visualized her bedroom; white lace curtains blew softly in the night breeze and the treasured photo of her and her parents at the beach sat on her bedside table. She opened her eyes again. She was still in the unfamiliar room, laying on the cold metal gurney.

Sharay thrashed, chafing her arms against the leather restraints. Purple bruises were already forming underneath the grip of the leather. The clicking sound of a key in the lock and the opening of the door startled her into silence. She licked her lips, her tongue rough as sandpaper. A nurse walked over to the side of the gurney.

"Hello, Sharay. I'm Claire," she said.

Sharay looked up at her. Dark curly hair framed her round face, and her skin, the color of rich ebony, creased in tiny worry lines across her forehead. Not the frenzied kind of worry lines like Aunt Phoebe's. More the kind of someone who might be concerned about your welfare. Slightly plump, the nurse's rounded figure bulged at the waist of her blue uniform, hospital issued blouse and pants.

"Where am I? What day is it?" Sharay asked. Her tongue felt thick, her words sounded slurred to her.

"You're in the hospital. It's Tuesday and you've been here almost a full day now. I know you might not remember much, but there's no need to be afraid." She smiled at Sharay, her worry lines smoothing out with the gesture.

"How did I get here?"

"Ambulance. You fought us tooth and nail when you arrived."

Sharay frowned. She had no recollection of fighting anyone.

"That's why you're in restraints," Nurse Claire said.

"Take them off," Sharay demanded, then added a weak, "Please." Spittle dribbled from the corner of her mouth. What had they done to her?

She began to weep again.

"You might do better with another injection," Claire said.

Sharay shook her head. She didn't know what kind of injection they'd given her before, but she didn't want more of it. "No shots. Please. I'll be calm." She gulped back a sob.

"You're not acting very calmly, Sharay."

Sharay grabbed for the first excuse that came to mind. "It's the nightmare. I can be calm. Really I can." She forced back her tears, quieted her breathing, and composed her face the best she could manage.

Claire paused. "Maybe we can try unlocking your hands."

"Thank you," Sharay said quietly.

Claire pulled a ring of keys from her sweater pocket and unlocked and removed the restraints from Sharay's arms, but left Sharay's legs fettered. Sharay used her elbows to help her sit up. She rubbed her sore wrists and took the tissue Claire offered her.

"Now, tell me, what was this about a nightmare?" Claire sat on the end of the gurney.

Sniffling, Sharay hesitated. She thought maybe Claire's warm brown eyes reflected some measure of compassion. She wiped the spittle from the corner of her mouth with her tissue.

"Why am I drooling like an idiot?"

"It's your medicine. We can give you a pill to stop it."

"Why don't you just stop giving me the medicine?"

"I'm sorry, Sharay, but it helps to clear your hallucinations."

"I don't have hallucinations," Sharay said, metering out each word forcefully.

She threw the sheets off her body, found she was clothed in a thin hospital gown patterned in tiny blue flowers.

Sharay felt years of fury for her aunt rise like bile, causing her to sputter. "Aunt Phoebe did this to me. She's dreadful."

"Focus on the nightmare, Sharay," Claire said soothingly.

"Damn the nightmare. It never changes. The car is crashed. My parents are dead." Her words came out in choking sobs. "They were going to the store to buy me ice cream for my birthday. I begged them for chocolate ice cream." She paused for breath, fought back the images of her dream. "I should have been with them. . . ."

"Their death was an accident, Sharay."

"No. It was my fault. Aunt Phoebe told me so."

Claire shook her head. "I want you to listen to me. No matter what your aunt says, you didn't cause that accident."

Sharay's body shook. "Aunt Phoebe told me she wouldn't celebrate any of my birthdays and neither should I. That my birthday marked the day I killed my parents."

Sharay pulled on her legs, tried to free them from the restraints around her ankles. "I hate her."

Claire gently covered Sharay's hands with her own until she stopped tugging on the restraints.

"That's better. Maybe you can talk to me about your uncle," Claire said.

Sharay snorted. "He's almost as bad. He and Aunt Phoebe moved in the same day my parents died. At first he played board games with me. He read to me from this leather bound copy of *Alice in Wonderland* he'd bought at a flea market especially for me."

"That was sweet of him," Claire said.

"It didn't last," Sharay said with sarcasm.

Memories of her aunt and uncles' guardianship came in quick succession, an overwhelming flash-flood of despair.

She and Uncle Larry were sitting together in front of the fireplace, in the chair that had once been her father's favorite, the book propped in her uncle's lap. Aunt Phoebe sat in the settee across from them, filling in the squares of a crossword puzzle.

"Did Alice really jump into that rabbit's hole?" Sharay had asked her Uncle Larry.

"Well, yes, of course. See here?" Uncle Larry pointed to the picture of Alice with her long hair and petticoats flailing upwards as she dropped into the long tunnel.

Aunt Phoebe interrupted. "The girl's ten. Don't you think she's old enough to know fantasy from fact, Larry? I think it's time you stop reading to her."

Aunt Phoebe stared at Uncle Larry until he slowly closed the book and put it down. Later that night, as Sharay lay in her bed, she heard muffled shouts behind their bedroom door as they fought about her.

She pulled her special rose colored quilt over her head—the one her mother had made for her, telling her it would keep her safe and protected from bad dreams—and cried herself to sleep. Over the next few months their arguing continued. Uncle Larry paid less and less attention to her until he finally stopped, worn down completely under Phoebe's haranguing.

He never read to her again, didn't play games with her or take her to the local fairs. Without Uncle Larry's kindness, all hope of affection shattered, like the broken windshield of her parents car wreck.

Sharay grabbed a corner of her hospital bed sheet to wipe her tears. Claire handed her another tissue.

"Do you think I have hallucinations?" Sharay asked.

"What do you think?" Claire answered.

Sharay looked into Claire's kind eyes. She needed to tread carefully here.

"I see things. . . ." Sharay lowered her head. It was too risky. "No. I don't have hallucinations."

Still, Sharay clearly remembered her excitement spilling over when she told her aunt about her very first vision after she'd turned eleven years old. She'd woken from sleep to the sound of the Goddess's beautiful voice calling her name.

She'd told her aunt about it the very next morning. "The Goddess of the Stars and the Sea came to me last night and spoke to me. Just like mother said she would."

Aunt Phoebe stopped pouring her cup of tea. "Already? But . . . you're so young." She turned away and busied herself with the teapot. "What did this Goddess say? What did She look like?"

Thinking her aunt enthusiastic, Sharay said, "She was so beautiful. She traveled across a beam of moonlight on the ocean, and She wore shimmering blue and silver robes." Sharay hesitated. Something felt wrong. "You were a priestess just like mama. Have you never seen her, Aunt Phoebe?"

Phoebe shoved the teapot aside. "That's not important. What you saw is only your imagination. It's craziness."

Sharay's lower lip began to tremble, but she took a step forward, hand on her hip. "I *did* see the Goddess. Just like mother said I would."

She ran upstairs to her bedroom and threw herself onto her bed. Aunt Phoebe had to be wrong. Sharay's chin thrust forward in defiance. "I'm not crazy! I'm not bad!" she declared to her brave stuffed golden lion. The childhood toy still had a place of honor atop her bookshelf.

Nurse Claire interrupted Sharay's recollection. "Sharay?" she said gently. "You said you see things?"

"I don't see anything. My aunt's a liar."

Claire was quiet for a moment. "All right then. Can we talk more about your Aunt Phoebe?"

Sharay tried; she opened her mouth but no words came out. Claire watched her patiently. But to describe what was inside her couldn't be spoken aloud. How could she explain what happened after her aunt crushed her dreams?

Her aunt's disapproval had stalked her, tarnishing her longing for the Goddess's visits. Sharay had followed her uncle's example and retreated.

As she withdrew from her aunt's criticism, she began to feel much like Alice in Wonderland following the rabbit down the tunnel. But *her* journey down the tunnel wasn't fueled by adventure. Her descent was driven by guilt and grief, her fall carved by anger.

After months of her aunt's condemnation, her plummet steadily deepened until, one night, while crying herself to sleep, she found the end of the long tunnel. There, an empty black hole awaited her. Sharay burrowed into the black pit, searching for safety and protection, just like she'd once seen the tiny ants do when her father had long ago dug up the hawthorn hedge to free the rose bushes in the front garden.

Each time she sought the solace of the black hole, its attraction grew. At first, she had cowered within the refuge, bewildered and trembling. Later, she'd buried her growing resentment toward Aunt Phoebe in the black pit, covered it over with mud and sticky tar.

With bricks of locked away tears and mortar of defiance, she built her asylum's walls thick and high, a fortress of solitude. She hid, protected from her guilt, her outrage muffled behind her dark barricade.

And there she shielded herself from receiving the visions of the Goddess she once found beautiful, her aunt's accusations a potent seed of doubt, tainting her mind until she could no longer cherish the visions that came to her. No longer believe in them. No longer welcome them. Instead, she tried to smother them. And now the visions had turned against her, causing her to be committed in this horrible hospital.

Sharay's stomach twisted with her anger and fear, painful as if someone had kicked her with heavy winter boots. What if the visions came again while she was in the hospital? Dr. Deluth would keep her here forever. She had to get away from this place.

Claire broke the silence. "Well, at least you've begun to talk to me. It's a good start." She leaned over Sharay's legs. "The restraints have to stay on for now, but perhaps they needn't be so tight."

Claire loosened the buckles tethering Sharay's ankles. She laid a reassuring hand on Sharay's arm. Sharay shoved it aside, and with two violent, quick yanks, wrenched her slim ankles through the leather and buckles, scraping her skin raw in the effort.

"Please, don't do this," Claire pleaded.

Sharay slid sideways on the gurney, beads of blood from her ankles streaking the sheets, and jumped down to the floor.

"Oh, Sharay. I'd hoped you could do better," Claire cried. She raced to the intercom on the wall and pushed the speaker button. "Dr. Deluth, your help in Seclusion Room Two."

Sharay ran for the door. It opened before she reached it and could stop herself from careening straight into the arms of two male interns. Dr. Deluth was not far behind. She screamed her outrage. Several pairs of hands seized her, pressed on her arms and shoulders, forcing her to the floor, face first.

"Hold her firmly," Dr. Deluth ordered.

"Yep. I remember last time," a male voice replied.

"You don't understand," Sharay sobbed. "I can't let Aunt Phoebe win."

One of the interns swung her arms behind her, and tightly grasped her wrists. Someone's knee forced its way up her back, holding her immobile. Someone else held her legs down so she couldn't kick.

No one spoke to her. She felt a warm trickle of urine wet her underpants and the front of her blue flowered hospital gown. She tried to see who held her down, but the only thing she could make out were the green tiles of the floor. They were hard and cold and smelled of antiseptic cleaning solution.

Sharay gave one last heave before the surprise of the injection. The needle painfully pierced her tense buttock muscles. The weight of the bodies holding her down grew excruciating and her body spasmed its protest. But it was nothing compared to the weight of her humiliation and despair. Bitter grief wrapped around her heart and dug deep into her belly.

"I hate you, Aunt Phoebe. Forever," Sharay cried.

Chapter 3

The security guard slouched against his chair, absorbed with the hangnail he was chewing. Across the lobby, the manager of the Bank of Lloyds of England, Glastonbury Branch, opened his office door. Mrs. Phoebe Wentworth appeared in the doorway. The guard glanced up. Hangnail forgotten, he straightened his back, stood and openly eyed her, slowly, from head to red polished toenails.

Phoebe Wentworth paused to give the guard a sidelong glance, and stepped out of the carpeted office onto the marbled floor of the lobby. Her new Manolo open-toed high heels tapped loudly as she walked. Larry Wentworth followed, his hands shoved into the pockets of his dark blue polyester pants. He didn't care that the security guard ogled his wife. He was used to it. Phoebe was attractive. Not beautiful or sophisticated like her sister Blanche had been, but alluring and voluptuous. In her mid-forties, she still turned the heads of men years her junior.

He watched his wife strut before him, felt the familiar heat simmer in his groin. He liked how her red flowered dress fit tight. Her gold hoop earrings nestled against stiffly hair-sprayed curls—the dyed color was brassy, her blue eye makeup applied thickly. Larry sighed.

Who was he kidding? He knew Phoebe's pretty face was not what fascinated men.

Across the room, a young mother, waiting in line for her turn at the bank teller window, yelled at her child. "Behave!"

Larry watched the little boy yank free of his mother's hold. The boy ran through the lobby and bumped into him, staining his pants with caramel sticky hands.

"Now, now," Larry said, as he pulled a handkerchief from his shirt pocket. "I think your mother's looking for you."

The boy stopped when Larry pretended the handkerchief was a sailboat, floating on the water. He looked up at Larry wide-eyed and never protested when his hands were wiped clean.

The loud click of Phoebe's high heels on the marble floor had come to a halt. Phoebe looked back at Larry and sighed. Stuffing the handkerchief back in his pocket, Larry followed her across the lobby.

He had grown up fascinated with Phoebe. He lived in the house down the road from hers, went to high school with her, made sure he kept up contact after graduation. He never had the courage to ask her out, but he made sure he was always a part of her life. He took tennis lessons where she did, boarded his horse at the same stable as hers, went to the same parties she did, and gradually secured himself as her only dependable friend.

He was attractive enough back then, and made a good salary as the financial officer for a small law firm. He worked hard until he could afford to offer Phoebe a nice home and the financial means to support her capricious desires. Then, just as he hoped, one of her many affairs—an attempt to lure a wealthy judge into more than their weekly rendezvous—ended disastrously. Larry was waiting in the wings with comforting arms and a two-carat diamond ring. He took her to a seaside resort and made wild love to her for a full week, until she finally forgot why she was upset and agreed to marry him. That was nearly twenty years ago. As long as he brought home his paycheck, Larry knew Phoebe wouldn't stray far. But that was exactly where his current dilemma came in.

Lately, Phoebe's attention was absorbed in attending to the details of her deception. He'd compliantly agreed to the charade his wife fabricated. He'd joined in accusing Sharay of the hallucinations and homicidal threats that ultimately committed her to the psychiatric ward.

He wondered if Phoebe would still want him if she succeeded in getting her niece's fortune. Even with his concerns and despite his growing guilt, he still desperately wanted to hold onto his wife.

He bent his head and grimaced, rubbed his forehead with his palms. Yes, he would do anything for his wife. But this plan of hers was getting away from him, becoming too complicated. She was pushing him hard, and he was beginning to chafe under the strain of pretense. Larry's stomach churned out bile, and it rose, bitter in his mouth.

Phoebe stopped at the end of the bank lobby, in front of the last desk in a row of many. She handed over the paperwork the manager had given her to a woman with a name tag that read, "Susan Parker: Assistant Manager." Larry stepped up to wait alongside his wife.

"Hello Mrs. Wentworth," Susan said with a practiced smile reserved for the bank's wealthier clients.

"I'd like my withdrawal in large bills, please," Phoebe said.

Susan checked the paperwork Phoebe gave her, opened the cash drawer in her desk, and counted out the requested amount.

"Yes, that will do. For now." Phoebe took the cash. She daintily opened her purse, put the money inside and turned to leave.

"Thank you, Ms. Parker," Larry said politely.

Phoebe made her way out the door, held open for her by the security guard. She turned abruptly once outside.

"Will you get me some change, Larry?" She reached into her purse and handed him one of the large bills.

Larry headed back to Susan's desk, knowing Phoebe had probably spotted a teenage runaway outside, begging for money. He never questioned when she, almost compulsively, gave those kids a handout. She was usually drawn to the ones that looked about the age their son would have been.

Phoebe perched on the bench outside the bank, and waited for her husband to bring her the change she wanted. She watched the teenager sitting on the sidewalk in front of the grocer's across the road. He was about seventeen, dressed in dirty jeans and a t-shirt. A mongrel dog sat beside him, and on his other side was a hand written cardboard sign that read, "Hungry. Please help."

She couldn't bear to watch for long. Distracting herself, she reached in her purse and eagerly fingered the bills withdrawn from the account that had once belonged to her sister Blanche. Her sister had married into an affluent, old money family from London.

Blanche's husband Jarred was the sole surviving son and heir to his family's successful architectural firm. Upon their death, Blanche and Jarred's estate left Sharay a small fortune. As Sharay's only next of kin, Phoebe had made sure to be appointed her legal guardian. With committing her niece to the psychiatric hospital, Phoebe now had complete access to Sharay's inherited wealth. Soon it would be totally and legally hers.

Phoebe congratulated herself, proud of her plan's perfect execution. Beside the money left to Sharay, there was also the inherited title of High Priestess. The role had belonged to Blanche before she died. Their family bloodline could be traced far back to the first priestess, Geodran. Traditionally, the title should have gone to Phoebe until such time that Sharay, as first born daughter of Blanche, would come of age. Instead, the priestess elders had broken convention and chosen Rosheen. They denounced Phoebe for misusing her magical powers for personal gain, and for her forays into the dark side of magic. They had long ago tried to help her; had disciplined her, reasoned with her, given her extra loving attention, and numerous chances to redeem herself. But in the end, they claimed she'd exploited their love and efforts to help her regain their trust.

Phoebe scowled. The title was rightfully hers and she would have it. Once Sharay was declared incompetent by the courts, the elders would be compelled to call for an emergency assemblage. And this time, they would be obliged to uphold priestess lineage law. The title would have to be transferred to her. She would win, would have everything her sister Blanche once had. Except the talisman necklace.

Along with the coveted title of High Priestess came that ancient talisman necklace. As High Priestess, her sister had been entrusted to safeguard the necklace and would never reveal its whereabouts to

Phoebe. It was too powerful a talisman in hands other than those of the High Priestess, Blanche had said.

Phoebe glanced at her watch and over to the bank door. What was keeping Larry? She closed her eyes and inhaled deeply. The long awaited taste of the power within her grasp was intoxicating. She felt her loins throb and her face flush.

The bank door slid open and Larry exited. He walked over to Phoebe. "Here you go," he said, handing her the change she'd wanted. He dropped several pound coins in her hand.

Phoebe stood and looked across the street. But the boy had left. She couldn't spot him anywhere along the road. She glowered, disappointment picking at the old wound inside her. "What took you so long, Larry?"

"The line was long, I had to wait. Never mind, let's go celebrate," Larry said, his voice eager for his wife's approval.

Phoebe sighed. She put the pound coins in her purse and lifted out the bank account slip to read one more time.

"Phoebe?"

Phoebe raised her hand, motioning Larry to be quiet.

"The amount hasn't changed since you read it moments ago," he murmured under his breath.

Phoebe shot him an irritated glance. "Don't ruin this for me."

Larry didn't reply.

Phoebe faced him. "Now you're being sullen. Everything is working. No thanks to you." Her smile was derisive.

Larry felt her words slice through him, threatening to dissolve any remaining shred of his pride.

"You forget something, Phoebe," he snapped, surprised at the strength of his frustration and the tone of his voice.

Phoebe lifted an eyebrow, apparently amused. "Oh?"

"Remember—I know what you did to Blanche and Jarred." Larry's heart raced.

Phoebe's smile faded. When she finally answered, her voice was cold. "I don't know what you're talking about."

"Come on Phoebe. There's no point in lying to me now."

"Then you'd do well to keep quiet about it," she said icily.

"You know I'll never tell."

Her silent stare wore on him. He muttered, "I know the old story. Jarred, with all his money, should have married you instead of Blanche."

"And if you hadn't knocked me up, darling, maybe he would have."

"Jarred was in a class above you, Phoebe." Larry's desperation turned his tone spiteful.

"Not so. He married my sister."

"My point exactly." He swallowed hard, already regretting his words.

Phoebe fought the urge to fight. She needed Larry agreeable, faithful, willing to continue all she had put in motion. She tugged on his sleeve, pulled him into the alleyway at the side of the bank. She coaxed him into the shadows between the dumpster and a row of garbage cans.

"Phoebe, not here," he murmured.

Phoebe took her husband's hand, placed it on her buttock, and rubbed up against him. She pressed her leg between his. Phoebe knew exactly how to handle her husband. Nuzzling her lips into his neck, she lifted her other leg up on top of the garbage can next to them. The catch in his breath told her he would once more bend to her will and forgive her for everything.

"Wait." Larry stammered and pulled back.

"Hmm?" Phoebe murmured. She kissed his neck in the spot he liked the most.

"Phoebe. Stop."

"What?"

"I said stop." Larry pulled up his pants zipper and stepped away from his wife.

"What is it now?" Phoebe asked, exasperation edging her words.

Larry didn't answer and he didn't meet her gaze. His face was flushed and there were tiny beads of sweat trickling down his cheeks.

Phoebe grabbed his belt once more. Larry shook her hand off and stumbled out of the alleyway, leaving her to stare after him in surprise.

Chapter 4

When Sharay woke, her tongue felt larger than her mouth. Her muscles barely obeyed her commands to move. For an agonizing few seconds she looked around. Stark white walls, metal door with a small barred window. Beneath her a hard gurney, her arms and legs trapped in thick leather restraints.

"Oh, God, not again," she murmured.

A cold sweat formed on her skin and her heart pounded wildly.

For time that seemed without end she had wandered through this medicated maze. She couldn't think straight. The fragments of her lucid moments were impossible to hold onto. She would forget where she was and why, then would begin to remember as the sedation wore off, only to be injected with more medicine.

"Help," Sharay called out weakly.

No answer.

Her stomach grumbled in hunger, her bladder called for relief. She had blurry recollections of how two nursing aides would come and release her restraints, and guide her to the bathroom. When they returned her to bed, one of them would spoon feed her food she barely tasted and often choked on.

Another sob shook her, but her tears had long ago dried up. The taste of humiliation and frustration was sour in her mouth.

Her breath grew shallow. She felt her heartbeat slacken. Her attention sank into the pit of her stomach. Like suction, the black hole, the dark refuge from Aunt Phoebe's tyranny, drew her into itself. She burrowed into the hole's protective folds, descended through layers of blackness that silenced her anguish. She noticed that the pull was stronger this time, the darkness deeper. That was okay by her.

"Sharay," a woman's voice beckoned, soft and sweet, barely audible.

She looked around the tiny room. Who was calling her?

"Dearest," the voice called again. It was the same endearment her mother had always used for her.

Sharay tried to reach for the voice. But the black hole constricted and held her down. What was happening, she thought. She had always been able to emerge from the black hole at will before. Her stomach clenched with fear.

Sharay tried to concentrate. The medicine—that had to be it. The tarry coating on the walls of her inner refuge was Thorazine, and Nurse Claire had been injecting her with it every four hours, depending on whether or not she had become "agitated." Whenever she screamed and struggled, tried to fight her way out of the restraints and the hospital room hell, the reward for her efforts was more Thorazine. And the constant admonition to "calm herself."

Sharay panicked as she felt the walls of her inner refuge close in on her. Her mind searched frantically for a way out. Her awareness sped down the never-ending corridors of the black hole. She thrashed on her gurney. Her dark shelter no longer felt familiar. Molecules of Thorazine patrolled its perimeters like tiny Nazi soldiers, paralyzing her in bondage. Policing her thoughts and annihilating her willpower. Her hope was that the Thorazine would eventually wear off and withdraw its stringent occupation.

A cold sensation crawled along the muscles in her back. Sharay stopped thrashing and waited. The coldness slithered along her spine, crept up her neck, and traveled slowly over her scalp. It was crawling beneath her skin. She wanted to smash it, hit it, fling it off.

The sensation grew stronger, pulling her muscles taut. Railing against the restraints, she screamed for help.

Abruptly, her neck wrenched off her pillow. The slithering turned into agonizing muscle spasms, undulating up through her neck. Her head arched back uncontrollably. She could barely breathe.

Sharay heard the door to her room open, and footsteps hurried over to her bedside

"Here we go again. Get ready for a fight," a male intern said.

With the spasm gripping her neck, Sharay could only see his arms, clothed in a white lab coat, with stubby hands and nail bitten fingers. She recognized those hands. They belonged to the medical intern, the same one who took her down to the floor when she'd previously escaped from her leather restraints.

"Wait." Claire, bending over her from the other side, slid her hand under Sharay's neck, and cupped it with her palm. "Fetch Dr. Deluth. Tell him it is torticollis. A severe one."

The intern stood motionless.

"Now, Mr. Millworth!" Nurse Claire shouted.

The urgency in Claire's voice added to Sharay's terror.

She heard Mr. Millworth's hasty footsteps leave the room.

Claire leaned in close to Sharay. "You'll be all right. You're having muscle spasms. They're a side effect of your medicine. We're going to give you something for it."

Sharay was unable to maneuver her mouth to form words. By the time Dr. Deluth arrived, with Mr. Millworth close behind him, she felt as if her unyielding muscles would break her in two.

"We're going to help you, Sharay." Dr. Deluth's hand felt along Sharay's rigid neck. "We need to back off her dosage of anti-psychotics and start her on anti-cholinergics to inhibit the muscle spasms," he said to his intern.

A wide-eyed Mr. Millworth nodded his understanding.

Dr. Deluth reached into his lab coat pocket and handed Claire a capped hypodermic.

Claire lifted Sharay's gown, uncapped the syringe to expose a long needle, and plunged it into Sharay's left hip.

"There now. It won't take long for that to work," she told Sharay.

Through rigid eye slits, Sharay watched them surround her bedside and peer down at her. She wished she could disappear.

She reached for the black hole. Yes, she decided, it would be all right this time. The antidote they'd given her would weaken the Thorazine's tarry entrapment. But in truth, she no longer cared. Like an addict, she craved the numbing protection, regardless of the consequences.

Abruptly, her consent given, the black hole wrenched her down at a startling speed. She heard a sucking sound, and a mighty wind tunnel pulled her into itself faster and faster, absorbing her. It dragged her past the tortuous muscle spasms, past great swarming vortexes of red and gray fear, and into numbness.

The relief should have warmed her. Instead, she felt an icy chill wrap itself round her core. Sharay shivered but she didn't resist.

Suddenly, she felt something wrench her from her downward trajectory.

"Sharay, dearest," someone whispered.

From across the veils that separated the living and the dead, that otherworldly realm of the afterlife, a pair of strong hands forced Sharay to make a sharp turn away from her black hole. She was lifted up and out of its inky depths. The fragrance of roses drew near; her mother's favorite flower water, the one she sprayed on her skin and hair every morning.

In her inner vision, Sharay saw her ethereal captor. Her heart wrenched. Her beloved mother hovered beside her, surrounded in a haze of brilliant gold, even more beautiful than Sharay remembered. Long silver-blond hair softly framed her face. Her gentle features were filled with love and concern, her smile tender, her pale blue eyes pleading.

Sharay breathed in the reassuring scent of roses. She lifted her arms to hug her mother, but there was nothing substantial to hold onto. Seven years of desperate longing welled up, and poured out in her tears. She wanted to stay with her mother forever.

Blanche met Sharay's gaze, and slowly shook her head no, reading Sharay's thoughts. Sharay's breath caught.

She tried to clutch her mother's robes. She had to make her understand.

She couldn't return to her grief, to her guilt, to horrible Aunt Phoebe, to the hospital gurney and more injections of Thorazine. She couldn't go back to her physical body, contorted in spasm and pain.

"If I can't stay with you, mother, then I'll go back into my black hole." Sharay whispered.

Blanche tenderly pointed to Sharay's heart, and instantly Sharay understood. The black hole's sanctuary was not benign. Its seduction would demand more and more of her vitality. Sharay pushed the knowing away. She didn't care.

Blanche's eyes filled with regret and compassion. The shimmering vapor of her image began to slowly fade.

"No. Please don't leave," Sharay cried.

A tear rolled down Blanche's cheek as she blended into the brilliant gold light behind her and disappeared.

"I've lost you," Sharay whispered. "Again"

The black hole sighed, announcing its presence.

Black curling tendrils reached to pull her back in.

Chapter 5

After a few moments, or maybe an eternity, Sharay's muscles began to gradually unwind. She no longer gulped for air, and eventually the muscled vice that had twisted her neck backwards released. But the wound of her mother's death had split wide open after their brief encounter in the ethereal realms of the afterlife. Red and raw, the wound bled with renewed vigor. Sharay pounded on the walls of the black hole, begging for relief.

The black hole listened to her need. Her grief's demands were muffled under its protection. It accepted her back into its shadowy depths without question and hissed its promise of shelter. But this time on one condition. One mandate. What was required now was Sharay's soul.

Sharay relinquished it.

In her inner vision, she saw what looked like hawthorn roots twist tightly around her heart, solidifying her decision. In exchange, her sorrow was subdued. Along with it, Sharay's vitality withdrew and was replaced by a cover of numbness. Her warrior soul, the majestic lion her mother had once told her was her spirit guardian, opened its mouth and roared. But the sound fell on inner ears deafened by the pervasive numbness.

Sharay shuddered as a chill moved through her body, forming icicles in the tiny crevices of her cells.

"May I check the status of her torticollis now?" Mr. Millworth asked Dr. Deluth.

His inquisitive squat hands pulled aside Sharay's blanket and probed her neck muscles. The intern's prodding yanked Sharay's attention away from the inner territory of her body-mind.

Dr. Deluth's authoritative voice filled the room. "Finding the correct dose of anti-psychotic medicine is crucial to controlling hallucinatory symptoms," he instructed his intern. "Just enough to control her symptoms, but not so much as to cause side effects, like the torticollis you just saw." He didn't look at Sharay while he spoke.

Mr. Millworth nodded his head in apparent acceptance of his senior's medical wisdom.

"Has this happened to her before?" he asked Dr. Deluth while he scribbled notes into a notebook.

"No."

"Do you think she could feel the torticollis coming on?" he asked, peering at Sharay's neck.

Sharay turned her head away from him. She didn't understand the jargon the doctors used. They called her psychotic and schizophrenic.

Her body felt remote and alien to her. Her muscles, worn to exhaustion, called out for rest.

"It's all right now, dear. The muscle spasm is over." Claire plumped Sharay's pillow around her head.

"What other side effects should we look for?" Dr. Deluth asked his intern.

Sharay began to softly hum a tune to block out the doctor's conversation. The lyrics had once come to her in a dream when she was much younger.

I am the spring beneath the hill.
I am the waters of the well.
I am the lion's mouth.
I am the tree's roots.
I am the climber of the hill.
I am the descent beneath it.

Humming the tune lulled her. She lifted her hand and rubbed the back of her neck, tracing the outline of the tiny star birthmark that lay nestled at the nape.

A distant memory began to bubble to the surface of her mind.

"I don't want to remember anything else right now," Sharay said.

"Did she say something?" Dr. Millworth asked.

Sharay ignored him and talked to her black hole. "You buffer my feelings. Now do the same with my memories."

The black hole played tug-of-war to keep the rising memory buried. The memory won.

"She's responding to her hallucinations," Dr. Deluth confidently explained. "Sharay, focus on this room. Feel your body on the gurney."

Memory's images became too strong to resist. Dr. Deluth's voice receded to the far background of Sharay's attention. Her mother's voice vividly replaced the doctor's. Sharay saw herself at age seven, sitting on her mother's lap. Her mother was braiding her hair. She gently touched the birthmark at the nape of Sharay's neck, and stopped braiding.

"You're special, my dearest. Not only because I love you, but for even bigger reasons that you can't understand yet. All to do with an important Prophecy."

Sharay had felt a fluttering in her belly and, surprised, her hand flew to the spot. Her mother tenderly covered her hand with both of hers.

"When you reach the verge of womanhood, I'll teach you about your responsibilities as a priestess. When you're older, your visions of the Goddess will grow strong. I'll show you how to work with them," mother had said in her gentle voice.

Sharay had clapped her hands together, eager to learn all she could right then.

"Let's not wait. Please tell me now, Mother!" she exclaimed.

Her mother smiled at Sharay's exuberance. "We really must wait, dearest. I need to train you first." Her voice was soft and her eyes had a faraway look in them. "And help you grow strong so no harm comes your way."

Sharay must have looked frightened, for her mother stroked her cheek, and tucked a lock of her white blond hair behind her ear, saying, "You *never* need be afraid of the visions, Sharay. Remember, you're a priestess, just like me. And I'll be right here beside you."

Sharay had looked forward to the visions, a sort of ancestral rite of passage. But back then, her mother's stories were more like a fairytale, a make-believe world yet to be discovered.

Mr. Millworth's voice grew loud. It broke through Sharay's awareness. "She's not answering you. Dr. Deluth." he said.

"That's all right. The point is to gently coax her back to reality," Dr. Deluth replied.

Claire stood close to Sharay and held her hand. "Feel the warmth of my hand holding yours, Sharay," Claire said gently.

Sharay stared at the stark white walls and ignored Claire and the doctors. Her memories took full claim of her now. Her mother had promised to tell her something special about her visions once her bleeding times, the threshold to her womanhood, came. But the bleeding times didn't begin until after her mother died.

Her mother's best friend, Rosheen, did come to the manor home to try and speak with her on several occasions after her mother's death. Sharay remembered Rosheen's first attempt to visit. Sharay had crept out of her bedroom and onto the stair landing where she listened to the conversation in the foyer below.

"You know she *must* be trained or the visions will tear her apart," Rosheen said to Aunt Phoebe, desperation in her voice.

"Sharay can't have visitors. She's busy with homework," Aunt Phoebe replied curtly.

Sharay didn't understand why Aunt Phoebe would want to stop her from seeing Rosheen. Her aunt continued to thwart Rosheen's visits. During Rosheen's last attempt to see her, Aunt Phoebe locked her in her bedroom. But Sharay put her ear against the door so she could hear their conversation downstairs.

"If the girl is meant to be a priestess, she will learn on her own. Like I did," Aunt Phoebe said to Rosheen.

"That's not true, Phoebe. Your mother and I—in fact all the elders— spent just as much time teaching you as we did Blanche."

"Your memory serves you poorly, Rosheen. When the priest, Dillon, came to Glastonbury, I was all but forgotten." Aunt Phoebe's tone carried old hurt and resentments.

"It was you, not us, who made the choice to turn away from your lineage."

Sharay put her palms against the thick wooden door, her heart aching to speak with Rosheen.

Rosheen's voice turned angry. "Remember this—once Sharay comes of legal age, she'll own this house. You can't stop me from seeing her then. I'll teach her exactly who she is and what she's meant to become. Then, I'll personally give her the sacred talisman that's rightfully hers as our future High Priestess."

Phoebe's voice turned to ice. "It's I who'll one day own that necklace. Pray you don't die early, Rosheen, or it will fall to me sooner."

From her place behind her bedroom door, Sharay held her breath. She always cringed when Aunt Phoebe used that tone.

After this last attempt to see her, Rosheen telephoned her. She told her to lay low, that she loved her, and would find some way of training her. Aunt Phoebe listened in on their conversation from the phone extension, screamed at her afterward, and from then on began to monitor all telephone calls at home, censoring those from Rosheen. She forbid Sharay a cell phone. Her Aunt Phoebe drove her to school and picked her up, brought her straight home, and never allowed after-school activities or long term friendships. Sharay had grown too terrified of her aunt's harsh reprisals to attempt to contact Rosheen on her own. Phoebe finally severed any possibility of connection to Rosheen by filing a court issued restraint order based on deceitful accusations contrived against Rosheen and the other priestesses.

Still, Sharay often had curious dreams where Rosheen would come to her on clouds of rainbow colors, her hands outstretched, her eyes pleading. Rosheen would point to an image, a symbol of two intersecting circles with a straight line down the middle. And, though Rosheen's mouth would move to form words, and her hands would gesticulate wildly, Sharay was never able to hear what was being said. It was as if the sound was being intentionally blocked. As if Aunt Phoebe controlled her dreams, too.

Now, Sharay harbored no hopes of discovering her heritage. The ensuing years had muted the tales and promises of her mother.

Dr. Millworth prodded Sharay's neck once more. "The spasms are much better."

Sharay looked at him hazily. "Do you know where the talisman necklace is?" she asked him.

She didn't listen for his reply.

Sharay's mother had once told her the saga of the necklace. She'd said it was the sacred relic of their priestess community. Sharay had thought it was no more than a bedtime story, a legend meant to inspire. She hadn't comprehended the existence of the necklace as real, for mother had said that the necklace's secrets were right under her nose. Her mother had tweaked her nose at this point in the storytelling and Sharay had squealed with delight.

"The secrets of the necklace are right here," mother had said, suddenly serious, pointing to Sharay's chest. "Hidden in the center of your heart."

Sharay had looked down to where her mother pointed. "In my heart?"

"Yes, in your heart. Long ago, the necklace was magically forged by Theolon, the mate of the first priestess Geodran," her mother began, reciting the beloved story by memory.

"What's a talisman, mother?"

"It's a powerful charm, dearest. It channels magic. You might not understand all the words in my story, but I'll tell you the story again and again until one day you memorize and understand it. That's how I learned it."

Sharay grinned and jumped up and down. She loved stories.

"The necklace was made to enhance guidance from the Goddess. It's meant to be worn by the chosen priestess who is charged with being the Goddess's helper." Her mother paused, gazed at Sharay, and gently swept a lock of hair from her cheek.

"This chosen priestess has helped the Goddess before, in other lifetimes. She has helped the Goddess usher in the spiritual evolution of humankind during critical, dark times throughout human history. Like during the time of Atlantis. But that's another story for another time."

"Oooh." Sharay settled on her mother's lap, enraptured, her full concentration on her mother's words.

"The necklace is passed in guardianship from one High Priestess to the next. The reigning High Priestess protects the talisman as we await the chosen priestess who will be born again to help the Goddess. This priestess will wear the necklace and use its power at the appointed time. In today's world, when changes in human consciousness are crucial to our very survival on the planet, its help will once more be needed. Its power will be called upon to augment the strength of that special priestess who is heralded in our lineage's Prophecy."

Sharay interrupted her mother's story. "Can I see the necklace?" she asked eagerly.

Her mother's eyes clouded briefly. "It's kept with our other holy items, under my protection." Her mother paused and held Sharay's gaze. "But I've had to move it. That's a big secret between you and me, okay?"

"I promise I won't tell," Sharay said, trying to be her most grown-up. "Where is it?"

"I can't tell you just yet. . . ."

"I know. Not until I'm older," Sharay said, jutting out her lower lip.

Her mother smiled. "That's right. When you're a little older I will tell you. And I'll tell Rosheen, too," she added softly. "But for now, I must keep its location a secret. For its safety."

Sharay nodded solemnly. She loved secrets shared with her mother.

"You see, whoever guards the necklace until the time of the Prophecy's fulfillment has its magic at their disposal—in the wrong hands, that power could be misused."

"Who would do that?" Sharay asked.

Her mother had a faraway look in her eyes when she answered. "Sometimes the very people you thought you could trust."

Sharay thought her mother looked sad.

Her mother refocused her gaze and smiled gently. "But I've already told you the true source of its power."

"The Goddess?' Sharay asked.

Her mother pointed once more to Sharay's heart.

Sharay felt her tears spill with the remembrance of her mother's tenderness. She banged her fist on the hospital gurney beneath her. "Why did you tell me I could trust the visions, mother? Look where they've gotten me," she cried aloud.

Dr. Deluth called to her, his voice finally stopping the flow of her memories. "Sharay, listen to me. Only me."

Sharay closed her mind to the swirling blue mist and the achingly beautiful sound of a thousand bells ringing. She refused to let herself feel the presence of the Goddess.

"Leave me alone," she said loudly.

Claire glanced at Dr. Deluth and shook her head in pity.

Chapter 6

Two days later, after the episode of torticollis, when Sharay finally reached the state that Dr. Deluth called the "correct dosing"—meaning she had stopped fighting the medical team—she was taken out of restraints and allowed to leave her room to wander the rest of the psychiatric ward.

The black hole had done its job well. It stood between her and full participation in her life. But her feelings towards the black hole had changed since it had demanded she surrender her soul. She now found she both ardently desired it and fiercely hated it. Desired it for how it obliterated her rage and strengthened the hawthorn roots that covered her heart. Hated it for stupefying her, leaving her impassive and aloof.

All day long, for the next six months of hollow sameness, Sharay paced the psychiatric ward. Slowly, one slippered footstep followed by the next, under the custodial watch of the black hole. While the hole numbed her unwanted feelings, the Thorazine layered its own brand of oppression. It smothered her thoughts and propped her up like a puppet so her beleaguered mind would appear as what others might call normal. A drug-induced monotony. No more agitation.

Sharay traversed the long halls of numbered patient rooms with their iron-clad doors. When she reached the nursing station, barring her with its unbreakable glass, she would turn around and complete the same circuit in reverse. The halls were quiet, untouched by the crying, moaning, and occasional shouting heard in the large patient gathering room, called the dayroom.

"Save me, save me, save me," one patient repetitively called out from the dayroom, day after day.

"I want to go home," another cried out.

"Where's my doctor? I want my doctor."

Although encouraged by Nurse Claire to spend time in the dayroom, Sharay preferred to stay as far away as possible. Too many patients with broken spirits and anguished lives. She could hear their thoughts and feel their pain. She didn't know what to do with it all. Sharay covered her ears with her hands whenever she walked past the dayroom door.

Each day on the ward seemed just like the one before it. At seven in the morning, Sharay rose to shower, eat breakfast, attend group therapy led by Nurse Claire at ten o'clock, and art therapy at twelve noon. Twice a week, at two in the afternoon, she met with Dr. Deluth. Nurse Claire would accompany her out the locked ward, down the old-fashioned elevator shaft with its wrought iron gate, and through a cement tunnel with flickering fluorescent lights that connected to Dr. Deluth's office. His office was inside a small building that was much prettier and smelled much nicer than the green tiled floor and white dingy walls of the National Health hospital ward.

Dr. Deluth would begin her therapy sessions by asking, "How are you feeling today?"

In her very first session, when Dr. Deluth asked her to talk more about her parents, Sharay grabbed onto the rare opportunity to share her memories of them.

She knew just the story to tell him about who they were. "I remember the summer I turned five. Mother had complained about the hawthorn roots in our front garden."

"Go on," Dr. Deluth said.

Though she was young when it happened, the story was clearly etched in her mind.

"They're smothering my beautiful roses, Jarred," her mother had said to Sharay's father early one morning when the rain outside fell in a fine mist.

Mother pushed aside the sheer curtains from the dining room window and gazed across the front lawn to the rambling hedgerow that bordered the property. "See?" she said, pointing to a particularly gnarled section at the end of the driveway. "There's the problem. We've had no rose blooms because of it."

Her father swallowed his last gulp of morning tea and joined her at the window. "I'll take care of it," he promised.

Sharay bit into her toast and marmalade and climbed down from her chair, still chewing. She wanted to see what her parents were talking about. Edging between their legs, she stood on her tiptoes and pressed her face against the bottom of the window. She couldn't see what they were pointing to exactly, but nevertheless, she knew she wanted to be a part of whatever adventure they were planning.

That very afternoon, once the rain had stopped, Sharay slipped into her Wellington boots and joined her parents by the hedgerow at the edge of the driveway, her plastic bucket and shovel in tow. It was the same bucket and shovel she always took to the beach with her. She wanted to help. While her father dug up the portion of the hedge that threatened the roses, Sharay busied herself scooping up clumps of the excavated soil. When her father had finished, his digging left a gaping hole, a soggy earthen pit of truncated roots and squirming earthworms. Sharay covered her eyes with muddy hands and cried when she saw the empty, ugly hole. Her mother knelt beside her, gently swept her hair away from her tear-stained face, and kissed her forehead.

"Cutting away the hawthorn roots to save the roses is a good thing to do," she said reassuringly. "I'll tell you what. You and I can play a special game. I'll show you how to put that old dug-up bush to good use."

Sharay peeked through her fingers, looking once more into the deep hole. She got down on her hands and knees, just a tiny bit closer, and peered inside. Exposed to light and air, a whole city of ants scrambled frantically through the dirt. Hard-shelled beetles poked through soggy clods of soil.

With their hidden sanctuary disrupted, the tiny inhabitants of the underground quagmire all searched for familiar safety in the depths of the hole. Their panic made Sharay cry.

"There, there, dearest," her mother said soothingly.

Sharay stopped sniffling, and took her mother's hand. Making good on her promise, Sharay's mother picked up the wicker basket of pruned hawthorn boughs with her other hand, and headed for their huge kitchen. Her mother laid the basket of hawthorn boughs on the counter built especially for chopping and drying herbs to prepare them for making her special healing tinctures and teas.

"Hawthorn is actually a member of the rose family," her mother instructed as she set out a knife and bowl, a large pot, and a wooden spoon. "Some call the bush maytree or mayblossom."

Together, Sharay and her mother brewed a medicinal heart tonic with the bush's bright red berries. Her mother showed her how to gently harvest the young, shiny leaves to eat for their dinner salad. With her mother's hands over hers, they carefully cut the bush's thorny branches, laden with clusters of scented white flowers that blossomed only in May, and adorned their front door for good fortune and hearty welcome.

But the image of the empty black hole, that deep squirming pit, stayed with Sharay all day.

That night, for comfort, she chose her very best stuffed animal friend to cuddle in bed with her. She pulled her brave stuffed golden lion from her play chest. Her mother had bought it for her, telling her that the lion's soul was her "totem"—her personal guardian spirit that would lend her courage whenever she needed it. Sharay hugged him close, and, armed with her stuffed friend, she climbed into bed and soon fell asleep.

Still, she dreamt of the pit with its truncated roots. Sharay woke with her heart pounding and her blanket fitfully kicked to the floor. "Mommy!" she screamed.

Her mother rushed into her bedroom. "What is it, dearest?" She sat on the bed and stroked Sharay's forehead.

"I dreamt you lost me," Sharay wailed.

"I'm right here. See?"

"I was all alone in the hole. I couldn't find you."

"The hole?"

"The big hole in the garden," Sharay cried.

"Oh, my dearest. That hole is nothing to be frightened of. It's home to all the insects. It protects them and helps them feel safe. And when your father fills it in with compost, it will feed the rose bushes."

"It makes the insects safe?" Sharay asked.

"Mm-hmm," her mother murmured, kissing her cheeks.

Sharay reached up and touched her cheeks, exactly where her mother had once kissed her long ago when she was a little girl of five.

"So, you see, Dr. Deluth," she said, concluding her story. "Aunt Phoebe is nothing like mother. Mother loved me."

During Sharay's second therapy session with Dr. Deluth, he prompted her to tell him about the day her parents died.

Sharay felt hesitant, but told him nevertheless. "My mother's friend Rosheen was with me that morning. We were blowing up balloons for my tenth birthday party when we learned about the accident. Rosheen stayed with me after the news."

"My parents weren't dead an hour when Aunt Phoebe and Uncle Larry came knocking on the front door. I barely knew Aunt Phoebe before my parent's car crash. I remember holding Rosheen's hand when we answered the doorbell. My aunt and uncle stood in the porch shadows."

Sharay took a steadying breath and continued. "I felt Rosheen's hand jerk back when Aunt Phoebe stepped forward and said hello. Rosheen told them about my parent's accident. Aunt Phoebe didn't cry. She said that of course she'd take care of me, that I was her little sweetheart. I was *not* her little sweetheart. She patted my head. I shivered when she touched me."

Sharay could still feel that shiver crawl along her skin. She lowered her head and pulled her sweater closer about her.

"You were most likely still in shock when they arrived," Dr. Deluth said. "Keep in mind, your aunt and uncle were willing to sacrifice much to be your guardians."

Sharay raised her eyes in disbelief. "How can you say that?"

After that, whenever Dr. Deluth asked her how she was feeling, she gave the same answer. "I feel fine." With the medicine she was taking she really didn't feel much of anything. Except a smoldering flicker of hate for her Aunt Phoebe. But she never told Dr. Deluth that.

He had warned her—no, he ordered her—to never listen to her visions. He had another name for them. He called them hallucinations, and said they weren't real. Said they were dangerous. He claimed they were the reason her aunt committed her. That and her supposed threats to kill her aunt and uncle. So, afraid to trust the visions, afraid to let Dr. Deluth know they hadn't completely gone away, Sharay never told him about any of the times that, through a crack in the Thorazine haze, she would catch a fleeting glimpse of blue and silver mist or hear the sound of a thousand bells.

Chapter 7

Sharay shifted position in her chair and squinted to see the new patient across the large expanse of the dayroom. The old man winked at her. Startled, she looked down at her hands in her lap, pretending not to notice him. She frowned. She shouldn't have given in to Claire's persuasion to come into the dayroom.

The large dayroom was protectively enclosed. There were three plain white walls, each having four narrow, barred windows. A sturdy, locked metal door was positioned on the fourth wall. The metal door led into a narrow corridor where more metal doors housed patient bedrooms, lined up along both sides of the hall and numbered like the rooms in an inexpensive motel.

To the right of the dayroom door the wall stopped at about the height of Sharay's waist. From there to the ceiling was a barrier of shatterproof glass that allowed for patient surveillance by the medical team who gathered at the nursing station. It provided for distanced observation, void of interaction unless there was commotion in the dayroom. It made Sharay feel like the tropical fish her father had kept in a huge aquarium. She expected the nurses to tap on the window and coo, pursing their lips in imitation of the fish, just as she used to do.

The dayroom was full of idle chatter, some nonsensical, along with the monotonous blare of a morning television talk show. Cigarette smoke wafted upward, trapped by the closed and barred windows, as much prisoner as all the patients committed to the hospital against their will.

Sharay looked up and feigned a casual glance around the room. Her gaze compellingly rested once more on the old man. He caught her eye and winked again. The corner of his mouth lifted in a hint of a grin, noticeable more by the pronounced lines formed in the craggy skin around his lips. The deck of cards he held shifted clumsily from one hand to the other. Staring at Sharay, his eyes never lowered as he laid the cards out in a pattern of three triangles on the table before him. One card at the top, followed by a card to the bottom left, and another to the bottom right, repeated three times.

Sharay glanced around and back again, unsure his wink was meant for her. The old man continued to stare. His gray hair, the same color of his eyes, was thin on top and hung loosely about his shoulders. His knobby hands scratched his scrubby gray beard, then, index finger curled, he motioned for Sharay to join him at his table.

Sharay hesitated. The old man pointed to the spread of cards before him and chuckled. He held one up for her to see, and furtively laid it back down again. Curious, Sharay stood and scuffled across the room, the closest she could come to walking while on her medicine, making her way past the vacant gaze of a middle aged female patient. She sat in a worn wooden chair across from the old man, the table and mysterious cards between them.

"Dillon." He proffered his weather beaten hand in welcome. "Dillon Emrys. Born in the North of Wales, high in the mountains in a town no one has ever heard of. Born and raised there." His voice was deep but carried the musical lilt of a heavy Welsh accent.

Sharay extended her hand and watched it tremor. Another side effect of her medicine. She quickly withdrew it, embarrassed.

"The shaking is nothing to be ashamed of. Easy to remedy. Here, try again." Dillon's hand hung over the cards, waiting for hers.

Timidly, Sharay offered her hand again. She was surprised at the strength of the old man's grip. He pressed his thumb against the top of her index finger and held on as if he awaited a return gesture.

"Ah, I thought perhaps you remembered the greeting of the ancients, but sadly not."

Sharay leaned her head to the side, wiped the drool from her mouth against her shoulder, leaving a wet stain on her sweater. The old man must be crazy, she thought.

"Sure, some call me crazy. Others call me wise." Dillon smiled, a full grin this time. Two dimples appeared in his deeply creviced face.

Sharay pulled her hand away, her eyes opened wide. How did he know what she was thinking?

"Nothing to be afraid of. Anyone can learn to read another's thoughts. You've done it sometimes, too."

Sharay didn't answer. She wondered if she could get away from Dillon without creating a scene.

"All right, I'll give you this piece of advice, and then maybe you'll trust me." Dillon leaned in close to Sharay. "Cheek your medicine," he whispered.

"What?"

"Cheek it. Take the medicine in your mouth, roll it with your tongue to the back of your cheek, near to your gums. Nurse will check your mouth but won't see it. Then spit it out when she leaves." Dillon leaned back, obviously pleased with himself.

"Nurse won't see it?"

"No. Just do it. It will stop that silly drooling of yours."

Sharay giggled nervously. Of course. It was so simple. "How did you learn to do that?"

Dillon shrugged and stroked his beard. "I know many things. Take this card for example." He held up the card he had tried to show her before.

"Tarot cards," Sharay said, recognizing the trump from a similar deck her mother had allowed her to play with as a child.

The cards were divinatory. When shuffled and laid out in a pattern, they could be interpreted, often giving readings that made accurate and profound pronouncements about one's life situation.

Sharay took the card he offered her. Its edges were worn, the colors faded. It showed the picture of a young man and woman facing each other with hands clasped, standing under a rose trellis and being blessed by a hooded figure of a Goddess. The word LOVERS was printed across the bottom of the card. Sharay felt a fluttering in her womb, as if the card fanned the flames of the burnt out embers of her inner strength there. She had almost forgotten about this power spot in her body, hadn't felt its heat since the day she met Dr. Deluth a full six months ago.

"Yes, Tarot. But this is a very old deck, a special deck. That card is for you. Keep it with you. Sleep with it under your pillow." Dillon lowered his voice. "Don't show it to anyone else."

Sharay touched the outline of the figures with her fingers, inexplicably intrigued by the faded picture.

Dillon coughed. Sharay looked up to see Dr. Deluth walk toward her, clipboard in hand, two interns following obediently behind. She shoved the card under her sweater and tucked it inside her bra. Dillon laid a magazine across the top of his card spread, his movements betraying none of the anxiety Sharay felt whenever she saw Dr. Deluth.

"How are we today, Mr. Emrick?" Dr. Deluth looked down at his clipboard notes as he spoke.

Sharay stole a quick glance at Dillon. She thought he had told her his last name was Emrys.

Dillon smiled, looked over at Sharay, and in a soft voice intoned, "Lamou dei tu wantna se de tu."

"What did you say?" Sharay cocked her head, forgetting all about Dillon's last name.

She had never forgotten that phrase, the exotic words spoken by the Goddess on the day she was committed to the hospital. But Dr. Deluth had told her that the vision, everything she had seen, heard, and felt, was all a part of her illness. Confused, Sharay pushed down her excitement, swallowing it back as dutifully as she swallowed her pills every morning and evening. She would block out what she had just heard Dillon say. Just as Dr. Deluth and Nurse Claire had taught her she should do.

"Mr. Robinson, your observations of Mr. Emrick, please," Dr. Deluth said brusquely.

Intern Geoffrey Robinson, red haired and freckled, and at the young age of twenty-five already touting a protruding belly and drooping jowls, stepped forward. "Mr. Emrick is perseverating."

Sharay stared at the way Geoffrey Robinson's cheeks wiggled as he spoke. She watched him intently, hoping the curious movement of his chin would preoccupy her mind.

"Wrong. Care to try, Mr. Millworth?" Dr. Deluth turned his back on Sharay to face his interns.

Mr. Millworth proudly stepped forward. Sharay shuddered as she always did when she encountered this intern. His muscular arms and his stubby fingers were a reminder of the purple and yellow bruises she received from the struggle to pull her down to the floor and restrain her when she first came to the psychiatric unit.

"Mr. Emrick is speaking in neologisms," Mr. Millworth said. "To be precise, word salad."

"Correct. Now, Mr. Robinson, define the terms," Dr. Deluth said.

Geoffrey Robinson blushed and stammered his response. "Neologism—the coinage of new words having special meaning to the patient. Word Salad—neologisms used exclusively and in sequence."

Dillon looked up and patiently waited for Sharay's returning gaze. "Lamou dei tu wantna se de tu," he repeated slowly. This time his soft, rich voice was firmer.

The doctors' conversation faded from Sharay's awareness. There was no mistaking it. Dillon spoke the language she had heard in her vision. Or hallucination. She pushed her chair away from the table and stood. Someone in the dayroom moaned loudly.

"How did you know, Dillon?" she whispered.

Dillon turned his face toward the interns and mumbled gibberish. Sharay shook her head and tried to clear her thoughts. Had her conversation with Dillon been just another hallucination? She stared hard at Dillon, half expecting him to disappear. Instead, she noticed drool sliding down his chin. Sharay put her hand to her bra, felt for the card he had given her. She hadn't imagined it. It was still there.

The card was surprisingly warm to the touch. She stepped back, knocking her chair over.

Mr. Millworth spoke, his words commanding Sharay's attention. "Dr. Deluth, I believe Mr. Emrick is agitating Sharay."

Sharay panicked. Anytime the word agitation was mentioned, injections were sure to follow. Her instinct screamed for her to run.

"Must stay in control," she murmured to herself.

She clutched the table edge in front of her. Her knuckles grew white with her grip. The Lovers card tucked inside her bra grew even warmer. She glanced from Dr. Deluth to Dillon and back again.

With all the will she had, she drew herself up tall and took a deep, shaky breath. "I am fine, Dr. Deluth. Thank you for your concern, Mr. Millworth."

Dr. Deluth turned and eyed her, his gaze a well-practiced assessment. Before anyone could speak, Dillon's voice rang loud and clear.

"I am oldest of old
I am newest of form
I am the spring beneath the hill
I am the waters of the well."

The dayroom chatter subsided. Everyone's attention, patient and doctor alike, focused on Dillon's thunderous recitation. Sharay was all but forgotten by the medical team.

"Thomas, calm down now. Lower your voice," Dr. Deluth ordered.

"Thomas? Your name's Thomas?" Sharay asked without getting a reply.

The two interns cautiously surrounded the old man. Several patients began to cry, softly at first, then more loudly.

Sharay trembled, not from her medicine but, rather, from the force of the images that swam before her eyes with Dillon's poem. His words were a deafening roar that crashed on the shore of her consciousness.

"I am the sword of the male," he cried.

"That's enough, Thomas," Dr. Deluth said firmly. He nodded his head to his interns, sign to ready themselves to subdue the old man on his command.

Sharay's thoughts abruptly stilled. In a hesitant voice, with words prompted from some deep ancient place within her, she murmured the next stanza.

"I am the yoni of the women."

Dillon smiled, and continued in a calm low voice, ignoring the interns close by his side.

"I am the blood red birth

I am the duality of death."

The Lovers Tarot card hidden against Sharay's chest burned hot. She again surprised herself with her knowledge of the poem prayer. She spoke the next words, felt them poignantly familiar.

"I am the Lion's mouth

I am the tree's roots"

Pictures swiftly paraded through Sharay's mind, weaving a kaleidoscope of forms, images, and colors that quickly coalesced. She saw nine women dressed in white robes sitting round a well. They honored the gushing spring with flowers and prayers, their faces reflecting a serene joy. A familiar green terraced hill, enshrouded in mist, loomed behind them—the Tor of Glastonbury.

Dillon continued.

"I am the climber of the hill

I am the descent beneath it."

Nurse Claire, observing the dayroom from the nursing station, stood, and grabbed the overhead intercom.

"Dr. Deluth? Do you need assistance?" she asked.

Dr. Deluth's voice was barely heard above Dillon's. "Not yet, Claire." He signaled for his interns to slowly move in on Dillon.

The interns approached cautiously so as not to agitate the situation further.

"Come on, Mr. Emrick. You don't want to stir everybody up like this do you?" Mr. Robinson said in a persuasive tone.

Dillon stood from his chair, raised his arms, and continued his booming narration. The power of his bardic voice, the magic in his words, caused the interns to falter. Dillon's words pierced Sharay's heart. Great sadness, deeper yet than the grief for her parents, surged through her body, and expressed itself in a keening wail.

Sharay covered her ears, tried to blot out the lament, until she realized it issued uncontrollably from her own voice.

"I am the persecutor and the slaughtered," Dillon prompted.

Sharay couldn't help but respond.

"I am the vessel for the memories
I am the wail of the mourning
I am the vase for the healing
I am memory re-membered."

Several patients moaned, a choral response to the litany.

"Dillon, who are these women I see?" Sharay implored.

"Thomas, one last chance. You must calm yourself," Dr. Deluth commanded. He turned to Robinson and Millworth. "Hold onto him."

Mr. Millworth seized Dillon's upright arm and Mr. Robinson grabbed the left arm, rendering Dillon unable to move. Still, he resumed his bardic prose.

"I am the hope of my lineage
I am one who once were many."

Sharay's vision continued. The beautiful women in the white robes seated around the bubbling well looked up at her. They reached out with their arms as if they saw her as clearly as she saw them. Their serene smiles turned to cries of terror as swords sliced through the air, impaling their bodies on pointed blades. Sharay closed her eyes, trying to blot out the horrific scene.

Dr. Deluth, clipboard long since abandoned on the nearby table-top, held Sharay by her arms. "Sharay, you're hallucinating. Talk to me. Focus on me."

Sharay couldn't speak. The images felt real to her.

"Sharay, don't pay attention to anything but me. Nothing is real but this room, and me talking to you." Dr. Deluth's tone was strong, assured. Sharay could ride it like a lifeboat out of her confusion if she chose to. All she need do was take his hand and climb in the boat.

Dillon's voice grew louder, calling her in another direction. Sharay felt the poem grip her soul, compelling her to turn away from Dr. Deluth and toward Dillon. A moth to flame. They two completed the ancient prayer in unison.

"I am the Carrier of the Flame
I am the past and I am future
And my quest is now."

The poem finished in a roar, a command from the gods accompanied by the screaming chorale of the other patients.

Dr. Deluth looked up and nodded to Claire, who waited expectantly inside the nursing station. She pressed a red button on the wall and set off a buzzer that blared overhead. Its repetitive tone alerted all available personnel on the unit to come to the dayroom, their prompt assistance needed to quell the commotion. Claire dashed from the nursing station and opened the door to the dayroom, followed closely by three psychiatric nursing assistants.

Lost in her trance, the pictures in Sharay's mind grew more vivid, the women's' cries torturous. Crimson red stained their white robes in ever spreading circles. Their blood seeped into the ground beneath them. The soil received their lost life force back into its earthly womb.

"Remember us," the women in Sharay's vision cried.

Their pain became Sharay's pain. She reeled.

"Dillon. Please. Make it stop," Sharay pleaded.

"I am so sorry but I can not. Not until you remember," Dillon said resolutely.

Sharay cupped her hands over her ears, but the women's voices lingered on.

"Never forget us," they implored. "We are your lineage. Remember us, and you remember your destiny."

The vision was haunting. The acrid smell of the women's blood mingled with the loamy dirt that drank it in; an earthly commemoration, stored away in dust's memory for those of future generations with the ability to see what once was.

Sharay sobbed. "I see them. I remember my holy sisters, Dillon."

Dillon slumped into the arms of Mr. Robinson, quiet and subdued at last.

"Come on old man, that's better. Let's get you out of here," Mr. Robinson said.

The psychiatric assistants stood by Dr. Deluth and waited for his direction.

"Mr. Robinson and assistant Bill can take care of Thomas. Mr. Millworth, you help me with Sharay," Dr. Deluth said.

Dillon's gaze locked with Sharay's as he was slowly walked backwards out of the dayroom.

Mr. Millworth took Sharay's elbow, held it lightly, and waited to gauge her response to his efforts to contain her outburst. Sharay pulled back reflexively. Dillon's narration, along with her keening, had escalated the other patient's emotions to a fevered pitch. The cries of the women in white robes melded with the moans of the patients in the dayroom. Sharay wasn't sure which reality she belonged to, but her body grew certain in its response. She was not willing to submit as easily as Dillon to her restrainers. She struggled to pull free from the arms that would cage her once again.

"Sharay, please settle down. You saw how easy it was for Mr. Emrick." Dr. Deluth's tone coaxed her to give up the fight.

She knew if she could refrain from resisting she would simply be escorted back to her room as effortlessly as Dillon had been. But something within her could not allow it. Her totem lion leapt to life and rattled the caged walls of the black hole in which she had been living.

Sharay panted. The furor in the dayroom felt insignificant compared to the battle waged inside her. The force of it discharged through her flailing arms and legs with kicks and punches aimed at those that tried to hold her back. They had almost won, had almost convinced her she was wrong about everything. Her visions of the Goddess, her trances, her hate for Aunt Phoebe.

Mr. Millworth and Dr. Deluth gripped her firmly, squeezing the sensation out of her arms.

"Sharay, there is no need to fight. We are trying to help." Dr. Deluth's voice sounded far away, exceedingly slow and deep.

Sharay's rage hurdled against the bars of constraint. The awakened warrior lion inside her roared.

She didn't recognize her own voice when she shouted. "You're wrong about me. All of you."

Dr. Deluth sighed heavily, and with lips set in a grim line, lifted one hand to motion nurse Claire to come forward. She approached quietly from the side.

"Sharay, if you'd only learn to settle down there will be no need for this injection," she whispered into Sharay's ear.

Sharay growled an unintelligible response, twisted sideways and kicked Millworth in the groin with her knee. He released her arm, and with a painful groan, slid down to his knees. Feeling returned to Sharay's right arm, light prickles of sensation. Dr. Deluth quickly took over and deftly pinned Sharay into position with her arms behind her back.

"Get up," he said to Dr. Millworth.

Millworth moaned but slowly stood, hands over his groin. He pushed against Sharay from the front; his heavy thighs against her knees blocked her legs from further movement.

The sting of the inevitable injection jolted Sharay back into her unwanted prison with brute force.

Chapter 8

Orange and pink brush stroke clouds, herald of the rising sun, replaced the dark night sky. Gazing out her kitchen window, Rosheen couldn't help a bittersweet smile from forming. As distraught as she was, dawn was a good time, her favorite time. The most magical time in the small town of Glastonbury.

She poured steaming water over the teabag in her china cup and put the kettle back on the burner. The citrus aroma of bergamot wafted through the kitchen. Rosheen waited for it to steep to perfection.

Her kitchen was on the first floor of Little St. Michael's Retreat House, the four-hundred-year-old cottage that also served as bed and breakfast lodgings for pilgrims of the Chalice Well gardens. While the three-story cottage had been recently renovated, the kitchen still boasted the original oak beams across its low ceiling, their wood darkened with age and slightly bowed.

Rosheen lifted her cup and sipped the tea, her gaze fixed on the rose bushes outside the kitchen window. The unease in the pit of her stomach wouldn't allow her to eat breakfast, even if it was permissible before the morning's ritual. She had arranged for it take place at the wellspring on her land.

While she could not legally call Little St. Michaels or the Chalice Well gardens her property, she more often than not referred to it as such. It belonged to the Chalice Well Trust, whose job it was to uphold and beautify the gardens and ancient wellspring. In truth, it belonged to the pilgrims it served. And to the priestesses of the Goddess of the Stars and the Sea, who had been the wellspring's stewards for centuries. Rosheen was currently their High Priestess. The priestesses were the true guardians of the Chalice Well. It was they who appointed the members of the Trust to help ensure that the peace and sanctity of the site was maintained, along with its legal status as a Charity Trust.

Rosheen carried her cup and saucer through the dining room, intending to head upstairs to the cottage sanctuary called the Upper Room. She wanted to collect the items necessary for the upcoming ritual. Instead, she set her cup down on the small table near the staircase, sat on the inglenook beside the old stone fireplace, and took a steadying breath. She was frightened.

Within the hour, two other elders of the community, Catherine and Aneta, would be arriving. Rosheen would need to let them know she had sent Dillon to the hospital to help Sharay. She wanted their support for her unilateral decision. Their probable concerns and questions were not what frightened Rosheen. What frightened her was Sharay's predicament.

Glad there were no lodgers booked into Little St. Michael's for the day, Rosheen decided that what she really needed was to go outside and clear her head. She left the cottage through the back door in the dining room, bringing her cup of tea with her. Once in the fresh, warm air of the summer morn, surrounded by the luminous colors of daybreak, the knot in her stomach began to relax. She made her way through the long backyard meadow, and up the gentle slope of the Chalice Well hill. The hill sat directly behind the lodge and the gardens, and was really more of a rounded knoll. Atop its crest, looking back in the direction of the gardens below, the hill offered a panoramic view of the countryside.

To the south, far ahead of Rosheen, pearly white mists rode across the flat plains of Somerset. Their cascading waves of white cloud mystery enshrouded the once marshy landscape Rosheen had cherished for over sixty years.

The mists rolled swiftly forward then stopped, as usual, a few hundred feet from the edge of town. The tips of their coiled wisps bowed before her, as if awaiting appreciation for nature's performance, exquisitely staged.

As encore, the mists banked near the foot of Wearyall Hill to the west, where they fashioned white shadowed silhouettes from the winding streets, old gnarled trees, and rows of homes that surrounded it.

To Rosheen's left, the east, mists encircled the five-hundred-foot-high hill that the locals called the Tor. Many considered it to be a natural geophysical and energetic gateway between the worlds of the physical and the spiritual. Below the Tor, at the foot of the mound she stood upon, enveloped in white embrace, the holy spring of the Chalice Well gurgled as it had done for time immemorial.

The now fully risen sun painted the foggy land clouds to reflect the colors of the sky. Rosheen sat down on the sweet smelling grass of Chalice Hill, set her cup and saucer beside her, and ran her fingers through her freshly washed short gray hair. With her other hand, she absently brushed blades of grass off her beige linen pants. She would don her red ceremonial robes later for the ritual with Aneta and Catherine.

The quiet of early morning, before the public was allowed entrance to the gardens, gave Rosheen temporary reprieve. She cherished these few moments of dawn, when earth and sky joined to cast their protective misty net over the land, reminding all with eyes to see that Glastonbury was no ordinary town in the Somerset plains of England. Rosheen closed her eyes and used her inner vision to gaze into the soul of her beloved Glastonbury. Those with eyes to see could gaze beyond the mists into the true nature of Glastonbury. It was Glastonbury's heart that she most wanted to someday show Sharay.

Glastonbury was known to some by the magical name of Ynis Witrin, Avalon, or, by an even earlier name, the Enchanted Isles. It was sacred land, dedicated long ago to the Goddess of the Stars and the Sea by Her first priestess, Geodran, a survivor of the Atlantis cataclysm. Geodran had been chosen by the Goddess to carry on the flame of her spiritual heritage.

She, along with a small group of Atlantean survivors, had settled in Glastonbury, and seeded the wisdom of their star-borne legacy. It was here that the priestess lineage took root. The land's primordial wellspring had been venerated by the perennial community of priestesses as the 'Red Well' for eons. Its waters were not only curative but also potent transducers of the spiritual energy of the land.

Legends grew and were forgotten over the centuries, each in their time claiming the wellspring as their own. The most recent legend, two thousand years old, told of a chalice—Jeshua the Christ's drinking cup from his Last Supper, the one used to collect his blood as he died on the cross. The chalice was said to be buried by the well, thus giving the wellspring its contemporary name of 'Chalice Well.' Christian accounts blended with the Arthurian romances of the Middle Ages, to leave their mark on Glastonbury. King Arthur and his adored Guinevere were said to have been buried on the grounds of the Abbey ruins in the center of the town. A simple stone marked their gravesite. Despite the romantic and Christian overlay, the innate heart of Glastonbury belonged to the priestesses in service to the Goddess of the Stars and the Sea.

The New Age tourists, eager pilgrims who constantly streamed into Glastonbury, sensed the magic in Chalice Well. They stayed at Little St. Michael's Lodge, visited the well, and left honorings at the sacred site—flowers, crystals, and prayers printed on small, folded pieces of paper. Still, no one but the priestesses knew that it was not the chalice of the Last Supper that had been buried beside the well, but, rather, the holy talismanic necklace of the Goddess.

Rosheen had been taught about the necklace as a young girl, as had all the priestesses. She remembered sitting in a circle beside the Red Well over fifty years ago, with a dozen other girls in her class, all between the ages of nine and twelve. She always made sure to sit beside her best friends for class time—Catherine, who would tap her fingers on her thighs until the lessons began, and wide-eyed Aneta, who spoke only when spoken to.

The class always gathered at twilight. It was the time of day that was neither light nor yet dark, where the dying rays of the sun made the leaves on the trees glimmer, and shadows were not yet cast to trick the eye or frighten a young girl's mind.

Their High Priestess Dana told them twilight was when the gap between the worlds of the Inner and Outer Realms was the strongest. A time of enchantment Rosheen loved to share with her fellow students. She wished Sharay had known this kind of camaraderie.

Rosheen gazed down the hill at the Chalice Well gardens in spring bloom with vibrant lilac bushes, yellow daffodils, and purple hyacinth.

She sighed. Her appreciation of the gardens mingled with sadness. She wanted Sharay to enjoy this beauty as intimately as she did.

When she was finally able to contact Sharay, she would catch her up on all her missed training. While many priestesses answered the calling of the Goddess, only a few were the direct bloodline descendants of the first priestess Geodran, as Sharay was. Rosheen would help Sharay claim her bloodline ancestry. She would help her learn what it means to be a priestess, a conscious mediator of sacred energies between the world of the seen and unseen, the Inner and Outer Realms. She'd train Sharay in the ways of the Goddess—ancient chant and visionary meditation, ceremony, ritual, healing, dance, poetry, art, teaching, gardening, and service to humanity's spiritual well being. She'd show her how to use her Second Sight to go into trance and gather information as an oracle and seer.

But, most importantly, she would teach Sharay about the Prophecy and her role in it. She would tell her of the portends of the Prophecy—how the lineage had in the past, and once again through Blanche, birthed the one who carried, deep within her cells, the ancient secret that was vital to the spiritual evolution of humankind.

Rosheen envisioned how she would ever so gently share all of this with Sharay, so as not to overwhelm her. She would bring Sharay into the gardens, and they would sit in the back section near the Red Well. With its perpetual flow at their feet, she would start by telling Sharay the story of the necklace. In the same place and with the same words as it was recounted to the priestesses every Spring Equinox, a time of year when light and dark were equal in the heavens above.

Rosheen remembered well the Spring Equinox she turned sixteen and was instructed to properly memorize the legend as part of her priestess training. She'd already known it word for word for years, but was paying special attention to the nuances—the intonations and tones her High Priestess used that embellished its telling.

"The cherished relic of our lineage was brought into form through the magic of harmonic chanting." Rosheen could still see her High Priestess Dana, radiant with the joy of teaching. It was when Dana was still vibrant and healthy, long before cancer ravaged her body and took her life.

All of the women of the community, from infants to the older women, priestesses as well as those in training, were present. Rosheen remembered how the newborn Phoebe, nursing at her mother Dana's breast, had stopped suckling, as if listening.

"The necklace was forged of the purist gold and silver, and clear crystal," Dana told them all in hushed tones. "It never ages and never tarnishes."

"When can we see it and touch it?" Catherine asked eagerly.

"Only when you become fully consecrated priestesses. And then only once, on the day of your consecration," Dana replied.

A facsimile of the necklace's design was carved in wrought iron and fastened onto the wooden wellhead of the Red Well. Rosheen imagined pointing to its various symbols as she instructed Sharay. It was fashioned in the shape of a Vesica Pisces—two intersecting circles. The space where the circles overlapped represented the union of duality—the marriage of body and spirit, masculine and feminine, heaven and earth, conscious with unconscious. That almond shaped space formed a yoni, the symbol of a woman's vagina and the portal to creation. The sacred feminine. A straight line ran through the configuration of the Vesica Pisces on the wellhead. It was another symbol of the merging of the opposites, of masculine energy intertwining with feminine.

Ever since the garden grounds surrounding the well had been made open to the public many years ago, the necklace had been moved from its burial place beside the wellspring and sequestered away to a secret hiding place in the Upper Room of Little St. Michael's cottage.

What remained for the public to see was the wrought iron duplicate of the mystical Vesica Pisces atop the wellhead cover.

From her spot atop Chalice Hill, Rosheen noticed a couple walking toward the entrance gate of the Chalice Well gardens. She checked her watch. She still had a good fifteen minutes to enjoy the burgeoning of the warm summer morning before the garden volunteers opened the gates.

While the New Age pilgrims venerated the Chalice Well, the priestesses of the Goddess knew its real mystery. Modern day science may attribute the well's red tinged water to its high iron content, but the priestesses knew the water to be the blood of the Goddess.

She was embodied in the hallowed ground of Glastonbury. The Tor was seen as Her earthly breast, Chalice Well mound Her womb, and the well was the sacred feminine portal of fertility that spewed the red waters.

Rosheen leaned on her elbows and lay back on the grassy earth. She inhaled deeply, luxuriating in the scent of loamy, rich black dirt mixed with the sweet smell of high summer grasses. Feeling the Goddess's Presence in the soft body of the earth was exactly the balm the ache in her heart yearned for.

She'd never regretted accepting the responsibilities of High Priestess. She'd taken over for Blanche eight years ago, when she was fifty-six. Blanche, twenty years her junior, had functioned in the role for only fifteen years before she died.

Blanche had at one time been her student and they had developed a strong bond of friendship. Before Blanche's fatal car crash, she had confided in Rosheen. It was the last conversation Rosheen had with her alone. It was forever emblazoned in her memory.

Blanche had arrived on the porch of Little St. Michael's in the middle of the night, pounding loudly on the door. Rosheen woke with a start and ran to answer the insistent knocking before her lodgers were aroused. Fumbling with the ties on her robe, she opened the door to find Blanche with her clothes ripped and her arms scratched.

"I am in trouble," Blanche had said. Her long pale hair was disheveled, her blue eyes opened wide in panic.

"My God, Blanche, what's happened?" Rosheen held the door wide open, put her arm around Blanche's shaking shoulders, and ushered her friend inside.

"Something evil has attacked me, Rosheen," Blanche said, her voice low.

"What?" Rosheen asked. "Who attacked you?" She led her into the kitchen and fumbled in the cabinet next to the refrigerator until she found bandages, cotton balls, and antiseptic ointment.

With her first aid items in hands, she directed Blanche out the back door and into the Chalice Well gardens, away from the sleeping lodgers inside Little St. Michaels. Blanche allowed herself to be led, her normally confident stature limp, her shoulders drooped. Rosheen headed for the Red Well.

The moon was almost full, and cast a silvery glow over the flowers, plants, and garden pathway. Its luminescent face reflected silver ripples in the well waters. The two of them sat on the bench beside the wellspring in silence while Rosheen cleaned Blanche's scratches and dressed them. When she was finished, Blanche reached for Rosheen's hands and held them tightly in hers to stop from trembling.

"Tell me what's happened to you." Rosheen pushed down the dread rising from the pit of her stomach.

Blanche spoke in hushed tones. "I've been psychically attacked. During my moon meditations this evening." Her chin began to quiver.

The dread in Rosheen's stomach grew. She was not used to seeing Blanche distraught.

Blanche took a deep breath and continued. "At first it was just a vague sense of something hovering in the corner of my meditations in the Inner Realms. Then it came closer. And it grew. It took form right before it attacked me. It was horrible." Her voice cracked. "But there's more, Rosheen."

Blanche withdrew her hands and placed them over her womb. "My power spot burns hot. It's telling me something bad is going to happen. I'm certain of it."

Rosheen desperately wanted to say something reassuring, something to minimize the terror in Blanche's eyes. She wasn't sure if it would be for Blanche's sake, or her own.

Blanche continued. "Years ago, I had a frightening premonition about this. Remember?"

"I remember. You reported it to the Council of Elders. Was this what you foretold?"

"It must be. I didn't know exactly what to expect back then. But I do know this attack was just a warning." Blanche's voice grew shrill. "I fear for my family. I fear for Sharay."

"Are you sure it's about your family?"

"I'm sure, Rosheen," Blanche replied vehemently. "This is personal. You must believe me." Her blue eyes pleaded with Rosheen.

Rosheen swallowed thickly. "Of course, I believe you. But you're scaring me."

"Goddess, Rosheen! One of us has to be strong. Be strong for me. When it comes to my husband, my daughter Sharay, I lose my center. I can't be much of a High Priestess if I lose my center."

Blanche turned to face Rosheen straight on, and grabbed her by the shoulders. "Whatever threatens me also threatens our community. Rosheen, you must be strong for me."

Rosheen nodded her head, wanting to be all that Blanche needed.

"I'm going to activate strong magical protection, and I need help. You must gather the other priestesses for an emergency meeting. Tomorrow. At high noon." She paused. "I have something very important to tell you about our talisman, too. But I'll tell you then. I'm much too weary now."

Blanche released Rosheen's shoulders and covered her eyes with her hands. "Goddess, it's Sharay's birthday tomorrow."

Blanche looked up, her mouth set in a grim line. "There is no time to physically gather with the other members of our lineage around the world. But you can contact the other High Priestesses for me. Wherever they are, ask them to tune into the Inner Realms at the appointed time."

Blanche's voice grew stronger. The sound of it reassured Rosheen. "We'll form our protection, and together see what menace attempts to intimidate us through threatening my family."

"We'll get to the bottom of this," Rosheen said with as much reassurance as she could muster.

"Promise me something, Rosheen." Blanche's voice broke.

"Of course. What is it?"

Blanche's tone grew demanding. "If anything should happen to me, you must promise to watch after the hope of our Prophecy. Look after my daughter. Look after Sharay."

"Nothing will happen to you. We'll see to that tomorrow."

"No. Promise me, Rosheen. Swear it!" Blanche gripped Rosheen's shoulders.

Rosheen felt her heart pound. "I promise you."

Blanche let out a heavy sigh. Her shoulders drooped with exhaustion. "And if anything should happen to me, you are to be our next High Priestess until the time Sharay can claim her rightful role. I've made my wishes known to the elders for a long time now, but I'll officially declare that tomorrow."

Rosheen drove Blanche back home to her husband and daughter. As soon as she returned to Little St. Michael's lodge, she contacted the nine priestesses who lived in Glastonbury, as promised. She informed them of the gathering, instructed them to meet for the ritual of protection, set for twelve noon the next day. She alerted all eleven of the other High Priestesses across the globe, asked them to lend their support in the Inner Realms.

The next day at ten o'clock, on a bright, sunny morning, Blanche and Jarred drove into town to purchase chocolate ice cream for Sharay's tenth birthday party scheduled for later that afternoon. Rosheen had offered to stay behind with Sharay at the manor home until Blanche returned. She would then accompany Blanche to the scheduled meeting.

At ten thirty-three, a police officer came to the house to report that a sudden torrential storm had caused Blanche and Jarred's car to crash. A piece of Rosheen's heart died along with her High Priestess and friend. Bad magic was stirring. Nothing she could prove, but she smelled its stench.

Rosheen stayed to comfort Sharay. She phoned Catherine and asked her to take her place at the meeting, and announce Blanche's death. The emergency council meeting was held without her, at twelve noon. Albeit too late for Blanche and Jarred, the rituals of protection against the evil Blanche had discovered were initiated. And a new High Priestess was selected.

Phoebe, the next in bloodline as Blanche's sister, was not seen as suitable to take up the role. Phoebe had rejected her spiritual inheritance when she was a teenager, in favor of charting her own twisted way in the world of magic. The elders honored Blanche's request, and determined Rosheen would become the temporary holder of the title High Priestess until Sharay came of age and completed her own initiatory rites.

Atop the grassy Chalice Hill knoll, Rosheen turned onto her stomach, lowered her head into her hands, and let out the sobs she had long held in. Eight years of guilt emptied through her tears. She felt she had betrayed Blanche's friendship. More than that, she felt she had betrayed her lineage. She had tried to do the right thing, by the gods she had truly tried. But she had failed in her efforts to maintain contact with Sharay.

Goddess only knew if the girl received the messages she had sent to her through dreams, in desperate attempts to reach her when Phoebe issued the restraining order against her visiting. Rosheen couldn't stand by any longer while Sharay languished in the psychiatric hospital. She felt she had to make up for her failures. That was why she had contacted Dillon and sent him into the hospital, to pose as a psychiatric patient. To help Sharay. If anyone could do it, he could.

She would right this wrong, rectify her omission to Sharay's well being, and make good on her promise to Blanche. Rosheen's chest felt tight and her heart ached.

She stood, knocked her teacup over, spilling its contents onto the grass of Chalice Hill. Swearing, she wiped at her tears with the back of her hand. How could she have allowed things to go this far? She should have stepped in sooner, been more forceful. She should have removed Blanche's daughter from Phoebe's clutches despite the legalities, and most of all, despite the priestess community's rules which barred anyone from interfering with the initiation of another priestess.

The rules dictated that a future High Priestess, even the prophesied emissary, would be given proper training, but must still make her way to her destined role in her own way, in her own time, with her own capabilities. The rules upheld the law of free will.

The process constituted first initiatory rites, testing the individual's character and abilities, her worthiness and strength. Rosheen sighed. In hindsight, she wished she had defied the rules.

Rosheen bent over, picked up her cup, and headed down the Chalice mound toward the cottage. Her remorse clung to her.

While Sharay's birth had been long awaited in their spiritual tradition, there was something important the Prophecy hadn't foretold, Rosheen thought with sadness. What she now knew was that on the day Sharay was birthed, two seeds blossomed. One seed was tender love, nurtured in the hearts of her parents. But the other was of resentment, and it bloomed bitter and dry in the heart of Sharay's Aunt Phoebe. Sharay had come to know the flowering of both.

Still, Rosheen was convinced Sharay was hope for the future. Somewhere within the young woman's tormented mind was a special ability to assist the Goddess. Within her lay the powers to help humanity in their spiritual and physical evolution. But for now Sharay was committed in a psychiatric hospital. Diagnosed schizophrenic. And accused of being a danger to herself and others.

Chapter 9

Rosheen pressed her palms against her red and swollen eyelids before she opened the back door of the Lodge. There wasn't much she could do to hide the fact she had been crying. She sighed, ran her fingers through her disheveled hair, and stepped into the dining room. Catherine and Aneta had let themselves inside and were seated at the dining room table, waiting for her.

Rosheen greeted her fellow priestesses with a forced smile. Catherine was the first to notice her distress. Her brown eyes pierced through Rosheen's facade. Aneta, seated with her back to the door, stood, and spoke before Catherine had the chance to ask questions.

"Rosheen, how peaceful the cottage is today without lodgers." Aneta offered her left hand, waiting for the traditional gesture of blessing and greeting from her High Priestess.

Rosheen returned Aneta's hand gesture, placing her thumb atop the woman's index finger. Aneta fit her index finger on the inside of the Rosheen's palm, the power spot of initiatory transmission, appendage of the heart. Then Aneta opened her arms and hugged Rosheen. Rosheen returned the hug, felt her friend's relaxed nature warm her soul.

It was no accident Aneta's name meant "Celtic water goddess." Along with Aneta's predisposition, she looked the part of a water deity. Now in her early sixties, her wavy long hair was still streaked with ash blond; she had green-blue eyes, a lithe body, and a broad, enchanting smile.

Catherine, appropriately nicknamed Catherine the strong, silently moved into the embrace of her friends. Her appraising gaze never left Rosheen. By contrast to the long-limbed Aneta, Catherine was short, stocky, and athletic. She, too, was in her early sixties. Straight salt-and-pepper hair cut in a bob framed her round face, highlighting her deep set eyes.

Of the three, Rosheen was the oldest by one year. Still, she looked more the age of the priestesses a decade her junior. Perhaps it was her smooth, scarcely wrinkled skin, her slim physique, or rounded bosom. More so it was her spry manner, her lively demeanor. No one but her late husband and her best friend Blanche had known that her seeming vigor was fueled more by nervous energy and an overly critical conscience.

Rosheen leaned away from her friends, but kept her arms around their shoulders. "Thank you for meeting on such short notice. I know my urgency must have been an inconvenience."

While widowed for almost five years, and recently retired from school teaching, Rosheen still appreciated the demands of a busy life.

"It's never an inconvenience when it comes to the affairs of our lineage," the always practical Catherine replied. She pulled away and headed toward the back door, ready to make her way to the Red Well.

Rosheen reached for Catherine's elbow and gently stopped her. "We're not going to the wellspring after all."

Catherine turned, a puzzled expression on her face.

"We'll do our ritual in the Upper Room. There's something there I must show you," Rosheen explained.

Catherine and Aneta exchanged glances. The Upper Room was the space normally delegated to pilgrims with scheduled appointments who wished to meditate or pray in silence. The priestesses rarely met there, preferring to uphold the tradition of ritual held at the Red Well.

When they did use the Upper Room, they did so only for the most critical meetings when they desired utmost privacy.

Rosheen would not disclose more until they were in the seclusion of the Upper Room. Catherine and Aneta followed her up the staircase and past the second floor landing. They stopped at the very top, in front of the aged door to the Upper Room. Rosheen reached up and fumbled for the old brass key left on the top of the doorframe.

She unlocked the creaking door and entered, followed closely by her companions. The perfume of freshly cut white and red roses, placed in vases the day before, mixed with the heady residual of previously burned incense.

The Upper room had the slanted walls of an old attic space, its low roof supported by dark wooden beams that rose at forty-five-degree angles to give a stark triangular outline to the garret. The walls of the long and narrow room were painted a luminous hue of muted gold, and there was a matching amber glass window on the left wall.

The priestesses made their way past two rows of cushioned meditation chairs that faced each other, their chair backs pushed up against the slanted walls. A large pile of brightly colored floor pillows was stacked neatly to the side of the chairs. This section of the room formed a sort of outer sanctum.

A waist-high wooden rail and red curtain divided the room in two. Situated beyond it, in what was considered the middle sanctum, was a rectangular shaped wooden table with twelve wooden stools. The set up fell in theme with the contemporary legends surrounding the wellspring, the ones that had a more Christian overlay. The table commemorated the Last Supper, complete with plates, pottery water pitcher, and a reproduction of the renowned chalice, the Holy Grail.

But it was to the far back wall, towards a three-foot-wide niche, that the priestesses headed. Rosheen pushed aside a tall, potted rubber plant, and stepped on a plank of flooring with the ball of her foot. The back wall of the niche slid open, revealing an unlit room behind it. This was the secret inneher daughter Sar'h from the land of the Jews and settled on Beckery Island in refuge from those who sought to harm her. She venerated a Mother Goddess very similar to our Goddess of the Stars and the Sea. The Magdalene was a priestess of

Isis from the mysterious land we call Egypt. And Egypt was one of the six countries settled and seeded by followers of our Goddess after the demise of Atlantis."

"Oooh!" the children exclaimed. As a student Rosheen had heard the tale many times before. Still, she couldn't stop herself from exclaiming along with the children at Dillon's masterful rendition.

"Mary Magdalene's tradition included many of the teachings of our Goddess. The initiations of Sacred Union and the Sacred Marriage. But because of her physically intimate association with Jeshua the Christ, her lineage was purposefully suppressed by the Christian Church, and driven underground. On Beckery Island, it was eventually replaced by the convent of St. Brighid."

Rosheen inched closer to Dillon, her imagination alive with the magic of the stories. The wellspring gurgled in the background, its perpetually flowing waters bestowing their own form of enchantment.

"During the time of the high priestess Rhianna, the plains surrounding the island of Ynis Witrin grew dry during the summer months. But throughout the winters, the plains were inundated by seawater. The flooding ocean water formed seven islands. The two most notable islands being Beckery and Ynis Witrin. It was during these winter months that the islands were most vulnerable to the raiding parties from across the sea to the west, the tribes of the Irish. It was these Irish marauders who one day landed their boats near the small community of priestesses of the Red Well. It was their first stop on their way up the coast to pilfer and thieve."

The small group sitting around Dillon grew somber.

"The raiders disembarked, leading their shaggy horses offr sanctum of the Upper Room; the concealed section only the priestesses were privy to.

Rosheen ducked under the low doorway and entered the small, ten-by-ten foot space. Her fingers searched along the wall to her left, found the familiar metal ledge that housed a candle and matches.

Once lit, the candle flame illuminated mahogany paneled walls bereft of windows, three unadorned wooden chairs, and a heavily polished, square wooden table of burled oak. A second beeswax candle was positioned on the table's center. Catherine, the last to enter, slid the concealing wall closed. The room smelled of old wood and candle wax.

Rosheen held the candle high, and stepped aside to reveal an unframed scroll, set in a small alcove. The scroll was one of the three prized possessions of the priestesses; the talismanic necklace and the Prophecy parchment were the other two. Fashioned in metal, the words of the scroll had been carefully etched by a blacksmith's hammer and awl seventeen hundred years ago, during the time of the high priestess Rhianna. It commemorated the lives of over fifty priestesses on the horrific occasion when the lineage had nearly been extinguished.

Rosheen remembered well one particular time she'd heard the history of the scroll memorialized. It was the most beautiful commemoration she'd had the privilege to listen to, before, or since.

She was sixteen, and, Dillon, a young bardic priest, was visiting from the mountains of Northern Wales. He was twenty-eight, the age of an apprentice turned full-fledged bard. The Goddess community in Wales recognized his bardic talent and sent him to the all-important Red Well for his official blessings and consecration as a priest. He had been well trained to practice his prose, refining his telling of the stories of the Goddess heritage to preserve the cherished oral traditions.

"What was Glastonbury called during the time of Rhianna?" Aneta had asked Dillon on a cloudless twilight eve over forty-five years before.

A small group of students, along with several consecrated priestesses, including Sharay's grandmother the High Priestess Dana, sat encircled round the Red Well, enjoying Dillon's enchanting rendition of their legends.

"Glastonbury was known as Ynis Witrin back then—it means the isle of glass—because it was surrounded by misty waters that came in from the sea. Even then, Ynis Witrin was sacred land, much like it is to us, today," Dillon replied.

"Tell us about the misty waters, Dillon," Rosheen had eagerly demanded.

"Shh!" cried the other students. Dana put out her hand and smoothed Rosheen's long hair. "Let Dillon finish, Rosheen. There will be plenty of time for questions after he's completed his tale."

Dillon smiled at Rosheen. "Questions are a sign of a keen mind."

Dillon continued, with his practiced bardic intonation. "This land has been sacrosanct to our lineage since the priestess Geodran first led her refugees here upon the Goddess' bidding, after the cataclysmic demise of Atlantis." Dillon paused, winked. "But that is another story for another time."

The children moaned. Dana smiled at their response.

Dillon's gray eyes twinkled. "While the priestesses flourished and kept the lineage of our Goddess alive, other orders of holy men and women also developed their own communities on the island of Ynis Witrin. The powerful Druids made their home here. They worshipped atop the Tor, the same hill that sits right beside us, to the east." Dillon pointed to the Tor, a few hundred yards from the Red Well. "The Druids were stewards of the labyrinth embedded in the very banks and steep slopes of the Tor."

While she couldn't see the Tor labyrinth from where she sat, Rosheen imagined the spirals of the ancient path of initiation she would one day traverse when she became a priestess.

"The Celtic Christian church built its impressive Abbey between the Red Well and Wearyall Hill." Dillon directed his listeners' gaze to the small hill in the distance behind him. "And Wearyall Hill was where Joseph of Arimathea first landed by boat in Ynis Witrin, after the death of his nephew Jesus. Joseph brought the first seeds of the new religion of Christianity to ancient Britain."

Dillon lowered his voice for dramatic effect. "The followers of Mary Magdalene, the beloved wife of Jesus, thrived on the mound west of our Red Well, a place called Beckery Island." Dillon pointed to the area far across the moorlands. "It is said Mary Magdalene traveled with their ships and onto land. Discovering that their landing point was home to a community of priestesses did not stop the Irish bandits from attacking. They raped and slaughtered the women of the Red Well. They nearly decimated the entire community in their massacre. If you listen carefully, and feel very closely, you will find that the land still cries with the remembrances of that day." Dillon put his hands on the ground, closed his eyes, and bent his head down over his knees, so that his forehead touched the earth.

Rosheen followed suit. When she put her forehead to the ground, she saw women clothed in white robes and heard the stamping of horse hooves. She lifted her head quickly to see if anyone else had seen anything. Many of the older priestesses wiped teary eyes.

After a few moments, Dillon resumed his tale. "Rhianna was one of only four survivors. She was entrusted by the Goddess to safeguard the lineage's ancient secrets—secrets passed down from the time of Atlantis. Rhianna was the key to protecting the lineage after the raid; she was the key to strengthening the lineage before the dark times of the Middle Ages ensued, the times when the Goddess was denounced and women were burned for worshipping Her. Rhianna placed a magical veil of mist over the realm of the priestess community in Ynis Witrin to guard its physical safekeeping. In doing so, she protected the continuation of the lineage of the Goddess of the Stars and the Sea. Our lineage survived, and the veil has long been withdrawn. Today we are strong, not only in Glastonbury and northern Wales, but across the globe. Across the globe in each spot where the original six ships from Atlantis had been dispatched to seed new lands with their ancient wisdom."

Dillon's voice rose, carrying with it the waves of emotion he had elicited with his rendering. "We must never forget our purpose. We must always remember our history. Our sisters' blood was shed on this very land. Rhianna fought to be the bridge, the keys to retaining all we had built for eons in service to the Goddess."

Dillon finished in a soft, reverent voice. "The prose of our metal scroll was penned by the high priestess Rhianna as sacred homage to our lineage."

Now years later, in the small inner sanctum of the Upper Room, Rosheen repeated Dillon's concluding words. "We pay homage to our lineage."

She looked deeply into the eyes of her two fellow priestesses, compelling them to remember, too. "Let's read Rhianna's scroll aloud. Let's remember, and in our remembering, acknowledge our lineage and all we strive for."

The three women raised their voices, strong and resonant, and sang out the poem of Rhianna.

I am oldest of old
I am newest of form
I am the spring beneath the hill
I am the waters of the well
I am the sword of the male
I am the yoni of the women
I am the blood red birth
I am the duality of death
I am the Lion's mouth
I am the tree's roots
I am the climber of the hill
I am the descent beneath it
I am the persecutor
I am the slaughtered
I am the vessel for the memories
I am the wail of the mourning
I am the vase for the healing
I am memory re-membered
I am the hope of my lineage
I am the one who once were many
I AM THE CARRIER OF THE FLAME
I am the past and I am future
and my quest is now.

The poem filled Rosheen and washed through her despair. She could almost see the high priestess Rhianna standing before her, red hair blowing in the strong breeze atop the Tor; could feel the rage and anguish that must have torn at Rhianna's heart when her sisters were slaughtered.

She hoped Catherine and Aneta felt as inspired as she. She wondered what Rhianna would do if she were High Priestess now. What would she have done about Sharay?

It was a few moments before any of them spoke. Rosheen lowered herself into one of the chairs and motioned the others to join her. It was time. She had to set things right.

Placing her hands over her heart, Rosheen chanted the opening invocation, her eyes closed, her heart yearning for comfort. "In the name of She whom we honor, we commence our gathering. In devotion, we dedicate ourselves in service to the Goddess of the Stars and the Sea."

Rosheen raised her right hand, placed her index finger and middle finger on her forehead. "We come together in the light of truth." The other two women followed suit, their voices joining with Rosheen's.

"The depth of regeneration." Her fingers moved to touch her pubis.

"The cleansing purification." Lifting her fingers to her right shoulder.

"The expansion of mercy." Fingers to her left shoulder.

"All beings as One." Her fingers drew a circle, beginning from her left shoulder, moving up to her forehead, connecting to her right shoulder, down to her pubis and back up the left side of her body, ending on her forehead.

"In the love and transformative power of the One Heart." Her hands back in their starting position over her heart.

Normally, drawing the circle of invocation on her body catalyzed Rosheen's connection to the Goddess and drew her deeper into the Inner Realms. This morning, her worries wrestled her focus away from the power the invocation raised. She let go of trying to make it work and surrendered herself to it. She began to see and feel the tingle of the outline of the circle traced on her body, a faint electric blue that shimmered and pulsated. Finally, she felt the union of her heart with the One Heart, a warm, expansive sphere of golden energy that radiated from her chest, into her hands, and filled the small room.

She reveled in the golden energy before she opened her eyes and lit the central candle on the table. Its flame was symbol of the central flame present in the core of her being. Again, she breathed deeply, and with her inner awareness, she searched inside herself for the resonance of her central flame with that of the external flame. She felt the warm spark within her core and sensed her connection with every priestess who had ever lit a candle to the Goddess. She was ready.

"There is a matter of urgency," she began.

Her two companions watched her, faces expectant. She knew they trusted her. Rosheen licked her lips, her mouth suddenly dry, and began again. "Allow me to come straight to the point. I'm afraid Sharay's not doing well at all."

"This is why your eyes are swollen and red," Catherine speculated, pointedly.

Rosheen paused before responding, carefully choosing the words that would reveal what the priestesses needed to know. "Yes, Catherine, that's what troubles me. I'm afraid I've made a huge decision without consulting you."

"But that's your prerogative," Aneta said.

Rosheen looked at Aneta. "I sent Dillon into the hospital to help Sharay." There. No longer a secret. Rosheen felt a small measure of relief. Still, guilt refused to release its grip on her stomach.

Aneta's mouth dropped open.

"You sent Dillon?" Catherine's voice did not conceal her surprise.

"Yes. I sent Dillon. It's time to help Sharay. It's long overdue."

Catherine leaned forward. "Rosheen, you know it's not up to us. Sharay will come to the Red Well when she's ready. When she's able. Then we can step in. Then and only then."

"Yes, I know that even our long-awaited priestess must show herself willing and capable of stepping into her responsibilities," Rosheen said.

Catherine interrupted, her brow wrinkled. "It's a matter of free will, a crucial choice not to be tampered with."

"I know the rules of first initiation well enough," Rosheen replied, keeping her voice even.

Rosheen's conscience needled her, her stomach churned. Her pledge to watch over Sharay rang loudly in her ears and echoed in the recesses of her heart. "I promise you, Blanche," she'd vowed. She'd let Blanche down. Aneta and Catherine *must* understand what was at stake. If they would only align with her decision to break the tradition of first initiation, the rest of the priestesses would follow their lead.

"That's why I haven't intervened, magically or practically, until now. But even my most fervent prayers haven't been answered. You see, I've been remiss in a higher obligation. Sharay is our prophesied emissary." Rosheen's voice was no longer able to mask her desperation.

"But what if Sharay can't live up to what we believe her to be. Look at Phoebe. She never measured up. Consider that, Rosheen," Catherine countered.

Rosheen paused and gazed at the candle flame in the center of the table. True, young Phoebe had been expected to become a priestess of the Red Well when she began her bleeding times. But Phoebe grew twisted with resentment and never followed through with her training. Her jealousy over Dillon's predictions that Blanche would be the one to birth the prophesied child poisoned her.

Her meditations grew degenerate, and in her envy, she turned away from all that she was born into. The same power that flowed through the veins of Geodran, the first priestess of the Red Well, ran through Phoebe, as well as it did through Blanche. The difference was that Blanche embraced it.

Rosheen looked up. "Yes, Phoebe was a great disappointment. And now she's let Sharay's raw powers go untamed and untrained, causing imbalance in the one we've long awaited."

"Is it possible Sharay is not the one?" Catherine asked.

"No," Rosheen answered firmly.

She continued. "Phoebe casts a web of deceit I never dreamed she was capable of. But I adhered to our tradition. I convinced myself that when the time was right, Sharay would answer her call to destiny. I waited." Rosheen looked directly into Catherine's eyes. "I was wrong," she said, her voice resolute.

Aneta reached out and took Rosheen's hand. "You did what you thought best."

Rosheen didn't feel reassured. "Blanche begged me to watch over Sharay. I should have been more forceful in my attempts to reach her when Phoebe took guardianship. I should have invoked powerful magic. Sharay was too young when Blanche died. She doesn't have the proper preparation to harness the power that surges through her," Rosheen said.

"If only Phoebe had stayed true to her lineage," Aneta said.

Catherine folded her arms across her chest. "We mustn't interfere. It's imperative Sharay comes to us on her own. Meddling will only serve to force her before she's ripened."

Rosheen shook her head. "We need to get Sharay out of that hospital before it's too late."

Aneta's gaze moved from Rosheen to Catherine and back again.

Rosheen felt her frustration mounting, the sting of tears in her eyes. "Sharay carries the ancient remembrance of the starlight initiation. She's the only one who can invoke it."

Catherine paused, sighed. "Rosheen, I can't deny that. But first things first. Let's focus on your reason for gathering us—your decision to send Dillon into the hospital. You sought my opinion. With all respect, sending Dillon in to help Sharay is intervening, plain and simple. We must stick to the wisdom of our tradition."

Rosheen didn't wish to quarrel further. She would use her last and best argument.

She stood. "I want to show you something."

Aneta's brow furrowed and Catherine's arms remained crossed over her chest. Rosheen reached underneath the lip of the table edge, found the small silver key nestled in a groove. She slid her chair back and knelt on the floor. A precise sequence of numbers ran through her mind. One, two, three, five, eight . . . the Fibonacci sequence, the numbers of the golden ratio. Crawling on her hands and knees, index finger pointed, she silently counted the narrow floor planks in accordance with the number sequence paired with a memorized pattern of directions—forward one, left two, forward three, right five, forward eight.

She finally stopped at a point to the left of Catherine's chair. The eighth floor plank in the sequence was loose. Wiggling it to and fro, Rosheen lifted it. Underneath was a metal box, tarnished with age. Rosheen reached in, picked it up, and lifted it onto the table. She stood, her trembling hand resting on the lid.

"Rosheen?" Catherine's tone was questioning.

Rosheen lifted her hand, palm forward. "Trust me."

Aneta's eyes opened wide with surprise. Every priestess knew of the contents of the silver box, but had seen them only during their initiation into the priestesshood. Due to the sanctity of the items within, and their age, further viewing was a privilege reserved only for a High Priestess. The box had held two ancient relics of the lineage— the talismanic necklace, wrapped in deep blue silken gauze that had not disintegrated in the thousands of years since its creation, and the

Prophecy parchment that predicted humanity's emergence from dark, tumultuous times into an era of great brilliance and peace, an era of spiritual and physical evolution.

The parchment itself, though inscribed onto a thin piece of leather, was nevertheless delicate. It was kept in an airtight box, inside the larger silver one. Rosheen unlocked the box with the silver key. She slowly lifted its lid, retrieved the pair of white gloves nestled on top, and wriggled her hands into them. Gingerly, she lifted the airtight container that held the parchment, and carefully opened it. Inside, rolled cylindrically, lay the revered Prophecy parchment. Rosheen had only seen the parchment twice before. It made her heart race each time she viewed it.

Delicately, she unrolled the parchment. Her breath caught in her throat with the weight of what she was about to do. Aneta and Catherine stood alongside her and edged in close.

The parchment represented the hope of the lineage, what they all aspired to partake in. It held everything Rosheen was fighting to preserve. She read it aloud—reverently, firmly, lovingly.

I am old and I am new
I am sister of the suns, mother of the moons
I am Geodran, first priestess of the Goddess
I am Rhianna, vessel to preserve the ancient memories
I am yet to be reborn.
I bring forth the Divinity within form
the Sacred Feminine, Divine Mother
I carry pearlescent seeds of star light
within my flesh
I answer the ancient call
of She who sees to the spiritual evolution of humankind,
beloved Goddess of the Stars and the Sea
I am yet to be reborn
When darkness reigns
and chaos seems to rule the world
I will return
Portent of the rightful destiny of humanity,
of the era of peace

of the perfected body of starlight
born of the Love within all matter
I am yet to be reborn
I am emissary of the Goddess
I beseech you, daughters of my lineage,
anticipate my arrival
For I herald the advent of She who will light our
way
Merging the infinite above
with the infinite within—
the Goddess of the Stars and the Sea.
I am mid-wife to this new era
I am yet to be reborn.
I beseech you—look for me
I will be born silver of hair
I will bear the mark of the Goddess;
the six-pointed star upon the nape of my neck
I hold the knowledge to awaken
the power of the stars
the power of love
within the body
I am the awakening
I am the keys to remember
I answer the ancient call
I herald the shift of the ages
I call upon you
as the Goddess has called upon me
Together we will serve Her
Together we will birth a new humanity
Together we will carry on the flame
to a new dawn.

Energy filled the small room, a palpable presence that made it almost difficult to breathe. The power spot in Rosheen's womb burned hot, her feet and legs tingled. Warm tears left a salty track down her cheeks. She hadn't realized she had been crying. She lifted her gaze, looked at the others. Aneta silently sobbed, her hand covering her mouth. Catherine's lips were gently parted.

Rosheen spoke softly. "The signs are clear. We live in dark, chaotic times. The silver-haired Sharay has been reborn with the star shaped birthmark on the nape of her neck. The degeneration we witness in the world is presage to a new dawn. Sharay is critical to this shift. With her, with the help of the lineage and the guidance of the Goddess, humanity can step fully into an era of spiritual development. We can face our darkest challenges and deepest fears and make this a better world."

Rosheen meticulously rolled the parchment, placed it in its container, and removed the white gloves from her hands. She waited for the others to respond to her plea.

Aneta was the first to speak. "What has Dillon found out about Sharay?"

Rosheen smiled. At least Aneta aligned with her now. "He does all he set out to do. He reports Sharay has the memories and hears the calling. But instead of using that to garner her strength and prove herself sane and capable, she doubts herself and her visions of the Goddess. The medicine and the hospital wear her down. I'm afraid Phoebe's plan to weaken Sharay is working."

"Don't you see you could be making things worse for Sharay by intervening? She can't be forced before her time." There was no contentiousness in Catherine's voice, only compassion.

Rosheen closed her eyes, remembering the ominous images that had plagued her meditations for weeks now. "I've felt something in my meditations. We need to get Sharay out of that hospital and away from Phoebe."

"I support your decision, Rosheen. Phoebe has pushed too far. We need to help Sharay," Aneta declared.

Catherine shook her head slowly. "I respect you, Rosheen. And your guidance. But, I'm afraid I don't agree. This may be Sharay's greatest challenge, the test to fortify her. She must overcome her hardships. She must win over Phoebe and take on her own inner demons."

"Of course. But she doesn't have to do so alone, poor girl," Rosheen said. "If we lose Sharay, we all lose. Our lineage fails in its purpose. More importantly, humankind loses."

"I need to know one thing for certain." Catherine looked Rosheen square in the eye. "What motivates you? Is it guilt, or is it guidance?"

Rosheen took an involuntary step back. "It's true, Catherine. I've felt guilt." She swallowed thickly. "But I've felt guidance, too."

Catherine's gaze remained on Rosheen.

"Look inside the box," Rosheen ordered, her mouth set in a grim line.

"But only you can handle our cherished possessions," Aneta said.

"Today is a day for breaking tradition," Catherine said.

"Look inside the box," Rosheen repeated.

Catherine stepped forward and peered inside the large metal container. She raised her head, a startled look upon her face.

"To my knowledge, the box hasn't been opened for almost eighteen years. Since Sharay's birth," Rosheen said quietly. "I checked the box two days ago. I wanted to read the Prophecy parchment. I wanted to validate my intuitions, my ominous dreams, my worries." She paused, her gaze level with Catherine's. "That's when I made the discovery."

"Who'd do such a thing?" Catherine asked.

"Do what?" Aneta asked.

Catherine answered, her tone soft for the first time. "The box is empty."

"What?" Aneta cried.

Rosheen nodded and replied, her voice hollow. "Our talisman necklace has been stolen."

Chapter 10

"Ouch!" Sharay woke with a start.

Nurse Claire bent over her and detached the Velcro closure on the blood pressure cuff, releasing its tourniquet effect on Sharay's arm.

"I'm glad to see you're awake. You've been asleep for most of the afternoon."

Sharay rubbed her upper arm and allowed Claire to put her fingers on the inside of her wrist to take her pulse. She noticed, with relief, there were no restraints binding her arms and legs.

Fully awake now, memories of the strange encounter with Dillon earlier that morning flooded in. She recalled the old man's thunderous recitation of the mysterious poem and the surprise of her voice joining in. Images paraded before her eyes—the Tarot card, the Red Wellspring, and the women in white robes with their blood seeping into the ground beneath them.

Sharay squirmed in her bed with a gnawing sense of unease and urgency. She had to speak with the old man again. While she wasn't sure if she was furious or fascinated by him, she knew he held answers to questions she didn't even know she had before she met him.

"Is something wrong, Sharay?" Claire asked.

"I want to get up," Sharay replied, her words slurred from too much medicine. She wondered if her tongue would ever fit her mouth again.

"All right, but let me help you." Claire put her arm under Sharay's back and helped her to sit up.

The room spun and swirled around Sharay. Closing her eyes only made things worse. She slowly edged over to the side of the bed.

"Easy does it," Claire advised, her hand still around Sharay's waist.

Feeling lightheaded, Sharay's frustration mounted with her leg's failure to cooperate. She heaved an exasperated sigh. The warrior lion that had sprung to life inside her—her totem that she'd unleashed during the dayroom melee—growled. It was growing strong, fueling her courage. While part of her craved the safety and protection of the black hole, her totem insisted she stand up and find Dillon.

"Where is Dillon?"

Claire looked at her blankly. "Dillon?"

A vice-like grip clenched Sharay's heart. Had she hallucinated the whole incident? "Dillon Emrys. The old man in the dayroom," she stammered.

"Sharay, you must've gotten his name wrong. The man's name is Thomas Emrick." Claire paused. "Perhaps you should stay clear of him for a few days. The two of you didn't mix very well. Do you remember any of that?"

"Of course I remember," Sharay snapped, confused yet relieved Dillon was real.

The nurses couldn't keep her from Dillon or Thomas or whoever he was. She needed explanations—the meaning of the visions the poem catalyzed, the haunting familiarity of the poem itself.

Sharay took a deep breath and stood. Her legs promptly buckled under her. Damn the injections, she thought.

"Whoa, Sharay. This isn't such a good idea yet," Claire cautioned. She held Sharay by the elbow, her strong arms supporting her so she didn't slide to the floor.

Sharay shook her elbow free. She had to climb up and out of the medicine saturated black hole in order to get to Dillon. In her mind's eye she could see the golden eyes and tawny mane of her lion totem and could hear its roar encouraging her to fight the black hole.

Claire spoke to her. Sharay wasn't listening. Inch by inch, she clawed her way up the slippery walls of the black hole. Her effort reminded her of clutching the bushes and brambles on the steep hillside she used to climb when her father took her hiking. One hand at a time, one foot slowly placed above the other. But the black hole wouldn't relinquish her easily, and the medicine patrolled the hole's perimeter.

Sharay slipped, her hands groped the slick walls of the hole, her feet searched to find a toehold. The lion roared in her mind, energizing her efforts to try again.

The room spun. Sharay felt the black hole seize her legs with wraith-like tendrils. Claire forced her to sit back on the bed. She pushed against Claire's grip. A voice caught her attention. She stopped resisting, and tilted her head to hear more clearly. It was a man's voice.

"Don't fight." Unmistakably Dillon's voice, yet Dillon was nowhere to be seen.

His booming voice spoke again. "Settle down and I'll give you your answers."

Feeling compelled to obey, Sharay clung to the totem lion's thick mane within her.

"Everything will be okay. Just follow what I say," Dillon's voice instructed.

Sharay leaned back against her pillow. In her mind, she saw her totem lion curl next to her side.

"Apologize to Claire."

The lion's eyes told her to trust the voice.

"I'm sorry Claire. I'm okay now. I won't fight you."

Claire hesitated. She kept her hands on Sharay's shoulders.

"Really, Claire. You can let go of me. I promise I'll rest here until I am stronger. I won't fight you."

A brilliant plan. The sooner Claire left, the sooner she would be free to find Dillon.

Claire hesitated and tentatively smiled. "There. You see? It is so much better when you don't struggle."

Sharay forced herself to smile back. She was learning the game. She would appear to cooperate. Claire fluffed her pillow, gave her a glass of water, and made small talk. Sharay nodded her head at the appropriated points and bided her time. Finally, Claire picked up her stethoscope and left the room, saying she would return later to check on Sharay.

Sharay waited a moment for Claire to clear the hall and then moved with resolve. Ignoring her lightheadedness, she again fought the pull of the black hole.

A strong hand, the wrinkled hand of Dillon, reached down the hole. Sharay stretched toward him, let him pull her up and out of the hole.

The hole was displeased. It reminded her she'd sworn allegiance to its shadowy protection. Sharay didn't care. She didn't care if she drooled like an idiot or shuffled like an old lady. She was out of the hole for the time being and she was standing. She made her way to her bedroom door. She felt the cold touch of steel as she put her hand out to steady herself. Once in the hall, she checked to see if anyone was there. All was clear. She shut her door behind her, and slowly tottered past the patient bedrooms. Cautiously peeking in each one, she searched for Dillon, hoping he hadn't gone into the dayroom yet. Praying Claire wouldn't catch her, her heart racing, she was halfway down the hall when she spotted him. He was sitting in a chair, his back to the door, staring out the window.

"Took you long enough," he said, keeping his back to her.

His nonchalance angered her. The lion inside her stood to attention.

"What do you mean?" she retorted in her medicine induced slur. "It is because of you I was jabbed again with enough medicine to down a horse. I'd like to see you walk in my condition."

Dillon turned to face her, the wrinkles round his eyes creasing, though he didn't laugh aloud.

Sharay entered the room and closed the door behind her. "Who are you? Thomas or Dillon? How'd you talk to me when you weren't in my room?"

Dillon raised his hand, motioning for her to be still. He stared hard at her, his gaze reached deep inside her. She felt the pit of her stomach contract; the black hole closed in on itself, hiding from his scrupulous appraisal. Sharay gazed back in fascination. His deep set eyes held a depth of being. A reflection of experience in the magical Inner Realms that crossed beyond the borders of everyday existence.

"You've no right to stir me up so . . ." Sharay's voice trailed off. She sat on his bed, her anger at him suddenly dissipated. The totem lion of her soul curled at her feet.

"Now then. The name is Dillon, just like I told you. What else would you like to know?" Dillon crossed one leg over the other and folded his hands on his lap.

"Well, for one thing . . ." she began. Much to her surprise and horror, Sharay began to sob.

Temporarily outside the boundaries of the black hole, years of grief and pent up rage emptied through her tears. Finally, after several minutes or several hours, she couldn't be sure, she reached emptiness.

When she lifted her head, she realized she was kneeling beside Dillon. He gently stroked her hair.

"I know," he said.

Sharay felt cleansed and fresh, for the first time in a long time. She hiccupped.

"Tahnea," Dillon murmured.

"What?"

"It means, silver haired one."

Sharay hiccupped again, wiped her wet cheek on her sleeve. "What am I to do, Dillon?"

"About the hiccups?" The smile in Dillon's twinkling eyes reached his lips, his mouth curving into a wide grin.

Sharay rolled her eyes. "No, silly. What am I to do about this?" she said, spreading her arms wide open to indicate the room, the psychiatric hospital.

"Simple. You're to go on an Imram."

"On a what?" She leaned back on her legs, and sat on the floor, her spine against the side of Dillon's bed for support. She was exhausted, and Dillon was talking in riddles.

"On an Imram. It's an important journey. A physical journey navigated by your soul."

"My soul will navigate a journey?"

"Yes—it will be both an inner and an outer journey. The Imram is the outward form of an inner mystical journey. It's much like a vision quest. You'll travel the land, and as you do, you'll visit the Inner Realms of your dreams and visions."

"But they call my dreams and visions hallucinations."

"They know nothing."

Sharay stared, wide-eyed. "I'm not hallucinating?"

"Of course not."

Sharay noticed how his dimples burrowed deep within the crevices of his cheeks.

"The Imram will be a splendid adventure. Just like it was for our ancestors, the Celts. They crossed the seas on mythic travels to foreign lands. They went on the Imram."

Sharay imagined huge wooden boats, mermaids carved on the bow, sailing by star navigation across deep blue waters, heading far into the west. She shook her head. "I'm afraid I'm in no shape to go on a sea voyage. I don't see how your Imram will help me."

Dillon chuckled. "The Imram is not limited to the sea. It's not about where you go but how you get there."

"So, how do I get there?"

"Trust the Imram. You're in good hands with your soul as your navigator."

"How can I go on an Imram? I can't even leave this hospital," Sharay said desolately.

"Indeed, you've been made a prisoner." Dillon's face grew serious. "Still, the grimmest place you are imprisoned is in the depths of that black hole inside you."

The tendrils from the black hole reached out seductively.

"You don't need the black hole, Sharay. It will do you more harm than good. But I'm afraid extricating yourself from it will prove even more difficult than freeing you from this hospital."

"I can be free of it if I want to," she said defiantly. She didn't for a moment believe her own lie. The hole was strong on its own now, but especially so when combined with the medicine. Sharay swallowed, remembering her promise to it.

Dillon gazed at her intently and then waved his hand. "First things first. We have your Imram to plan."

Despite her unease, Sharay felt excitement flutter in her chest.

"We won't use a boat. A van will do nicely. We're no longer in ancient times, you know." He winked at her.

"I'm going on an Imram, traveling through my dreams and hallucinations . . . I mean, my visions . . . and I'm going in a van?" Sharay asked skeptically.

"Yes," Dillon answered matter of factly. "Now, how do we get you out of the hospital?" Dillon pulled on his beard, deep in concentration.

"Who's the *we* you're referring to?" Sharay asked, dabbing spittle from the corner of her mouth.

"Well, I suppose this is my idea alone. Rosheen only asked me to come check on you, nothing further."

"Rosheen?" Sharay asked eagerly. "You know Rosheen?"

"Why, yes, of course. I've known Rosheen since she was a child."

"You must have known my mother, too," Sharay said with longing.

"Indeed," Dillon replied gently. "She was an incredible priestess."

A thought suddenly occurred to Sharay and it sparked her anger. The lion inside her lifted its head. "If Rosheen knew I was in here, why didn't she help me?"

Dillon waited a moment before answering. "I'm afraid that is a long story, a complicated one fraught with tradition and rules. And your Aunt Phoebe's meddling. But, Rosheen sent me here, and I'm with you now. And I'm going to get you out of here."

Dillon grew quiet again, deep in thought. Sharay put her head in her hands. Her thoughts jumbled, this new information stirring up the remnants of her old life, when her parents were still alive. A time when visions were accepted as commonplace, expected and encouraged. No one called her psychotic and dangerous then.

"Aha," Dillon cried.

Sharay lifted her head and found Dillon gazing at her, a mischievous grin spreading across his face. "To plan your escape, I'll need the help of my grandson." Dillon beamed. "Yes. I'll call on Guethyn to help us."

Sharay began to worry about the mysterious plan Dillon was making. Imrams and soul journeys and grandsons with odd names. "What kind of name is Guethyn?"

"Welsh, of course. As I told you, I come from the north of Wales. My daughter and my grandson have Welsh names. None other would do."

Dillon's eyes appeared unfocused and he gazed far into the distance. He whispered. "Yes. Best to act normal, like nothing unusual is happening. We should leave soon."

"When?"

"Within the next few days. A week at the most. Oh, one more thing. Remember to cheek your medicine. You need to be as clear of head and light of foot as possible."

Amidst the first hope she had felt in years, a shudder ran down Sharay's spine. "Are you really going to help me escape? Or, are you just crazy?"

Dillon answered with another of his mischievous grins. "Both."

Phoebe entered the reception area and closed the door behind her. The room hadn't changed much in the last six months since she had delivered Sharay into Dr. Deluth's care. The same three floral pictures yellowed with age hung on the far wall. There was the receptionist's desk and the odd assortment of worn leather armchairs. Mrs. Hansen was at lunch and Phoebe waited on her own for the doctor.

Everything was going as planned. Dr. Deluth's medical evaluation had recommendation long term treatment for Sharay. As such, the courts found her incompetent to handle her legal affairs. Phoebe now owned full rights to Sharay's inheritance.

Even Larry was quiet and cooperative. She just needed to take care of the small matter of Dr. Deluth's latest phone message. He'd informed her he had noted some minor improvements in Sharay's condition.

He'd requested she and Larry come to his office to discuss the new developments.

Phoebe picked up a magazine, tossed it back on the end table, and sat in one of the leather chairs. She tapped her foot impatiently and stopped to admire the gold bracelet she had purchased yesterday.

Hand extended out, she noticed the letters S-h-a-r-a-y etched into the mahogany surface of the chair arm.

Phoebe frowned. She felt a compulsion to rub out the name. Taking a handkerchief from her purse, she folded it in half and rubbed it over the letter S. A sensation of warmth emanated from the carved letter through the folds of the handkerchief. Phoebe dismissed it and rubbed again. It was definite this time. The letter radiated subtle warmth. She pulled her hand away and stared at the letters with a furrowed brow. The girl had magical protection. It was new, a strong force that hadn't been there before.

"Who watches over you, Sharay?" she murmured.

Her mouth set in a determined line; she wadded the handkerchief in a ball and tried again, this time rubbing harder. The crudely etched letters refused to be worn down.

"Don't mock me, Sharay," she cautioned in a harsh whisper.

The letters remained, taunting her.

"All right. I'll fight magic with magic. When I return home," Phoebe muttered.

"Mr. and Mrs. Wentworth?" Dr. Deluth's brusque voice called to her from the inner office.

Phoebe startled when she heard him.

"Come," he said curtly.

She fluffed her hair with her fingers and entered the doctor's office. Philip Deluth stood beside his file cabinet, Sharay's chart in hand. Good, Phoebe thought, moving forward quickly, hand extended. Best to keep him from sitting behind the desk that would only separate the two of them. Dr. Deluth shook her hand cordially, his eyes coming to rest on her ample cleavage. He coughed and averted his gaze.

"Is Mr. Wentworth not with you?" he asked, glancing behind her.

"He couldn't come this time. Work conflict. Oh, good, you have Kleenex," Phoebe bent over and reached for a tissue on his desk, angling her chest to give Dr. Deluth a more generous view.

Dr. Deluth's face reddened.

Phoebe pulled a tissue from its box and faced him. "Doctor, I do apologize. I'm just so worried about Sharay." She sniffled and dabbed her eyes with the tissue. "I'm afraid my concern overwhelms me at times. You understand, don't you?" She placed her hand on his jacket lapel.

Dr. Deluth grabbed the edge of his desk. "Mrs. Wentworth, let me come to the point," he stammered. "In our previous meetings, I'm afraid all I could offer you was bad news. Now I finally have something positive to share about Sharay."

"Positive?" Phoebe asked, feigning an optimistic smile.

"Yes. It's a small gain, mind you." Dr. Deluth paused. "Over the last few days, Sharay has been more cooperative. Perhaps now, after six months, she's finally beginning to respond to treatment."

Phoebe stiffened. "She is?"

"Most of my patients do, eventually. Some just take longer than others." Dr. Deluth slowly edged his body along the desk, sliding away from Phoebe.

Phoebe stepped closer, leaned into the doctor, and allowed her tears to flow more freely. "I'm so relieved," she said. "You don't know what it's been like to worry. And to fear for my life. Do you really mean the danger is over? Sharay will no longer threaten to kill me?"

Dr. Deluth patted Phoebe awkwardly on the back. "You're safe with Sharay in the hospital, Mrs. Wentworth."

"Call me Phoebe."

Dr. Deluth ignored the request. "If Sharay dutifully stays on her medicine, those threats may subside. I can't promise anything, but she might eventually be able to return home."

Phoebe lowered her head against the doctor's chest, hiding her alarm. "Can you guarantee me she won't harm me ever again," she said.

"Ever again?" Dr. Deluth asked. "I thought you told me she had threatened you, not actually physically hurt you."

"I was afraid to mention it, afraid it wouldn't look good on Sharay's record. But, yes, she beat me more than once in a crazy rage. It was only Larry's intervention that stopped her." Phoebe lifted her head and raised her chin so that her mouth was inches away from the doctor's. "Do you see now why I'm so frightened?"

Dr. Deluth took in a sharp breath.

Phoebe slipped her arm around his neck. "Please assure me, doctor. Tell me she won't hurt me again," she pleaded. She brushed her lips against his, tasted his desire.

Dr. Deluth pulled away. "Mrs. Wentworth." His face was flushed. "I can't promise you. All I'm saying is, based on Sharay's recent behavior; she's finally showing some progress."

Dr. Deluth quickly moved to the opposite side of the desk. "In due time, if she stays on her medication, there is a good chance she'll never hurt you again."

He looked down at his paperwork.

Phoebe clenched her fists at her side. The insult of his rejection was nothing compared to the immense problem she now faced.

"I'm sorry, Dr. Deluth. I lost myself in the strain of all I've been through. I don't find the reassurance I need in my husband, and now I'm so embarrassed. I should never have turned to you as I did. Please forgive me." Phoebe smoothed out the wrinkles in her skirt and folded her hands demurely in front of her.

The doctor slowly looked up. "Nothing happened here. You're merely under great tension," he said in a clipped tone.

"Yes, I am. But I must admit I'm still very frightened of what Sharay is capable of."

Dr. Deluth impatiently shuffled the pages he held. "I would never release Sharay from her commitment papers if I believed she was dangerous."

"Of course not. Then I look forward to the day when Sharay is cured."

"There is no cure for schizophrenia, Mrs. Wentworth. But I am more hopeful we may be able to manage her symptoms."

Phoebe nodded, smiled sweetly. "I'm delighted."

Dr. Deluth stared hard at her, said nothing. Phoebe met his gaze.

He took his glasses off and laid them on his desk. "I understand you're concerned for your safety, Mrs. Wentworth. But I have to say, I'm somewhat puzzled by your response to Sharay's updated prognosis."

Phoebe reached for the door handle behind her. "Please understand—after what I've been through, I'm afraid I find it difficult to trust her." She added, in her most gracious tone, "I sincerely appreciate the excellent medical care Sharay's receiving. Now, good day."

Swinging the door shut behind her, Phoebe pushed aside her panic. She couldn't let Dr. Deluth's latest prognosis stop her now. She exited the reception area and marched resolutely down the tiled halls of the medical building. Her mind was already formulating plans to make up for today's loss. Phoebe's mouth pursed tight. Yes, this had been a major setback to her plans. But the battle was far from over.

Chapter II

Rosheen was jolted from sleep. Her cry echoed throughout the empty house, floated out her open bedroom window. Though the night air was mild, the chill in her room was unmistakable. She pulled her covers tightly about her as if their cotton threads could weave a protective shield.

Steadying the scream that caught in her throat, she peered into the darkness of her bedroom. The new moon's crescent cup barely illuminated her reading chair and lamp, her chest of drawers, her looming wardrobe. It was into their shadows that she cast her practiced gaze, looking for signs of who had invaded her dream state, clawing at her through the gateway of sleep.

Rosheen was well trained, had paid scrupulous attention to the magical arts of psychic defense after Blanche had been pursued and murdered. She suspected her friend's death was no accident. She could never prove it by the investigative methods the police employed. Still, she knew what she knew. Tonight she sensed the same menace that had shadowed Blanche tracking her through her own dreams. The fetid smell of a conjured demonic entity tainted her nostrils and choked her supply of fresh air. She raised her hands from under the covers to cough, to banish the stench.

Hands covering her face, a sticky wetness trickled down her right arm and pooled in the inside curve of her elbow.

Rosheen leapt out of bed and switched on the tiny lamp beside her reading chair. Her body trembled uncontrollably and she sank slowly into the chair. She pushed back the now tattered sleeves of her nightgown, exposing her arm to the stark lamplight. There were three deep scratches on her forearm. Just like on Blanche's—the night before she was killed.

Sharay crept quietly down the hospital hallway towards Dillon's room. She had been cheeking her medicine as Dillon taught her and could already feel a small measure of her surreal, medicated haze lifting.

The Thorazine fashioned police guard that had patrolled her black hole had thinned. Her thoughts were clearer. Voices sounded less like they came from inside tin cans, overhead lights didn't bother her as much, she could form a cohesive sentence without garbling her words, and best of all, she didn't drool nearly as much.

Sharay stopped when she heard conversation from inside Dillon's room. The nurses didn't want her to associate with him, and Sharay didn't wish to give them cause to watch over her any more closely than they already did. She was about to turn away, but paused when she heard her name mentioned.

"You mean I drove all the way from University of Wales to help you free a crazy woman?"

Sharay didn't recognize the man's voice but it was definitely Dillon who responded with a chuckle.

"Sharay is no crazier than you or I. Well—no crazier than you at least."

Sharay imagined Dillon's eyes twinkling, his dimples forming two deep crevices in his cheeks. His humor seemed to have no effect on the man he was talking to.

"That's not funny, grandfather."

"Hmm. When did you lose your sense of humor?"

"This isn't about me." Sharay heard an exasperated sigh from Dillon's visitor. "I can't believe I drove here for this."

"Well, you're here now. So, you'll help me?" Dillon asked.

"I didn't say that," the man replied, his voice gentle but resolute. "I'm right in the middle of my graduate thesis.

"I wouldn't have called unless it was extremely important."

"Important to you hasn't always meant urgent." The man paused. "The final draft of my thesis is due in two days. Now, that's important. Can't this wait?"

"No."

Sharay peeked around the corner of the metal doorframe. Her gaze tracked a long black scuff mark across the tiled floor, ending at the heels of the visitor's polished leather boots. His green flannel shirt, sleeves rolled up on sunburned forearms, was tucked into long-legged, tight-fitting blue jeans. Sharay liked how his tawny hair was tied into a thick ponytail. It reminded her of her totem lion's shaggy mane.

Dillon, facing the door, spotted her. He crossed his arms over his chest, and slowly circled round his visitor, his movements compelling the young man to turn with him. Though maneuvered to face the door, the visitor's face was still blocked from Sharay's view.

"I can't help you this time. I'm sorry, but I've got too much at stake to go on another quest with you."

"You're already here."

"I'm leaving."

"Wait." Dillon stepped aside.

Sharay pulled back. Too late to go unnoticed.

"Guethyn, meet Sharay."

Sharay stepped out from behind the door, suddenly conscious of the spots of dried spittle on the shoulders of her sweater. She bent her head downward and her long hair draped over her face.

"Oh, come on grandfather, this isn't fair." Guethyn proffered a reluctant hand in Sharay's direction.

Sharay stole a look through her hair at Guethyn. He was the image of a young Dillon—the same thin face, the same deep set dimples. Only Guethyn's dimples weren't in smiling mode. But it was his eyes that riveted her attention. Blue. The color and depth of a sun caressed ocean. She wanted to say something intelligent or witty but nothing came to mind. She lifted her head and held out her hand in return instead.

When Guethyn's fingers met her handshake he cried out. "What the hell?" He swiftly pulled his right hand away, rubbed it with his left. "What's going on here?"

Sharay had felt the same jolt charge up her arm. Guethyn's handshake inexplicably drew her into a strange and different reality.

Before she could stop it, she saw herself career head first into this alternate reality, and plunge into the interior of an immense conch shell. She spiraled around, shimmied faster and faster through curving cylinders of seashell passageways. With each encircling turn, she pulled out traces of ancient memories until finally, she dropped into the shell's center. There, the ancient memories sprang to life.

Full color images of a man with the same blue eyes as Guethyn. Images of herself with the same silver-blond hair but wearing flowing robes made of a mysterious blue cloth. The two of them, lying entwined in each other's arms on the shoreline of a vast ocean where the gentle lullaby of the waves kissed the shore as tenderly as the man kissed her body.

The ache of sexual desire, fulfilled in the arms of the man with blue eyes. The sound of a thousand silver bells infused the sea mist.

"Sharay?"

Dillon's voice startled Sharay back into acute awareness of Guethyn's presence, close beside her in Dillon's room. She couldn't help but stare at him. His eyes held frustration and confusion. So different from the loving gaze of the man she'd just seen in her inner vision. The contrast pierced her heart. She reeled back against the door, hand over her mouth. Uncontrollable sobs rose up from the poignant ancient memories.

Dillon stepped toward her and folded her in his arms.

"Hallucination," Sharay murmured into the curve of his shoulder.

"No hallucination, Tahnea. It's real," Dillon whispered.

"Real?" Sharay looked up, searched for reassurance in Dillon's eyes.

"Is there a problem?" a curt voice asked.

Sharay froze and belatedly tried to compose herself.

"No problems here, Mr. Millworth. Sharay is fine." Dillon's tone was firm.

Mr. Millworth's hand unconsciously went to his groin, his body remembering the painful kick that landed there the last time Sharay was uncontrollably upset. "She doesn't look fine. I thought she was supposed to stay clear of you."

Sharay clutched Dillon's shoulder. When she spoke, her voice was tremulous. "Mr. Millworth, there's no need to be concerned."

Mr. Millworth hesitated for only a moment. "To be sure, let's take you back to your room."

In Sharay's mind's eye, the totem lion inside her raised his head high. "I'd like to stay here," she said, her voice now steady.

"I said, you need to come with me," Millworth said determinedly.

"Enough, Dr. Millworth." Dillon's tone was commanding.

Millworth's head jerked up. His demeanor registered anger and shock. "I'm afraid you're not the doctor here, Thomas." He reached out for Sharay's elbow.

"Who's Thomas?" Guethyn said, turning to Dillon.

"Let go of me." Sharay jerked away from the intern's grasp. "One more move like that, and I'll let the lion loose."

"The lion? Okay. I've heard all I need. You're hallucinating and you'll be better off in your own room. Really, Sharay." Dr. Millworth leaned back into the hallway, raised his hand and beckoned a psychiatric assistant from the nursing station, who promptly rushed to his aid.

Wordlessly, the intern and assistant each took one of Sharay's arms and pinned them to her back.

"Wait. She's done nothing," Guethyn said.

Dillon put a restraining arm on his grandson's shoulder and leaned over to Sharay. "Don't put up a fight," he whispered.

Her best efforts to subdue herself warred with her rage. Rage won.

Guethyn heard her scream all the way down the hall to her room. He turned to his grandfather.

"I'll help you."

Chapter 12

Dillon sat on the tattered sofa in the dayroom beside fidgety Mrs. Feeney, conversing with her in whispered tones. He stole a glance at her wristwatch. Seven o'clock in the evening. The height of hospital visiting hours.

At the nursing station, the young ward secretary smiled. "Hello Guethyn. Thomas will be glad to see you. I thought . . . I mean he thought you might not be coming this evening."

She handed him a pen so he could sign the visitor log-in sheet. She let her fingers graze his before she let go.

Guethyn looked up, still not accustomed to his grandfather's fabricated name, even more surprised at the ward secretary's flirtations.

"Hello, Connie," he mumbled.

He glanced down at the desk, noting she pushed a red buzzer right beside the phone to unlock the dayroom door. He turned away from the nursing station without signing in.

Waiting alongside a small group of visitors, Guethyn mentally marked the short distance between the elevators to his right, the nursing desk to his left, and the barred door leading into the dayroom straight ahead of him.

The buzzer sounded again and the lock clicked open, allowing entrance to the latest batch of the patients' family and friends.

Dillon noted his grandson's arrival with a nod. He got up from the sofa and moved toward another patient, the edgy Mr. Grammercy. Guethyn poured a soda from the refreshment table and by the time he brought it to his grandfather, Dillon had moved on again. He was quietly speaking with John Jones. Dillon had saved him for last, knowing him to be the most volatile. The perfect kindling for the smoldering fire he was laying. Dillon's hands gestured as he spoke to John, moving back and forth in a methodic tempo, metered by the ticking of the dayroom clock, which read seven-fifteen.

Sitting on the edge of the bed in her room, Sharay's foot wiggled up and down. She uncrossed her legs and jumped up to check the clock above the door. It was time. She didn't bother with one last glance round her bedroom. She didn't have anything of value to take with her. All she owned during her six-month confinement was what she was wearing. Tattered jeans, short sleeved black tee shirt, and frayed green sweater. She reached for the hospital issued comb, slid it into her back pocket, and left her room, heading for the dayroom.

Guethyn felt her presence before he saw her. He dismissed the pre-sentience. She entered from the patient corridor and sat in front of the television set. Exactly seven-seventeen. She glimpsed Guethyn, then quietly reached for the television remote, gently removing it from the lap of the snoring Mr. Newsome. She thumbed the volume button, turning it up.

Hearing the pre-planned television prompt, the abrupt roar of canned laughter from reruns of "The Golden Girls," the obedient Mrs. Feeney stood and belted out a round of "one hundred bottles of beer on the wall."

The exuberant John Jones leapt up and joined her, took her hand and waltzed her around the refreshment table. Sharay inched the volume up as loud as it would go, then slid the remote back onto old Mr. Newsome's lap, who was, to her amazement, still snoring. She crept to the back of the dayroom, deliberately placing herself outside the growing fracas. Dillon and Guethyn unobtrusively joined her.

Dillon acted the part of orchestral conductor, maestro of the song, and created an ever-quickening tempo, flailing his arms up and down for the singers to follow. Pimply faced Bobby giggled nervously, and Mr. Grammercy added his voice to the chorus.

Bill, a young psychiatric aide, opened the door and peered nervously into the dayroom. Dillon's hands immediately fell to his side.

Bill strode over to John Jones, the loudest of the singers, and put his hand on his shoulder. "Mr. Jones, help me calm the others. Would you stop singing?"

John stole a sly look at Dillon and grinned mischievously. Dillon nodded his head and smiled back.

"I'm the maestro now," John declared. He raised his hands and led the singers in their ongoing refrain.

The rounds of the tune were catchy, and soon most of the other patients had joined in. The singing fever substantially escalated, reaching "eighty-six bottles of beer on the wall" by the time two other nurses dashed into the dayroom.

"All right, that's enough everybody," Nurse Claire ordered.

Mrs. Feeney, unnerved by the onslaught of medical staff, began to whimper. The others kept up their rousing performance. A quick triage by the nurses had most of the loudest singers surrounded. The previously snoring Mr. Newsome was well awake, but the raucous singing left him agitated. In his confusion, he dropped the remote down the side of the couch pillows and the television continued to blare. Visitors looked around apprehensively.

Huddled in the corner of the dayroom, Sharay's breath came in shallow gulps, her body recalling the last time she was involved in a dayroom melee. Her gaze darted from Claire to Bill. She reassured herself with the knowledge that doctors and interns weren't on duty in the evening hours and that the nursing staff was preoccupied isolating the loudest of the perpetrators. She would be safe if she remained quietly in the corner with Dillon and Guethyn.

"We need to clear the dayroom," Claire called out.

"Would all visitors please come with me?" shouted Bill.

He was soon lost amidst a throng of over thirty visitors who seemed all too eager to leave the confusion. Guethyn moved swiftly, herding

Sharay and his grandfather into the swelling crowd. He pulled a tam from his coat pocket and put it on his grandfather's head, and took off his hooded jacket and flung it around Sharay, drawing the hood up with one quick tug. He pushed down a fleeting urge to run his fingers through the length of her hair, to gently brush the stray strands that always seemed to cover her face.

"Tuck your hair in so you won't be noticed," he said instead.

Slipping his arms around his charges, he moved them into the center of the crowd. Sharay held tightly onto Dillon's hand, realized it was Guethyn's. She didn't let go.

"I'm ready," she whispered in Dillon's ear.

There were fifty-five bottles of beer on the wall and John Jones sounded determined to get them all down. Medical staff shouted above the contagious crescendo of the song.

"Get the buzzer."

"Round up the patients."

"John, let go of Mrs. Feeney. She doesn't want to dance any longer."

"Get help."

The overhead alarm rang out a repetitive call for the assistance of health care workers from the other psychiatric units. Sharay hated the sound of it.

The buzzer at the nursing desk released the lock on the dayroom door, and the pressure of panic-filled bodies swept her through her first gateway to freedom.

"All visitors, please gather here with me," Bill called out.

Someone pushed the elevator button. At a snail's pace, the doors squeaked open. Dillon hurried inside and made room for Sharay. As she was about to step in, she felt the pointed elbow of a frantic visitor poke in her side. She lost her balance and fell side-ways, just outside the elevator door. The weight of the crowd pulled her to the floor. A woman screamed. Guethyn was over her in an instant, arms and torso impeding anyone from stepping on her, a mixture of frustration and protection visible in his clenched jaw.

"Dillon," Sharay called.

"Shh. We'll be noticed," Guethyn chided.

"But we're supposed to be in the elevator with Dillon. We've got to stay with Dillon if this is to work," Sharay said.

She heard Dillon's voice. "Take care of her, Guethyn."

Guethyn lifted her to her feet with one arm and looked nervously at the elevator. The small elevator cubicle was filled beyond capacity. The crowd of visitors pushed forward.

"Stay back. This one's full. Another lift will be here soon," Bill called out to the remaining crowd.

Sharay searched the sea of faces for Dillon, her gaze finding his right before the doors clanked shut, severing her tether to confidence.

Guethyn's gaze searched around the small foyer. "This way."

He dragged her past the remaining cluster of visitors, one of whom repeatedly pressed the elevator button.

Another anxious looking woman slapped her palm on the closed dayroom door. "I want to see my son. I want to make sure he's okay," she demanded.

"He'll be fine. The nurses will take care of him," Bill said. He laid a reassuring arm on her shoulder and turned her toward the elevators.

The nurses' station was empty. All available staff were helping with the dayroom chaos. With his gazed fixed on Bill's back, Guethyn held onto Sharay with one hand and leaned into the nurses' station, his fingers fumbling until he found the button he was looking for. Sharay prayed Bill wouldn't spot them.

The buzzer beside the phone sounded, the dayroom door clicked open, and the anxious female visitor dashed back inside amidst Bill's urgent protests. The uproar swelled out into the vestibule. Teenaged Bobby tried to leave the dayroom, and Bill fought to corral him back inside.

"Get the visitors out of here." Claire snapped.

"I'm trying," Bill shouted back, caught in the middle of the escalating hysteria.

"Forty-five bottles of beer on the wall. . . ."

Guethyn tapped Sharay's shoulder and pointed to the stairwell.

Sharay shook her head, whispered, "What if it's locked from the outside and we can't get out?"

Images of being trapped in a dimly lit stairwell, high up on the fifth floor, helpless until the nursing staff found her and forced her back to the psychiatric ward, made her nauseous. Suddenly, the stairway door flew open and two male nurses rushed into the small vestibule. Guethyn discreetly stepped in front of Sharay and pulled her close, blocking her from view.

He raised one eyebrow. "I guess we won't have to worry about locked stairwell doors."

"Right," Sharay stammered, distracted by the musky smell of his skin.

"Forty-four bottles of beer on the wall. . . ."

Bill grabbed the newly arrived nurses by the arm and pointed into the dayroom. "Go help in there. I can take care of the visitors."

While Bill ushered the nurses inside, Guethyn steered Sharay through the stairwell door and softly shut it behind him. Sharay's eyes tried to adjust to the dim lighting. A large white "5" indicating the fifth floor was painted on the door.

"Now run," Guethyn demanded, pushing Sharay in front of him.

Sharay grabbed the handrail to guide her way. "One-two-three-four-five. . . ." Twenty steps down to the fourth floor. Sharp turn around, another flight of steps. The hard thump of her tennis shoes landing on linoleum stairs kept count with her thundering heartbeat.

By the time she'd reached the third floor, her breath had quickened to keep pace. Raspy exhalation, padded thump, syncopated heartbeat. Another twenty steps down. Sharp turn round to the next stairway.

The sudden clink of metal on metal signaled a door opening on one of the landings above them. Sharay hesitated, cocked her head toward the noise. The resounding overhead alarm filled the stairwell. She froze.

"I don't care if it's your dinner break. Hurry!" a female voice said.

The hard thud of two pairs of footsteps competed with Sharay's pounding heartbeat.

"Be quiet. Stand still," Guethyn hissed in her ear.

She felt his hand grip her arm and she screamed. The sound had barely escaped her lungs when her mouth was covered by his other hand. Sharay smelled musk and mint and sweat. And her own fear.

"Did you hear that?" a voice, now several landings above them, asked.

The thumping footfalls stopped. Sharay held her breath.

"Probably coming from the fifth floor."

"Sounds like they could really use our help up there."

The sound of thumping footsteps resumed. A door opened and clanged loudly shut. Silence.

Sharay shoved her elbow backwards into Guethyn's ribs. "Don't ever do that again," she sputtered.

"Would you have rather been caught?" Guethyn argued.

Sharay repeated her demand. "Don't ever restrain me."

Guethyn paused. "Just try not to scream again. We still have to stay clear of any security guards outside."

She didn't reply, just turned and ran down the remaining steps with Guethyn close behind. When they had reached the last step, Guethyn stepped in front of her and cautiously opened the door. He held his arm out behind him, stopping her from coming closer.

After a moment he whispered, "We're clear."

The pair crept out the door into a narrow alleyway. Guethyn flattened his body against the side of the building and motioned for Sharay to follow suit. "Stay in the shadows. Against the wall so we won't be seen," he whispered.

The heady scent of flowering jasmine from the hospital gardens wafted faintly from the back of the building, and mingled with the smell of stale garbage bins. Sharay wrinkled her nose, pointed in the opposite direction, toward the front of the hospital complex and the main street. "Parking lot's that way," she whispered.

They crept along in silence, clinging to the alleyway shadows, until they finally reached the front lawn and the parking lot. It was still filled with cars. The security guard at the front door paid no attention to them, too busy helping the onslaught of visitors leaving for the night. Guethyn led her to a tan colored van. Dillon leaned against the van door, waiting for them.

Sharay cried out, "Dillon," and ran into his arms.

Two women, parked two cars down, turned and looked in their direction.

Guethyn scowled. "Are you *trying* to attract attention?"

"Of course not," Sharay shot back.

Dillon glanced back and forth between Guethyn and Sharay. His breathing was loud.

"Are you all right?" Sharay and Guethyn asked in unison.

"The excitement," he said with a dismissive wave of his hand.

"You shouldn't be dallying in magical adventures any longer, grandfather."

"Nothing magical about escaping from a hospital." Dillon winked at Sharay.

Sharay studied his face, his breathing.

"You know what I mean. I'm talking about your heart," Guethyn said.

"My heart's been duly considered," Dillon said. "Now let's get out of here."

Guethyn reached inside his pocket for the keys, unlocked the van door, and climbed into the driver's seat. Dillon shepherded Sharay through her second gateway to freedom, the back seat of the van, and joined her there. Sharay curled next to him and listened intently to his chest. His breathing had become quiet and regular. Guethyn turned the key. The engine sputtered twice then dutifully started up.

He turned to face his passengers. "Ready?"

Dillon nodded yes. Sharay let out a sigh, all too ready to expel the anguish of her hospital confinement and the tension of her escape. She surrendered to the unaccustomed feeling of being taken care of, something she hadn't felt for a long time. Sweet exhaustion came with the release. She touched her hand to her chest and frowned. Dillon's mysterious gift, the Tarot Lover card, wasn't near her heart. She had left it under the pillow in her hospital bed.

Chapter 13

"Wake up," Dillon whispered. He gently nudged Sharay's shoulder.

Sharay was captive inside dreamtime's trance. She ran down dim stairwells that twisted and turned and carried on for eternity, all the while hunted by some malevolent force she couldn't see. A piercing bell rang overhead, alerting her unrelenting pursuer.

Dillon shook her shoulder once more. "Wake up, Tahnea, my silver-haired one."

"What?" she mumbled. She was panting hard.

"Wake up. You're dreaming. We're here."

"Already?" she said, pushing aside the nightmare's haze.

Dillon rubbed her shoulders, helped her sit. "We've been driving for nearly three hours. You've been asleep the whole time."

Guethyn parked the car and looked over his shoulder from the front seat. "Everything okay back there?"

"Nightmare," Dillon murmured.

"I'm sure I'd have them, too, after what she's been through" Guethyn replied.

Dillon got out of the van and held out his hand to help Sharay. Still groggy, she stretched, took his hand, and stumbled out the side door. Even under the dark cycle of the moon, she recognized where she was. Glastonbury.

Guethyn had parked the van on Wellhouse Lane, the narrow country road that divided the unmistakable conical hill, the Tor, from the rock walled gardens surrounding the Red Well. The Tor, to Sharay's left, reached high into the night sky, a lofty beacon to Glastonbury pilgrims. Its terraced slopes outlined the shape of a spiraling labyrinth. From where she stood near the foot of the Tor, the traces of the labyrinth's pathways appeared to faintly glow. Sharay blinked hard.

"Dillon?" She wanted his solid reassurance. "I'm not sure what's dream or vision or real."

"What you're seeing now is real. Trust it."

Guethyn drew up beside his grandfather, "Is she all right?" he whispered.

"She will be."

Sharay leaned her back against the outer rock wall of the Red Well gardens and managed a weak smile. She felt the rough edges of rock poke into her back. "Too many months of that horrible medicine."

She leaned further into the stone wall, grateful for its pointed pressure. The minor discomfort helped her focus on a physical reality she could touch and feel. She hoped the sensation would keep her bound to her body, away from her recent nightmare, away from seeing things she didn't yet trust. Behind the rock wall, in the center of the gardens, the Red Well gurgled noisily. She thought she heard her name spoken softly in the water's perpetual burble—"Sharay"— a faint whisper of long awaited welcome. Her heart ached with the inexplicable familiarity of the gurgling well waters.

"What's that I hear?" Guethyn asked Dillon.

"It's the Red Well."

Guethyn's eyebrows knit in confusion "Did you ever bring me here, Grandfather?"

"No."

"You're sure I've never been here?"

"I didn't say that."

Guethyn was quiet for a moment. "I know this place," he finally said, pensively.

"It's the Red Well of the Goddess," Dillon said.

Guethyn's jaw clenched. Sharay touched his shoulder reassuringly, empathetic with his bewilderment. Guethyn looked down at her, puzzlement clouding his blue eyes. She sensed an undercurrent of deep emotions in him, something tender and open. Swiftly it changed, all signs of tenderness sealed away.

His tone was hard. "I don't believe in the Goddess any longer."

Sharay knew he wouldn't tell her why, even if she asked. But she really wanted to ask.

"Come. Rosheen waits for us," Dillon said after a lengthy silence.

The small party silently made their way down Wellhouse Lane, the nighttime quiet broken by the sporadic conversation of pilgrims making a late night excursion to climb the Tor. The whir of an occasional car told them they were close to Chilkwell Street, the main crossroad to Wellhouse Lane. The entrance to their destination, Little St. Michael's Retreat House, was off of Chilkwell Street, to their right.

Sharay felt a cool mist spray her face and hands. She turned to her left, to the foot of the Tor. There, a chalky white spring tumbled out a rocky fountainhead. The font was banked against an earthen wall that sprouted a living, perfumed tapestry of hundreds of delicate purple and yellow flowers. The branches of a gnarled apple tree hung low to the ground, brushing against the sides of the font. A pathway to the left led into a small café and gift boutique, set into the banks of the Tor. Both shops were closed for the evening.

The milky waters of the White Spring prompted unexpected memories for Sharay. She crossed the narrow Wellhouse Lane and sat on the rocks that enclosed the small spring. She remembered splashing her hands in its waters when, as a child of five, she had visited it with her mother and Rosheen.

In the glimmering light of that early summer day, she had sat in the exact spot she sat now. Her mother, close by her side, had readied bright red ribbons to string on the nearby apple tree branches. The sun had dappled the water into diamond hued clusters of bubbles, colored just like the ones she used to make when she blew soapsuds through her fingers during her bath time.

"Make a wish," her mother had said, handing her a ribbon. "And bind your prayer to the magic of the apple tree with your ribbon." She helped Sharay tie a silken knot around the branch above.

"I wish. . . ." Sharay had closed her eyes tight, silently wishing she would grow up to have a laugh just like her mother's. Light and lilting, her mother's laughter made her feel warm inside, warmer even than when she drank a cup of her favorite hot cocoa.

On that day long ago, Rosheen had joined company with Sharay and her mother, as she often did. Her long brown hair caught the sun's rays and shone like new spun silk loosely woven with fine strands of silver. Sharay thought it was almost as pretty as her mother's light blond hair.

Rosheen had sighed contentedly. "Now this is what magic is all about. The Goddess orchestrating the White Spring to flow so close to our own Red Well."

Always ready to teach, she had pointed her fingers for Sharay's sake, first to the White Spring beside them, then to the Red Well a mere fifty yards across the lane, gurgling behind the rock wall that enclosed the well and flower gardens.

A car's headlights flashed along Chilkwell Street, but Sharay was so lost in memory she barely noticed, incorporating their high beam into her recollected images of that dazzling bright day with her mother and Rosheen.

"Let's sing the Beltaine song, Blanche," Rosheen had said, her face lit with enthusiasm.

Rosheen and Sharay's mother began to sing the poem in unison. Sharay loved the tune, and the sound of their voices singing was high and pure. The words they sang rose up in Sharay's memory—words heard repeatedly as a child, mysterious words she hadn't understood then, but did now. She softly sang along with the memory of her mother and Rosheen.

"Milky white water,
fluid male seed,
vitality of the Father,

springs from deep within the Tor,
releases near rounded womb of Mother.
From the earth we see Her bleed,
Red Well water
joins with the seed.
In coupled chorus they sing,
and dance in harmony.
Male and female unite!"

The masculine White Spring rippled in harmonious compliment to the feminine red water, the Red Well of the priestesses, bringing Sharay further memories of that bright sunny day.

"What's male seed, mama?" Sharay had asked after the song had completed.

Her mother had smiled at her, that special smile saved for Sharay alone. "Well . . . it has to do with the rites of Beltaine."

"Rosheen taught me about Beltaine," Sharay had said, proud she remembered Rosheen's teachings.

"And what did I teach you?" Rosheen asked.

"Beltaine's one of our holy days," Sharay had replied dutifully.

Rosheen beamed. "That's right, Sharay. Beltaine is a special time of the year. It's the time of year when the star formation called the seven sisters rises low on the western horizon. Remember, we showed them to you last night?"

Sharay nodded yes, recalling how she'd marveled when the seven sisters twinkled and pranced across the night sky.

"Beltaine is when the first white hawthorn flowers bud, just like this one." Her mother plucked a cluster in full bloom from the bush next to her and lifted it to Sharay's nose for her to smell. Its many blossoms tickled Sharay.

"We celebrate the fullness of the flowers and the fullness of being a woman," Rosheen said.

"It's when the well waters rise high. The young men and women make their plans for the passionate Beltaine holy day," Sharay's mother added.

Sharay's attention drifted from her mother's voice and was drawn to a shiny black beetle crawling through the delicate white bloom of the hawthorn. It fell upside down on the rock she sat on, its legs wiggling wildly as it tried to upright itself. She touched her finger to its feathery legs and it lay still. She tried to help it stand.

"I remember my first Beltaine," her mother reminisced, turning to face Rosheen. Her back was to Sharay, which usually meant adult conversation.

"I wasn't with Jarred, but I was taught the pleasures of the Goddess."

Sharay wanted to be included, wanted her mother and Rosheen to teach her some more. "What does that mean . . . the pleasures of the Goddess?"

Her mother smiled. "It means the depth of sexual union offered up in Her name. Something I'll teach you about later."

She picked up the hawthorn bloom, tickled Sharay's nose, and turned to Rosheen once more. Sharay watched the beetle crawl slowly across the valleys and hills of the small rock enclosure around the font of the white spring.

"Jarred certainly benefited from what I learned on that Beltaine," her mother said to Rosheen, her rich, lovely laughter punctuating her words.

Rosheen sighed wistfully. "And I remember my first Beltaine."

Her mother grew serious. Sharay looked up from the beetle when the tone of the conversation changed. She wanted them to laugh again.

She pulled eagerly on her mother's skirt. Her mother reached down and stroked her hair, tucked a lock of it behind her ear, then turned to face Rosheen.

"I've heard from Dillon. We received a note this morning."

"How nice. What news is there?" Rosheen's voice was high and bright, almost forced.

"He says his grandson's magical training is coming along nicely. That the boy is talented. Quick to learn."

"I'm not surprised." Rosheen looked down at her hands. "Will he visit us?"

"He didn't mention that he would."

Her mother paused. Sharay carefully pushed the black beetle away from the spring water where she was sure it would drown without her help.

"Oh, Rosheen. I take it Dillon stopped writing you?" her mother asked.

Rosheen nodded. "There's really nothing more he can say, Blanche. We took each other as Beltaine lovers to honor the Goddess. That was a long time ago. You know there's no more to it than that."

"Don't minimize the power of your union, Rosheen. You honored each other in the Beltaine ritual. That's a very special bond."

"Yes, I know. And he's always been extremely dear and kind since then. It's just that . . ." Rosheen wiped a sudden tear from the corner of her eye. "It's just that I managed to fall in love with him, and he managed to fall in love with another." She shook her head and smiled. "Look at me. Years gone by. Me married to George. I really do love George, you know. Yet I still shed tears over Dillon."

Sharay traced her finger along the rocky crevices of the White Spring well's enclosure where the beetle had crawled that day long ago. Conversation that had little meaning back then, suddenly brought her new understandings. Dillon and Rosheen. The true meaning of Beltaine.

Another set of bright car lights flashed along Chilkwell Street, and the footstep of a late night pilgrim crunched the underbrush of the nearby path that led up the side of the Tor. Guethyn called to Sharay from across Wellhouse Lane.

"Sharay? Shall we move on?" His voice sounded impatient.

Sharay wondered how long she had been sitting by the White Spring, lost in reverie. Though Guethyn and Dillon stood only a short distance away, for a moment, they appeared far less real then the memory she'd just recollected. Sharay stood, crossed the lane, and joined the pair.

She turned to face Dillon. "I remembered my mother speaking of you," she said softly.

Dillon nodded.

"I remembered Rosheen speaking of you," she added gently. "And I remembered them talking of Beltaine."

Dillon smiled.

"It felt so real. I could almost hear my mother's laughter."

The memories brought fresh grief. It swelled up, caught on the unyielding hawthorn roots round her heart, and was swiftly quarantined by the black hole. Dillon watched her intently, his eyes reflecting keen observation and compassion. Sharay bent her head, swiped at her tears, and walked rapidly ahead to Chilkwell Street. She rounded the corner and strode up the driveway leading to Little St. Michael's where a silver Airstream motor coach took up most of the space in the tiny front lot.

Sharay's companions soon caught up with her. Dillon faced the silver motor coach and made a grand sweeping gesture with his hand. "This trailer will be the ship of our Imram."

"I thought you said we were taking a van." Sharay said.

"Now that would be entirely up to Guethyn." Dillon glanced questioningly at his grandson.

Guethyn frowned, vehemently shook his head no. The front door of Little St. Michael's opened, silhouetting Rosheen in the soft porch light. Sharay's first glance startled her. Rosheen had changed of course, grown older. There was stark contrast between the young Rosheen's silky brown hair of Sharay's recent memory, and her current short gray hair, stylishly combed back away from her face. Rosheen was a handsome woman, and though her skin had weathered with age, she had the same bright eyes that promised warmth and perennial wisdom.

"Ah." Dillon smiled broadly when he saw her.

Rosheen focused on Sharay, put a bandaged hand to her mouth, and wiped her eyes with a handkerchief she clutched in the other. She stepped forward, her arms opened wide in welcome. Sharay wrapped herself inside Rosheen's greeting.

"My poor darling." Rosheen leaned back, looked Sharay up and down. "Goddess, Sharay. I'm so sorry."

Sharay hadn't realized how much she'd missed her mother's best friend, her childhood teacher. Dillon and Guethyn waited patiently close behind.

Rosheen looked past Sharay. Her heart clutched, and the speech she'd practiced caught in her throat. Finally, she simply said, "Hello, Dillon."

Dillon came forward and kissed her on both cheeks.

"It's been too long," Rosheen murmured.

"The miles too far," Dillon replied.

She turned to Guethyn, with a sharp intake of breath. "You two are most certainly related."

"My grandson, Guethyn," Dillon said proudly.

"He looks so like you at that age."

Rosheen stared for a long moment, eyes unfocused, remembering another time and another place. Dillon's mischievous eyes, and deep set dimples, his dark tawny colored hair spilling over his shoulders as he slept beside her in the woods the morning after the Beltaine of her youth.

Guethyn glanced from his grandfather to Rosheen. Rosheen sighed, patted Guethyn on the back, then swiftly ushered the small party through the front door and into the dining room.

"I've brewed some tea. I've no lodgers this week, so we're alone," she said over her shoulder, to hide her nervousness.

Once she'd made sure everyone was seated comfortably around the table, and she'd set out cookies and cups of tea, Rosheen said, "I received the call from the hospital a little over an hour ago. Let's see . . . that would have been about half past ten."

"The hospital called you?" Sharay exclaimed.

"Yes. We expected the medical staff would eventually check here. Of course, they phoned Phoebe first. When they found you weren't there, Phoebe didn't waste any time informing them to try phoning here at Little St. Michael's," Rosheen replied.

Dillon noted Rosheen's bandaged arm and looked into her eyes.

Rosheen felt the intensity of his penetrating gaze break through her well-constructed wall of false bravado. She sighed, surrendering her feelings to his scrutiny. "I've taken care of things, Dillon. But first, let's make our plans for Sharay's safety."

Dillon nodded for her to continue.

"It's obvious she can't stay with me here," Rosheen said.

"Don't talk about me as if I weren't sitting right here." Sharay immediately regretted her harsh tone.

Sharay's response caught Rosheen off guard. "You've every right to be angry."

"If you can't stay here, where do you plan to go, Grandfather?" Guethyn asked.

"Sharay and I will use the silver motor coach for our Imram."

"You'll be tracked down quick enough if you use Rosheen's motor coach," Guethyn said.

"Then we'd better go in your van," Dillon countered.

Guethyn put his hand up. "Oh, no you don't, Grandfather. You're not tricking me into this. I'll be driving my van to get back to the university."

"Wait. The caravan coach isn't even registered to me. It's registered to a friend, to Catherine," Rosheen said.

"There you go. That'll work to hide your trail," Guethyn said, crossing his arms over his chest.

Dillon didn't reply.

"I remember our Imram, Grandfather. Quite an adventure, but do you think it is a good idea? I mean with Sharay in the condition she's in. . . ."

Sharay bristled. "I'm not crazy, Guethyn."

"I know that," he stammered. "I only meant . . . you said it yourself . . . you're still not fully recovered from your whole experience in that hospital. Maybe it would be safer if you took her straight to Northern Wales, Grandfather. The hospital doesn't know your real name or address. Hell, I never signed in at the desk when I visited, so they won't find you through me, either."

"Another good reason for you to join us," Dillon said doggedly.

Guethyn shook his head. "The only place I'm heading is back to Aberystwyth and the university."

Sharay's heart sank. The feeling surprised her.

Rosheen interrupted. "Sharay, I completely trust Dillon to take care of you. And right now, you *must* be protected."

Something about Rosheen's tone prickled along the back of Sharay's neck. "Is there something I don't know about?"

"This is serious, Sharay. Please know that we'll safeguard you. From the police. From your Aunt Phoebe. I promise." Rosheen's face was suddenly lined with exhaustion and worry. "You'll soon learn how important you are to our lineage at the Red Well. But because of that, there are people, there are forces, that would like to stand in your way."

"Are you trying to scare her on purpose?" Guethyn asked.

"No," Rosheen replied firmly. "I'm sorry, Guethyn, but this is a matter for Dillon, Sharay, and me."

"I see. More magic. More about the Goddess. Well, I'm out of here then. I've done my bit. I have my life to get back to." Guethyn pushed his chair back and stood. "Sharay, I wish you the best." He walked over to where Sharay sat and offered his hand.

Sharay lifted her hand in return. She found Dillon's grandson annoying. But his striking blue eyes pulled her in. Into that other reality where Guethyn was someone else, someone she knew very well, and had once loved in lives shared long ago. The certainty of that feeling both frightened and intrigued her.

"Guethyn, before you leave us, will you load the motor coach for me?" Dillon asked. "Rosheen has gathered together some supplies for us."

Guethyn had not let go of Sharay's hand. She didn't want to pull hers away.

Dillon coughed. "Guethyn?"

"What? Oh, yes, sure. Supplies."

Rosheen gazed at the pair, her eyebrows lifted.

Guethyn slowly released Sharay's hand. "You take care of yourself, Sharay."

"Count on it," Sharay replied.

Guethyn left the kitchen to load the silver caravan. Sharay stared after him, felt a sudden longing for him to join her Imram. She sighed loudly. "I need to freshen up, splash some water on my face."

"Bathroom's up the stairs to your left," Rosheen said. "I've laid out some clean clothes for you."

"Do I have time for a quick bath before we leave?" Sharay asked.

Dillon nodded. "Yes. The police aren't likely to be involved for a few hours yet."

"The police? A few hours?" Sharay asked.

"Sharay, there's the court order to consider. The hospital commit-ment papers. Phoebe will surely fight to have you found and legally re-committed. Eventually the police will be involved," Rosheen replied.

Sharay frowned. "Damn Aunt Phoebe."

Rosheen wished she didn't agree with Sharay. She stood, reached into the side pocket of her sweater. "Now's a good time for this." She offered Sharay a small gold ring.

Sharay took the delicate ring, put it in her open palm.

"It's called a Claddagh ring."

Sharay studied the shape of the ring. Its gold was carved into two outstretched hands clasping a heart between them, with a crown resting atop the heart. "How beautiful."

"The symbol comes from the Irish Celtic tradition. It means love and friendship shall rule forever."

"I like that, Rosheen."

"Yes, it's lovely, but that's not why I've given it to you. I've imbued it with magical powers. See, I have one, too." She displayed her left ring finger to show Sharay. "Dillon, I have a ring for you. And when you phoned me that Guethyn was going to help you escape, I imbued one for him, too."

Dillon held his hand out for his ring. "As you noticed, the boy has a sour taste in his mouth for magic."

"He certainly doesn't take after you then."

"He does, really. He's just never opened to his innate abilities. Doesn't believe in the Goddess. Says She was never around when he desperately needed Her," Dillon replied.

"Wait," Sharay said, staring in fascination at the ring cupped in her palm. "Back up. Tell me about this ring. What's it imbued with?"

"It's a magical amulet. I made them the other night after . . ." Rosheen paused, her face suddenly pale. "After I realized that you . . . all of us . . . needed special protection."

Shivers criss-crossed Sharay's spine, an ice cold feeling she couldn't shake. "Protection from what? The police? Aunt Phoebe?"

Rosheen sighed, not sure how to ease Sharay into her role as a priestess. "Sharay, perhaps it's best if you take your bath first. We can discuss all this when you're through," Rosheen suggested.

Sharay persisted. "Protection from what?"

Rosheen took the ring from Sharay's palm, placed it on the ring finger of her left hand. "Please? Give me just a little time with Dillon, first."

Sharay hesitated. "All right."

She turned, headed toward the stairs and the first floor bathroom. On the landing, she stopped, clutching her left hand in surprise. A tingling sensation radiated from her ring finger, up her arm, throughout her body; a halo of penetrating, golden sun rays. It was dizzying. A serene stillness permeated her being. The sound of a thousand silver bells echoed in the silence. It had been months since she'd had such a strong vision.

The Goddess enveloped her in soft arms and tenderly whispered her name. Sharay reveled in feelings of serenity before the harsh indoctrination of the last six months intruded. She could hear Dr. Deluth speak to her, as clearly as if she were sitting in his office chair during one of their sessions. "It's a hallucination, Sharay."

She shook her head in defiance. Her totem warrior lion growled.

Sharay imagined Nurse Claire's voice cautioning her. "Don't give in to the hallucinations, Sharay."

Confused, tired of fighting, Sharay scrambled back down the stairs, halted on the bottom step. She took a breath to collect herself. She knew she had to learn to trust herself but she still sought the comfort of Dillon's reassurances.

Rosheen's voice rang out from the kitchen. She sounded desperate. "Yes, Sharay needs time to recuperate, Dillon. But we must tell her about the Prophecy. And her role in it."

Sharay crept forward, hidden in the shadows of the hallway, and peeked into the dining room.

"Time enough for that. She's fragile right now. There's no Prophecy to be fulfilled if she doesn't build her strength." Dillon paused. "I've seen something in her. There's a darkness she retreats into, Rosheen. A dark abyss that ultimately only she can climb out of."

Sharay felt the pit of her stomach contract.

Rosheen's eyes opened wide. "Do you think we're too late?"

"No."

"It can't be the same as it was with Phoebe, can it?" Rosheen asked.

"No. Phoebe's out of control, her power's distorted. It grows from her twisted choices and feeds on her wounded emotions."

"Goddess knows Sharay has been emotionally wounded. From her parents' death, from her aunt, from her hospitalization," Rosheen said.

"Yes, but she has a strong destiny. It's hers to claim"

"She's got to claim it soon."

Sharay's stomach churned. Her mother's voice echoed in the halls of her memory. "I'll teach you many things, Sharay. But you are special, and there will come a time when it is you who will teach all of us."

Dillon's voice pulled Sharay back. "Give her time, Rosheen. You were right—she had to leave that hospital. It was wearing her spirit down. But she needs to heal in order to be all we know her to be. The Imram will help her. It will initiate her."

"I'm afraid we're running out of time, Dillon." Rosheen sounded frightened. "I've had dreams. . . ."

Dillon pointed to her bandaged arm. His eyes held unspoken questions.

Rosheen exhaled slowly. "The other night something intruded on my dream state. It was in my bedroom. Something horrible." Her throat went dry. "That's why I imbued the protection amulets."

The ring on Sharay's finger grew warm to the touch.

"What attacked you, Rosheen?"

"Something unnatural. It was dark and frightening. I couldn't make out its shape, but I did trace its energetic trail back to the one who sent it."

"Or created it?" Dillon suggested.

Rosheen nodded. "Yes. I believe it comes from Phoebe. I did a magical working to bind her powers the best I could. She's strong."

"She does carry the blood of our lineage."

"Yes, the pure blood. But a poisoned heart. Oh Dillon, Blanche was attacked in the same way I was. The night before she died." Rosheen's voice cracked.

Sharay's hand flew to her heart.

Dillon calmly reached for Rosheen's hand. "Is that what you fear?"

"No, I don't fear for myself. I sense it comes to me to find its way to Sharay."

"It could go to Sharay directly."

"I've thought of that. I believe it means to further break her spirit by going after those she cares about. Then it has easier access to her untapped power as the Prophesied one." Rosheen took a steadying breath. "There is more. Something of enormous importance."

Dillon waited for Rosheen to continue.

"It's about our sacred talisman."

"What about it?" Dillon asked.

"It's missing."

Dillon closed his eyes, stroked his beard in silence.

"Dillon, without it Sharay may be vulnerable. She needs it to fulfill her destiny. We have to find it before its power is misused . . ." Rosheen covered her face in her hands. Her shoulders heaved in a silent sob, straining to release the dread she'd held back since the night she'd been attacked.

Dillon reached for her, held her in his arms.

Sharay rubbed the birthmark at the nape of her neck. What was this destiny they were planning for her? She didn't like the sound of any of it.

Eventually, her tears spent, Rosheen wiped her wet cheeks with her handkerchief, dabbed at the tear stains on Dillon's shirt. "I've missed you," she said, not daring to raise her eyes.

"You're always in my heart, Rosheen."

Rosheen nodded. "I wanted more."

"I know," Dillon said gently.

Rosheen felt familiar disappointment wrench her heart. "You've always been kind to me. Even when you told me you were to wed Elana." Rosheen looked up, sympathy filling her. "I'm truly sorry you lost her. I know the pain. Gerald's been dead five years now."

"My marriage to Elana was precious even if it was short. And times change. What wasn't meant to be before may have its own time now."

Rosheen smiled softly. She lifted her hand to touch Dillon's craggy cheek and gray beard. "In my heart you haven't aged a bit." She sighed, a heavy breath filled with wistful longing. "But I have to lay my own desires aside right now and focus on Sharay."

Dillon was silent as he turned inward for guidance. Eventually, he spoke. "The necklace is not ours to find."

"What? But our lineage has never been without it."

Dillon leaned back in his chair. His eyes glazed over, his voice took on a resonant timber. "Sharay must discover the power inherent in the necklace first. It is her responsibility as future High Priestess and the Prophesied one. It is the era when the magic of the necklace must be brought forth from within."

"I've failed her—haven't I?" Rosheen asked. Guilty tears threatened to flow.

Dillon blinked, focused on her. "No, my dear one. This is part of her initiation."

"What if she doesn't succeed, Dillon?"

"She will succeed."

"She must. But can she?"

Chapter 14

Sharay put her hand over her mouth. She stole out the back door, and hurried through the gate into the Red Well gardens. There was no moonlight to guide her. Its dark phase reflected the bleakness inside her soul. She ran down the garden path by instinct, childhood memories stored in her body leading the way. The ancient lineage encoded in her blood compelled her to head toward the Red Well. Something inside her knew her salvation lay in the waters of the Goddess as they bubbled up from deep within the earth. She ran to the back of the gardens, threw herself prostrate beside the well, her own fount of emotion swelling upwards with an intensity that matched the potent surge of the gurgling spring water.

Talismanic necklaces, Prophecies, dangerous destinies forced on her without her consent. She had left the world of her lineage behind when her mother died. But she had never truly forgotten her roots. Still, what Rosheen and Dillon planned for her made her heart clutch and her head ache.

Her tears mingled with the spray of the fountainhead. The night air, heavily perfumed with the fragrance of white hawthorn flowers and lush red roses, blended with the scent of loamy dirt and dew-covered grass. Sharay burrowed her face into the soft lawn, seeking refuge in the ageless constancy of nature. Instead, the ground spoke to her in hushed tones and shadowy images of memories shrouded within the soil from a time long ago.

She began to hear things—at first, the whisperings of women's voices. Then she began to see things—the flash of a pointed sword bearing down, the outline of an arm raised in defense. The faint images and muted sounds grew louder, turned into the agonizing cries of massacred women. She saw the same white robed priestesses she had seen in the dayroom the first time she'd met Dillon. The familiar landscape of the isle of Ynis Witrin—the veiled Avalon of the priestesses, ancient Glastonbury—emerged from the recesses of collective memory buried in the earth around the Red Well. Sharay's bones resonated with memory's imprint embedded in the dark soil.

Admonished by Phoebe to distrust her Second Sight, programmed by Dr. Deluth to believe anything out of the ordinary was a hallucination, Sharay wrestled with the rising vision. But there was a stronger part of her that knew these images were very real. Were personal. Part of her past life history and part of the history of her priestess lineage. Collapsed on the ground beside the Red Well, she knew all at once who she was—who she had at one time been. The High Priestess Rhianna. She remembered intimately the lifetime she had led as part of a community of priestesses residing near the Red Well. Her community. She'd lived and worshipped among them, as healer and initiate, and eventually as their leader. And she remembered them all. Wise Cyrie, innocent young Ella, fragile Anna, carefree Dayanna.

She recalled one devastating day in that life long ago. She and three of her priestess companions had been collecting herbs far off in the woods when something portentous tugged at her power spot, her womb space in her belly. She sensed horrendous suffering amidst her fellow priestesses back at the Red Well.

Dropping her basket of carefully chosen plants, she ran toward the community, across faint dirt trails, past trees with sharp branches. Her three companions followed close behind. As they approached the community, the wails of the dying were shrill in the air. A party of marauding warriors had crept upon their settlement, taking what they desired, leaving their defilement behind. They had murdered and raped the women she had lived with, the women she had loved. The blood of her beloved sisters seeped into the ground and the soil soaked it up. The earth pledged to hold their memory.

Sharay saw herself as she was then, long red hair flying in the fury of a storm that matched her rage. "I promise you! You will not be forgotten my sisters. I vow to carry forth the secrets of our lineage."

Sharay's ancestral lineage called to her from that time long ago. Filled with sorrow, she lifted her body and stood at the side of the Red Well—head flung back, arms raised. The wails of the slaughtered priestesses rose from earth's catacomb, coursed up her legs, ascended to her heart, and exploded out her mouth in a resounding keening. "Nooooo!"

Her mourning silenced the song of the night birds. The liberation of her sisters' collective pain from earth and bones left her body emptied, pulled her down to the ground once more, onto her hands and knees.

Deeper memories spilled forth. Their torrential flood rent a tear in her unconscious, and flashes of places and times more ancient than Glastonbury broke through. Glimpses of a man who resembled Guethyn, with his tawny hair and clear blue eyes. Ethereal, flickering images of places she had heard of in the tales her mother once told her—tales of Atlantis with its crashing ocean waves and its towering pyramidal power source. Silver drenched shoreline of moonlight devotion to the Goddess of the Stars and the Sea. Sharay's lineage summoned her. But caught within the grief and rage of her present life, she recoiled.

"Where's my protection?" she called to her black hole.

Despite its promises, Sharay somehow knew the black hole could not rescue her from this ancestral anguish. The golden totem lion inside her lifted its head and roared.

The sound of a thousand silver bells rang loudly in her ears and reverberated throughout her womb. A blue and silver mist surrounded her so she could see no further than the Red Well in front of her. Spent, Sharay sank onto her belly, hands splayed before her.

"What do you want of me, Goddess?" she sobbed.

The voice that responded was honeyed salve to the bruises within her soul. "I want you to receive My love for you."

"I don't know how."

"I will teach you."

"Teach me?"

"First, to heal your heart."

"But what do you want from me?"

The Goddess sighed into the wind that rustled the apple trees in the garden. "I want that which you promised long ago."

"I remember no promise to you." Sharay lifted her head. "Besides, everything's been taken. I've nothing left to give."

"Then let me hold you in My arms. I will replenish you."

Sharay shoved her arms out in front of her in rejection. "No. I can't do this. There's been too much pain. Too much lost."

A soft summer breeze stroked Sharay's cheek. She brushed it away. The heavy scent of roses grew stronger, and the blue and silver mist cushioned her, cradling her in misty embrace.

"I will help you remember the promise you made Me."

Sharay felt her thoughts flash back through time, back through her life, back to her birth, and earlier yet. Her body was formless then, her mind still, her soul between lifetimes. She watched.

In Her velvet black womb, the Goddess of the Stars and the Sea carried the spark of a brilliant soul. She spoke lovingly to the spirit resting in the darkness of the midnight sky. "The needs of humankind call. The shift of the ages is upon them."

Her voice rang with the melodious echo of a thousand silver bells, song of the stars. "Are you ready to help Me once more?"

The sea, starlight's mirror, pitched and rose with urgent expectancy.

Without hesitation the soul within the womb of the Goddess replied. "Yes, I will help. I have given you my word."

"Then I am pleased." The sea quieted its eager swells, and the stars in the heavens glowed brighter.

The Goddess continued. "In your new life, you will forget this conversation with Me. You will forget who you truly are and all the other times you have assisted Me. Once born into the earthly realm, you will need to make this choice anew."

"I understand."

The wind swirled and pranced through the night clouds, and the full moon beamed.

The Goddess sighed, her breath a gentle breeze that caressed the yet formless soul. "It will not be easy. There will be those who will strive against you, even among those you might think to trust. But one day you will remember what you have learned in all the lifetimes you've assisted Me. You will hear the ancient call of your destiny. At that point the choice will once again come to you. To do what you were born to do and help humanity in its transition. Or to refuse, and make a different choice."

"But I have always chosen you," the soul said eagerly, perhaps even over-confident.

"Understand—this time your task is the hardest yet. The path of human evolution is to embody love. You are to be a catalyst to that end."

"I am to catalyze embodied love," the soul repeated, suddenly unsure. "I . . . I'm not sure I know how to do that." The brilliance of the stars grew unbearable. The soul shielded itself, turned in the womb of the Goddess and looked down, focusing on the depth of the heaving sea below and the roots of green leafed trees implanted in the fertile soil beyond the shoreline.

The soul's response did not go unnoticed by the Goddess. "My sweet child, embodying love is your calling. You will learn, and then teach others. It is yours to do—to carry on the flame to a new dawn." Her voice was kind. "I will show you how. But you must remain open to receive Me."

"How will I recognize you?" the soul asked softly.

"You will find me everywhere. Draw me into you as you walk upon my body, the earth. Taste Me in the salty wetness of your tears. Raise my power in your belly. Feel me in the chalice of your heart. And see me in the people you will grow to care about. I will wait for you with arms to soothe and heal you in the darkness of your suffering."

The soul was silent.

The Goddess smiled tenderly and said only, "In this lifetime you will be called Sharay." She then embraced the precious spark in Her womb.

The soul felt a quickening. The irresistible sensation to plunge down-ward. She frantically willed herself to remember everything she'd been told.

The last message she heard echoed through her descent. "Most of all, remember to love."

In a swirl of shimmering blue and silver, the Goddess of the Stars and the Sea breathed form into the soul. Her hands created life from the dust of loamy earth, the water of the seas, the fire of the stars. She sent Sharay's soul on angelic wings through the spiral of orgasmic ecstasy where it embedded into a human mother's womb, to be born in the earthly realm.

Sharay's formless soul lurched back into her physical body. "I remember," she whispered.

Sharay wiggled her fingers, touched the moist earth beneath her. She inhaled the scent of roses and grass, felt warmth and pressure on her skin, stretched against the strength of her bones and muscles, once more grounded in all her physical sensations.

The Goddess said, "They pay tribute to Me, those who have dwelled for eons at this Red Well. But among them all there is one whose return I have awaited. She who was known to me as Geodran. As Rhianna. And now known to Me as Sharay."

Sharay wiped at her sudden flow of tears. "Why must I relive their pain?"

"Their soul is your soul. Their lives, yours. All must be remembered for you to fulfill the Prophecy."

Sharay crossed her arms around her waist, small comfort, and closed her eyes. A white owl peered down from its perch in the apple tree branches above Sharay, calling, "Hoo-hoo!"

"Why did you abandon me?" she asked in a small voice.

"Never abandoned. You conceal Me when you refuse My Presence. When you shut out My Love for you."

The imagined sound of Dr. Deluth's orders admonished her. "Ignore the hallucination, Sharay."

Sharay put her hands over her ears, wanting to blot out his voice. But inside her, the golden lion stood regally, offering her strength. She rubbed her palms over her face, cleared her thoughts. No hallucination.

There had never been any hallucinations at all.

She sat back on her heels. "You *are* real."

"Yes. I am real."

"I am She who is called by the needs of humankind, at this turning of the ages. My heart aches with their cries."

"The Goddess of the Stars and the Sea," Sharay said softly, voicing the name for the first time in years. Pieces of her mother's stories, snatches of her visions prior to the hospitalization, came in rapid succession.

The sound of the silver bells grew louder in smiled response.

"Humankind is at the threshold of a spiritual evolution. Turbulent times always precede the next great leap in consciousness. I can assist. But to do so, I need the help of my priestesses."

"But I'm not a trained priestess. Why would you even want my help? I've only made a mess of my life so far." A soft breeze stroked Sharay's cheek once more. She didn't brush it away.

"It is the time of your calling. Of your destiny. You are one who holds the keys."

"Keys?"

"To remembering how to awaken the starlight within your body. Your true essence of Love. Your golden immortality."

Sharay was silent. She tried to perceive the keys the Goddess spoke about.

She felt into her belly but its fiery embers burned low; felt into her heart but the hawthorn roots constricted it. And the shadowy mist of the familiar black hole was tugging to pull her back into itself.

"I know I promised, but I can't find these keys you speak about."

The blue and silver mist gently held Sharay. "Know this. Love is a Divine substance that enlivens your body. It is My true essence."

"That's the key?"

"Yes. Allow yourself to receive more and more of My Love and the very substance of your body will transform. When you do this, others will awaken their remembrance of how to do so as well. You are a bridge to this new way of being. It is a great service, Sharay."

"This is how I'm to help? I don't even understand."

The Goddess replied with compassion. "Take one small step at a time. I will guide you. The answers are within the infinite depth of your cells, where I reside."

Sharay tried once more to feel the keys the Goddess spoke of, but still felt nothing.

The black hole inside Sharay broke through. It spoke to her scathingly. "You owe nothing to this Goddess," it scoffed. "She abandoned you to misery and pain. Come back to me. No confusion. Nothing to do. Simple refuge."

Its promises beguiled Sharay. The lion totem inside her growled, bared its teeth menacingly.

"I don't think I can do this."

"You are not alone."

Sharay felt only an immense chasm—the unprotected leap between the seductive black hole and the golden lion.

Her heart, heavy and aching, withdrew. "But I *am* alone."

Raw grief and red anger rose in jagged lightning flashes that seared her will. The lion roared its protest. Sharay whimpered. The black hole whispered its approval.

Chapter 15

A strong hand grabbed Sharay's shoulder. Dillon was on his knees facing her. His hands gripped both her shoulders, his eyes bored through her soul.

"Trust, Tahnea," he whispered.

The lion stood silently and the black hole cringed in the shadows in Dillon's company. The wind picked up, parting the silver and blue mist. The gurgling of spring water pierced the night. The presence of the Goddess was palpable.

"Dillon." Sharay wrapped her arms around his neck, laid her head on his chest.

Dillon cloaked her in his arms. "There's nothing to fear, Tahnea."

She looked up at him. "How can I help the Goddess when I can barely help myself?"

"Is it the black hole that stops you?" he asked, sitting back.

Sharay sighed, not surprised he knew about it. "Yes."

"That black hole only pretends to protect you, Sharay."

"It does protect me. I never feel sad or angry inside it."

"And you never feel alive."

Sharay fell silent.

"The black hole inside you is your own emptiness. Every one of us has one."

Sharay looked up in surprise. "You have one?"

"Indeed. But we must all sooner or later face the pain we hoped we could bury."

Sharay rubbed her Claddaugh ring. "There are so many things I don't understand."

"Then ask me."

Sharay thought for a moment. "Why does Aunt Phoebe hate me so?" Even as she said it, something slick moved along the inside of her gut.

Dillon rearranged himself to sit cross-legged. Looking up at the starry sky, he took a deep breath. Sharay swore he looked twenty years younger.

"Let me tell you a story. Do you see those stars?" he asked pointing upwards.

Sharay leaned her head back. A configuration of seven stars, patterned closely together, shone more brightly than the rest.

"Those stars are called the Seven Sisters. They rise up in full majesty in the late spring, around the time of Beltaine."

Sharay felt herself relax into the cadence of Dillon's voice.

"Those seven stars, along with all the other stars in the heavens, lie within the velvet womb of the Goddess—the night sky. The starlight pours down to earth from Her womb. On its way down, star light turns into the water droplets that make up our vast oceans."

"That's how both the stars and the sea are the realms of the Goddess?"

"Yes." Dillon's songlike Welsh accent deepened with the telling. "Descending far beneath the ocean, into the center of the earth, the water turns once again to fiery stars. Then they ascend back up to the heavens. The pattern of their travels from star to sea to earth's center and back up again, forms a figure eight." Dillon used his fingers to trace the figure eight pattern in the air.

The pattern glistened in shimmering iridescent blue. Sharay's belly grew warm. Her hand flew to the spot.

Dillon noticed and said, "The star embers are awakening within your womb space."

Sharay softly rubbed her belly.

"The figure eight is the pattern of the Goddess of the Stars and the Sea. This is just one of the magical teachings held by our lineage. *Your* lineage, Sharay." Dillon took her hands in his. "Remember what I've told you. Hold it safely in your heart."

Sharay nodded, memorized the figure eight Dillon traced in the air in front of her. "The liquid light of the stars and the sea."

Dillon studied her a moment. "Very good. You've understood the deeper level of the teaching." He smiled approvingly. "There are many more teachings. And one great Prophecy. One that involves being of assistance to humanity during a time of great need."

"You still haven't told me why Aunt Phoebe hates me."

Dillon stared off in the distance, recalling old memories, old hurts. "Your mother had everything Phoebe wanted and didn't have. Blanche had true love with a good man. She married into financial wealth. And although Phoebe also carries the true blood of the lineage, it was your mother who was destined to birth the Prophesied daughter."

"So, Aunt Phoebe resents me?"

"She's envious, yes."

"Grandfather? Sharay? Where are you?" Guethyn's voice carried across the garden, interrupting them.

"Well, that's enough for now." Dillon stood with a groan, held out a hand for Sharay. "Are you ready to go on your Imram?"

Sharay nodded. "Yes."

"Over here, Guethyn," Dillon called.

Guethyn was breathless when he reached them. "Come quick. Rosheen just received another phone call." His voice sounded urgent.

Dillon waited calmly for Guethyn to continue.

"We can't stay here any longer, Grandfather. We have to leave," Guethyn said.

"We? You're coming with us? What's the rush?" Sharay asked.

"I can't let you two go alone now. The police just phoned. They know you're here, Sharay."

"How do they know that?" Sharay asked.

"Seems your Aunt Phoebe told them. . . ."

"But Aunt Phoebe already told them to phone here earlier. They were satisfied when Rosheen reported she hadn't seen me."

"I think Rosheen should tell you the rest."

Dillon put an arm around Sharay's shoulder and they walked swiftly toward the house.

The back porch light flashed on, and Rosheen stepped onto the terrace. She flagged the small group, arms waving frantically.

"What's happening?" Sharay asked when they reached her. "I thought you said the police wouldn't be involved yet."

"There's been a complication." Rosheen shot a quick glance at Dillon. "A murder."

"Murder? What's that got to do with us?" Sharay asked.

"The police say Larry Wentworth's been murdered."

"Uncle Larry?"

"Yes. You have to leave this minute. Phoebe's told the police you showed up at her house late this evening and would probably head here next." Rosheen hurriedly put a jacket over Sharay's shoulders, and handed a large wad of money to Dillon.

She sighed, stroked Sharay's cheek. "Goddess, Sharay. There's so much I wanted to teach you. So much to tell you."

Sharay churned with longing. "Tell me, Rosheen."

Rosheen methodically buttoned Sharay's coat for her, her face tight with worry. "I can't. Get yourself to safety then we'll talk. I can telephone you." She grabbed Guethyn by the arm. "You have the rented cell phone I gave you?"

Guethyn nodded, patted his coat pocket.

"Sharay, you've got to leave. It's not safe here any longer."

"But. . . ."

"Leave here now. Your Aunt Phoebe's filed charges with the police." Rosheen swallowed thickly. "She's accused you of murdering your Uncle Larry."

Chapter 16

Phoebe stared at the knife, her hands trembling more now than when she had thrust it into Larry's chest. She still remembered the feeling of hitting bone, the knife sliding sideways, searching for its true mark, his wildly beating heart. She closed her eyelids, tried to blot out the images, the look of shock in Larry's eyes when he gazed up at her. He never did understand all that was at stake.

When she'd learned earlier that evening that Sharay had escaped from the hospital, her body had vibrated with fury, her thoughts had raced with panic. That's how Larry had found her. She was putting the phone receiver back onto its cradle when he'd walked in from his evening out at the pub playing darts. He instantly gauged her distress, and sliding his arms around her, he'd tried to comfort her. She'd pushed him away. She'd yelled, screamed that all was lost, that Sharay had escaped from the hospital. He'd tried once more to hold her. His pitiful attempts to ease her panic fueled her anger. She replayed their argument in her mind yet again.

"If you'd only been helping me all along, this wouldn't have happened," she said.

"I've done nothing but help you in this . . . this . . . charade," Larry stammered.

"How dare you call it that? You're useless."

Larry lost his temper. "Oh, I understand very well. Just leave the poor girl alone, will you? We don't need her money."

Larry rarely lost his temper and now it lit the kindling of resentment Phoebe had felt since she'd married him. "It isn't only the money. You bastard."

"I've had enough of all of this, Phoebe. Enough of your conniving." His thin lips were set in a determined frown. "If I'm not good enough for you, why don't you leave?"

"How dare you? I'm trying to make our life easier, and you decide to turn on me now?"

She raised her hand to slap his face.

Larry grabbed it, thrust it behind her back. "I've had enough of your deceit. I won't play this game anymore. I may even call Dr. Deluth. Tell him the truth"

"You wouldn't dare."

"Try me." Larry's eyes turned smoky and dark.

Phoebe recoiled in revulsion. More frightening than his rage was the look in his eyes. He pulled her to him and ripped open her blouse. Phoebe struggled, but Larry was stronger. She couldn't stop him. He raked her chest with his teeth, pressed his mouth to hers, bruising it, drawing blood with brutal force. His anger was fueling his arousal. She felt nauseous.

She shoved him. Her struggles made him stronger. She went still. She would let him think he could get what he wanted. She began to return his kisses, felt him release his grip on her arm and clutch her body closer. She lay back across the desk and let him mount her. She vacillated between forcing down the bile that threatened to fill her mouth, and cold, precise planning. Once Larry was lost in his pathetic thrusts, Phoebe made her move. She reached her arm over her head, her fingers fumbling around the objects on his desk. Searching for the scissors. Next to the phone, beside the letter opener. Larry always kept things in order.

Phoebe didn't hesitate.

Guethyn started the ignition in the silver motor coach and backed down the driveway. He didn't put the headlights on until he had pulled out onto Chilkwell Street.

Dillon had insisted on sitting in the back seat by himself, and even now was softly chanting, his eyes closed, his fingers moving about in subtle mudras. One of his fingers would alternately point, then curl under, while another finger raised and traced intricate geometric shapes in the air, all in a precise, measured flow. Sharay didn't know what the hand movements signified but was sure it involved something magical and protective.

"What's going to happen to your van?" she asked Guethyn.

"Rosheen said she would move it to her friend Catherine's."

Sharay vaguely remembered a woman by that name. A priestess who used to occasionally play with her as a child, swinging her around and upside down with strong arms until the ground spun in circles and Sharay begged for more.

Sharay suddenly careened against the passenger door. She frowned and hastily put on her seatbelt. Guethyn's foot was heavy on the accelerator. The caravan trailer skidded around corners and broke off bush branches in its hurried exit down the narrow, hedge lined country lanes. Every few minutes Guethyn looked in his rear view mirror. The gesture made Sharay far more edgy than the close turns. She began to stroke the base of her neck with her fingertips, softly tracing the indentation of her birthmark.

"Do you know your way out of here, Guethyn?" she asked.

"Rosheen gave me these directions." He held up a piece of paper with scribbles across it. "Would you navigate for me?"

Sharay took the paper, but couldn't see it in the dark. "Is there a flashlight?"

"I saw one in the glove compartment."

Sharay opened the glove box. Inside was a tire gauge and maps of England, Scotland, and Wales. She rifled through and underneath was a candle and votive holder, matches, a vial marked "Red Well water," a packet of what looked like dried herbs, and a deck of cards that looked suspiciously like the ones Dillon had shuffled when she first met him. At the bottom was a slender beamed flashlight.

"Did you find it?" Guethyn asked.

"Yes." She pulled out the flashlight, flicked it on, and decided she would investigate the other items later. She aimed the light and read the directions. "She's put her phone number here, too."

"Good."

"There's two numbers. One says it's for the Lodge house phone . . ."

Guethyn interrupted. "She doesn't want us to use that unless we have to. The police might decide to tap it."

Sharay continued. "She's also written down the code for the pre-paid cell phone card."

Sharay switched the flashlight off and looked at Guethyn. "Think the police will find us?"

"Not if I can help it." Guethyn swung the steering wheel sharply to the left. "Listen. The police don't have any leads on us, Sharay."

"But you gave Dr. Deluth and the nurses your real name."

"They don't know I have anything to do with you. Like I said, I didn't sign in at the nurses' desk. There's no official record of me being at the hospital last night." He paused. "Although that ward secretary, Connie, may remember me."

"So, they might think two patients escaped in the confusion at the hospital, separately from each other. Or they may connect the three of us."

"Hard to say," Dillon said from the back seat, his hands now neatly folded on his lap. "They'll explore all possibilities. So, we'll stay away from Aberystwyth and your university, Guethyn. We'll drive further up the Welsh coast. Then on to Scotland."

"Why the Welsh coast, Dillon?" Sharay asked.

"We need to stop and honor Beltaine."

"What?" Guethyn's voice rose. "Sharay's wanted for murder, and you want to play around with pagan holy days?"

"Things will be done the way I say."

Sharay noticed Dillon's commanding tone. Guethyn didn't argue further.

After a prolonged silence, Sharay asked, "What will you do about your studies, Guethyn?"

"I'll phone my professor, try to make different arrangements."

"I'm sorry about that."

He glanced at her. "I said I'd help. I'm in for the whole thing now."

Sharay couldn't help smiling. She covered her mouth and coughed, didn't want Guethyn to see her grin. She couldn't deny she was glad he'd joined her Imram, but what was puzzling to her was her sense of relief. It wasn't that she didn't trust Dillon to hide her from the police or the hospital authorities. She trusted him absolutely. But there was something about Guethyn, something she sensed in him that made her feel completely safe.

She remembered seeing the face that looked so like him in her visions beside the Red Well. She simply knew that man had protected her before, in lives long past, and in circumstances even more dire. And that he would do so once more. She sighed. She'd need to get comfortable with her Second Sight again, and with the flood of long forgotten memories. She didn't have much choice anyway. The memories seemed to inundate her.

The soft scraping of hedgerows against the side of the caravan made her look up. The country lane barely allowed passage for a small car, much less an Airstream caravan. She flicked on the flashlight again and aimed it at the paper Guethyn had given her. "Oh! Turn here. Now," she exclaimed, pointing to her left.

Guethyn veered to the left, making the turn barely in time to avoid driving into the thick hedge. "Bloody hell. Give me those directions. Let me navigate."

"No. I can do it." Sharay held firmly on to the paper.

"Fine. Have it your way."

She didn't speak for the next several hours, other than giving directions, making sure she gave Guethyn plenty of warning when he was supposed to turn. Her irritation had calmed by the time the sky was beginning to show the muted orange and pink of dawn's horizon.

Dillon gestured to the left, instructing Guethyn to pull off onto a small side road, its dirt entrance barely noticeable amidst the dense stand of oak trees. Guethyn was sure he would have missed seeing the side road if his grandfather hadn't pointed it out. He wondered if the road was charmed. He headed the caravan west.

"Where are we going, Dillon?" Sharay asked.

"We'll stay in the mid-section of Wales, along the coast, for a few days. Until we're sure we're safe. That will give you plenty of time to . . . well, we'll talk about that later."

Sharay wanted to push to hear more, but Dillon continued. "Guethyn, shortly you'll come to an area forested with birch trees. Beyond that is the ocean shore and a small cove I used to visit in my youth. It's extremely secluded, far away from the tourist areas to the south."

"Are we near your home?" Sharay asked.

"My home's farther north. In the mountains. We'll be avoiding it altogether. Just in case."

Within a half hour the silver caravan was parked as far as Guethyn could drive it into the woods. Sharay rolled down her window. The sound of waves breaking against the shore and the salty scent of seawater tugged at her.

"Time for this old man to sleep." Dillon yawned and stood. He moved to the back of the caravan and pulled down a seat cushion to form a narrow bed. He pointed to the seating area opposite him, indicating it would convert into a bed in the same manner. "That's for you, Sharay. Guethyn, you can sleep across the passenger seats or in a tent, if you don't mind."

Sharay said, "I'll sleep in a little bit, Dillon. First, I want to go to the ocean."

Guethyn looked up from the cooler where he was selecting a bottle of water. "Can't afford to have you out of our sight, Sharay."

Dillon laid down and pulled a blanket over him. "Then go with her," he said.

Guethyn rolled his eyes. "Can't this wait?" he asked Sharay.

"No," she replied, suddenly irritated again.

Guethyn gave an exasperated sigh, and followed her out of the caravan trailer. The pair walked in silence through the dense forest of birch trees.

The silver bark caught the last traces of faded starlight and reflected it back into the dawn. Guethyn stole a sideways look at Sharay, marveled at how the bark of the birch trees reminded him of the color of her hair.

Moist undergrowth softened their footsteps and tree leaves rustled in accompaniment to the ocean waves not far ahead of them. Guethyn held his bottle of water up and offered Sharay a sip.

Sharay took it gratefully, realizing how thirsty she was. When her lips touched the bottle rim he'd drunk from, she pulled back in surprise. Dream-like images formed in her mind's eye, shifting kaleidoscope patterns, all featuring the man she'd seen in previous visions. The man that looked like Guethyn, with the same vivid blue eyes. Again, Sharay's soul recognized them as one and the same man.

"Hey, leave some water for me," Guethyn chided.

Sharay sputtered, wiped her mouth on her shoulder. She stared at him.

"Don't get annoyed. I only brought one bottle," he said.

"That's not it. . . ." She sighed, waved him away with the back of her hand. She wasn't ready to share her remembrances. Yet.

Guethyn shrugged and carried on walking. He left the water bottle with her. Shortly, they reached the sandy beach. Sharay stepped out from the forest, her mouth parted in awe. The ocean was wild, primal.

It thrashed impatiently against the shore. Each ebbing inhalation and crashing exhalation spewed bits of sand and shell back onto the beach. Sharay tasted its watery spray on her lips. The sound of the waves, the smell of salty air, caught her off guard. The last time she'd been ocean side was with her parents. It was one of the happiest moments of her life.

She suddenly yearned for the framed picture of the three of them at the beach, the captured memory from her favorite vacation. She'd kept it at her bedside since her parents death, had gazed at it every night before she slept and every morning on awakening. She wondered if it was still on her bedside table. Silently, she vowed she'd someday get the photo back.

Taking a steadying breath, she picked a low-lying boulder to sit on. "Tell me about your dissertation," she said to Guethyn, hoping to keep her mind off the heaviness in her heart.

Guethyn's face lit up. "I'm getting my doctorate in Marine Biology at University of Wales, Aberystwyth." He dropped down on the sand beside her, resting back on his elbows. "I study ocean ecology."

"I've always loved the ocean," Sharay said, gazing into the misty horizon.

"Me, too. Fell in love with it when Grandfather took me there as a boy."

"See this?" Guethyn asked, picking up a handful of sand, letting it run through his fingers. "It's a miracle of nature how sand is created. Rocks and shells, pulverized by the ocean over years and years. Imagine all that power in an ocean wave pounding hard then lapping softly. It creates this." He held up another fistful of sand, stared at it, lost in thought.

Sharay glanced at him, noticed how his enthusiasm softened his eyes, and relaxed his jaw. She liked him like this. "You love what you do."

"Hmm?" he replied, bringing his focus back to her. "Yes." He rolled on his side, leaned on his elbow, and looked up at her. "Functional and behavioral ecology's my life." He smiled when she looked blankly at him. "Regional and local patterns of marine biodiversity. It means marine environments."

"It's nice you get to research something you love."

Sharay slid down onto the sand next to Guethyn and leaned her back against the small boulder.

"My parents took me to the beach on vacation once . . . and. . . ." She swallowed hard. "And, I thought I'd never seen anything so beautiful." She blinked back a tear.

Guethyn nodded, studied her face. "Yes. Beautiful."

Something in his voice made her turn to him. She suddenly wanted him to know. "I lost them you know. My parents."

"Grandfather told me."

Sharay considered Guethyn's features, found a certain strength of character in his unwavering gaze, the way he wrinkled his eyebrows together when he was serious, the way his dimples deepened when he smiled—just like Dillon's. His face was open and relaxed here by the ocean, none of the tightness in his jaw as when he was angry or tense.

"I'd like to study the ocean, too. But, I'd like to paint it." Sharay paused. "I have a photo of that summer at the beach with my parents."

"May I see it?"

"It's at my house. I mean the house Aunt Phoebe has now. I promised myself I'm going to get that picture back someday."

"I hope you get your wish."

He surprised her with his quick switches from brusqueness to kindness. She looked in his eyes, looked quickly away when she found him returning the gaze with unguarded intensity.

"Grandfather's all I have," he said.

"What do you mean?"

"The only family left to me. Father died in a mining accident. They called it the big explosion of southern Wales."

"I've heard of it. The one that closed down the mines?"

He nodded. "I was nine at the time. Mum moved us up to northern Wales to live with Grandfather and Grandmother. Mum hung on another twelve years, fighting her loneliness. For my sake. But she never got over losing dad. And once I was grown and off to university, I think her loneliness for him just took over. She died of cancer three years ago."

He sat up, picked up a small flat rock and threw it so that it skimmed along the surface of the waves. "Grandfather and mother taught me a lot about magic. I went on Imrams with grandfather, learned the chants, the prayers, the legends. And all about the Goddess. But you know what, Sharay? The Goddess wasn't there to save my father. She wasn't there to save my mother." His jaw muscles clenched. "I no longer believe in any of it."

He was offering her a piece of his soul, and Sharay struggled with the acceptance. It came too close to her well-armored grief. Still, something inside her loosened, a gnarled hawthorn root unwound. Just one tiny root, but enough for her to say, "I'm sorry."

"I just wanted you to know." His eyes never left hers.

She thought she'd drown in their blue depths. It was exquisite, and it frightened her. She became a fragile seashell, the ocean lapping over her sheath, then pounding hard. Pulverizing her armor into fine grains of sand. It was too much.

She broke the gaze, and argued within herself whether to re-weave the hawthorn roots around her heart or to let them unfurl.

"Sharay?"

"Yes?" She ventured a quick look at him.

"I'll help you get your photo back."

Chapter 17

Sharay woke with a sore back. Eyes closed, she reached around the nape of her neck and rubbed, found the indentation of her birthmark and traced its outline contentedly. The roar of ocean waves crashing onto shore and retreating back again lulled her, then her eyes flew open in surprise. She was still on the beach, only it was full daylight. The orange incandescence of late morning. She felt a jacket under her head. It was coarse denim and had the scent of musk and mint on it. Guethyn's scent. He must have placed it there after she fell asleep.

The sound of the deep, even breathing of slumber made her turn. Guethyn lay beside her, asleep on his side, facing her. Seeing him, his hair tousled by sleep, his jaw unclenched and relaxed, swiftly brought her dream back to her. Guethyn had been in it. His face had been different, his nose longer, his forehead higher, but he had the same long tawny hair, the same clear blue eyes.

In the dream she had also seen herself, just as she had appeared in her visions at the Red Well the night before. As the powerful silver-haired Geodran and the fiery red-haired Rhianna. Her dream had shown her hazy panoramas from these two prior lifetimes. Turquoise oceans, lush green forests, exotic marble and crystal homes, and a pyramidal tower glowing brightly in the horizon had flashed across the dream landscape of Geodran's lifetime in Atlantis. The recognizable conical hill, the Tor, towering above ancient Glastonbury, with the ancient Red Well gurgling at its feet, was the mainstay of Rhianna's lifetime. In both lives she'd been a priestess, just as the Goddess had told her. In both lives, Guethyn, or whoever he was then, stood staunchly at her side. Loving her. Supporting her. Protecting her.

Guethyn stretched, yawned. "Rhianna?"

"What? Who?" Sharay exclaimed, louder than she'd intended.

Guethyn bolted upright, dazed.

"What did you say?" Sharay repeated.

"I . . . I don't know. I was dreaming. I lost someone. I was calling to her." He looked at her, his eyes struggling to focus. "I was calling *you*."

"You had a dream about me?"

Guethyn blinked hard. "But not you as you are now."

Sharay chewed on her bottom lip. "Guethyn, I think we had the same dream."

"No. I don't believe in that stuff." He shook his head, got to his feet. "I haven't believed for a long time. I don't believe in Santa Claus or the Easter Bunny, either."

"Wait a minute," Sharay pushed herself up and stood. She faced him, his lean tall body silhouetted against the blue of the ocean. "I'm just as freaked out as you, but it looks like we were in each other's dream. Whether we like it or not." Sharay's words caught in her throat and her womb space burned hot as she glimpsed at what lay just behind Guethyn, apparent now only in day's full light.

The mouth of a cave, partially hidden by a sharp outcropping of rocks, beckoned her. Sharay peered over Guethyn's shoulder. It looked like low tide would allow easy entrance.

"Look." She pointed. She ran toward the opening, unable to deny whatever it was that compelled her to search inside. Guethyn was right beside her.

The interior of the cave was small, perhaps ten feet long by five feet wide. Its rocky roof was only a few inches above Guethyn's head. It opened out at the far end, a much smaller opening, barely enough to fit through. Beyond that opening would be the ocean at high tide. But now, with low tide, Sharay saw sandy beach and gently lapping waves. The sand glinted and the rocks hummed with the echo of the surf. Sharay stood still, cocked her head, sure she heard soft voices above the sound of the surf. She looked around her, seeing no one but Guethyn. The voices persisted. Many eager voices that all spoke at the same time so their words seemed to reverberate off the cave walls.

"Here. It starts here, Sharay," the many voices whispered.

"We'll teach you. We'll show you how," they murmured.

She looked at Guethyn, wanting a reality check, needing confirmation. His mouth was parted, his head inclined to the side, as if he, too, was listening. Sharay began to feel an unusual confidence—the voices she heard now, the voices she heard in the past and was told to suppress, the voices she was sure she would continue to hear—were all revealing inspired guidance. If she could finally accept it, Guethyn could, too. The warrior totem lion inside her stood tall, regal.

"It's all real, Guethyn." She looked up at him, put her hands on his arms. "Our dream was a message. Not meant to scare us."

"I told you I don't believe in all that anymore."

"Then why did you come with us, Guethyn?" she asked softly.

"Because you needed my help. Nothing more."

"Nothing more?"

Guethyn did what he'd wanted to since he'd met Sharay. He brushed aside a strand of her hair. The one that often fell over her cheek.

Sharay trembled at his tender affection, unsure of what to do. Her body had its own instinct. She lifted her chin, raised her lips to his. She now understood what Guethyn meant to her, how vitally important he had been to her before and could be again. But she wanted proof of it for his sake. When their lips met, she felt his warm and eager welcome, the heat of exploring his mouth with hers. In the next instant, all the images in her dream rushed back simultaneously and forcefully. She expected it, and still it stunned her.

More so, it filled her with longing for the love she shared with him in other lifetimes.

"Sharay," he whispered. Confusion warred within him at the strength of their rediscovered feelings, and mirrored itself in the lines of his jaw and the force of his grip.

She could barely see him through her tears. The intensity of lifetimes loving the man who stood before her exploded inside her. The strength of it brought her to her knees. He dropped down alongside her, and they clung to each other.

Sharay didn't know how long she held him. She soothed him, remembered him, wanted him.

Though he'd long ago rejected the Goddess, Guethyn couldn't fight the visions Sharay brought to life when he held her in his arms. The soothing sounds she whispered in his ear somehow helped him remember it all. The lifetimes together, the all-consuming love he'd felt for her for eons on end. Once out of her embrace, he might push aside the visions, he might question everything, but he knew what was real for him in this moment. The love he suddenly felt was more real than anything he'd ever experienced. His heart ached for her, rejoiced in finding her. Every cell in his body called out for her. A week ago, he might have rejected the jarring memories of this ancient love come to life again. But with Sharay's body against his and his arms around her, there was nothing to do but yield to the force of his feelings for her. No words passed between them; understanding bound them.

When she finally stood, released from his embrace, Sharay felt suddenly shy. She didn't know what to say. Something in her gut, something dark and slippery, tightened. The black hole rose up in shadowy warning, calling her back to safety, warning her she'd only be hurt by love.

Sharay shook her head, recoiled from the hole's enticement. It tugged at her belly, tightened the roots that bound her heart.

"Are you okay with all of this? I mean us?" Guethyn asked.

Okay? She was more than okay. She nodded yes and touched his cheek. She just needed to escape the black hole's grip. Fortified by Dillon's wisdom and Guethyn's love, on sheer will power she pulled away from the hole. It tugged on her once more. She yanked herself back. The effort left her shaking. Guethyn took her hand.

The black hole retreated angrily, its enticing whispers muffled. Its promises rang empty for Sharay. She no longer desired the isolation it offered. Still, she could sense it in dark recess, waiting patiently.

Still holding onto her hand, Guethyn moved to leave the cave. The pair ducked under the cave's low entrance, and emerged to find Dillon sitting cross-legged on the beach, munching lazily on a cheese sandwich.

He smiled at them.

"Here, you must be hungry." He pointed to a small wicker basket beside him filled with more sandwiches, apples, and bottled water.

Sharay wasn't sure she could eat with all she was feeling, but Guethyn sat down and dove into the small meal as if it were his last supper.

"You two have been gone a long time," Dillon mentioned casually.

Sharay looked up from the apple she'd chosen from the picnic basket.

"We fell asleep on the beach. We were exhausted," Guethyn said between mouthfuls of ham and cheese on whole wheat.

"I see." Dillon's eyes twinkled, his dimples slowly forming in his cheeks.

"What?" Guethyn sat up straight, threw his napkin at his grandfather in mock defense. "Not that it's any of your business, but nothing happened. Sharay's been safe in my care, rest assured."

"Nothing happened?" Sharay repeated, looking at Guethyn.

"Guethyn, there's no question that I trust you to take care of her," Dillon said.

"Nothing happened?" Sharay repeated.

"Well, of course something happened." Guethyn held out an imploring hand to Sharay. "I mean . . . but not *that*, grandfather." He looked over at his grandfather, and set his sandwich down. "Hell. I'm twenty-five and well old enough. Sharay's eighteen and knows her own heart . . . what am I doing explaining anything to you?"

Dillon grinned. "More to the point, why would an innocent statement get you so riled?"

Guethyn shook his head, rolled his eyes. Sharay stared at the two of them, aware of the affection they shared even as they sparred.

"Well, it just makes my job easier," Dillon said leaning back against the same boulder Sharay had rested upon earlier. "It's Beltaine in two days."

"You planned this," Guethyn said.

Sharay remembered the conversation her mother and Rosheen had about Beltaine when she was a child of five. The implications of it dawned on her. "What are you saying, Dillon?"

Dillon got a faraway look in his eyes. "Beltaine is a holy day. A time to honor the new life of spring, the fecundity of the Goddess, and the mystery of sacred union in Her name." A secret smile curved his lips, deepened his dimples. "Rosheen was the first to honor me with celebrating the rites. It was very special."

"Rosheen?" Guethyn asked.

Dillon turned his gaze back to the pair and winked. "Yes. And I would have asked her to honor me again this year if it was safe to bring her here."

"You old geezer," Guethyn teased.

"Never too old to honor the Goddess. But, Beltaine is more a time for youth to discover the path of sacred union."

Sharay looked over at Guethyn. His face was flushed, bright blue eyes clouded and smoky, his jaw set. "Wait a minute," he said. "You set us up. To use for your magical agendas."

"Now calm yourself, Guethyn. I didn't need to do anything. You've been searching for her for ages." Dillon gestured toward Sharay while his gaze remained steady on Guethyn.

"I told you, I want nothing of your magic. You've gone too far."

Sharay's heart sank. She'd felt the undeniable truth of Dillon's pronouncement, and was stung by Guethyn's rejection.

Dillon said, "Gone too far? Have I? I only ask you to participate in a holy rite that's as natural for the two of you as breathing. Tell me it's not something you desire?"

"That's not the point. . . ."

"Guethyn?" Sharay took a steadying breath and leaned over to speak quietly to him. "I would never beg you to be with me in that way." She stopped, swallowed. "Somehow, what Dillon says . . . feels . . ." she lifted her hand, searched for the word, ". . . feels right. It does seem quick for all of this, but it's bigger than the two of us. Our dreams told us that. And what he said is true. We've waited eons." Her words surprised her, but her certainty did not.

Guethyn felt torn between newfound tenderness and angry confusion, between his desire for Sharay and his distrust of magic and of the Goddess. He broke eye contact with Sharay. "Didn't you say we needed a few things from that small village we passed, grandfather?"

Dillon didn't answer.

"I'll make a quick run into that village, buy a few things, fill up on petrol. I'll phone Rosheen and let her know we're okay."

Guethyn needed time to think and he needed it now. Before his grandfather got him involved in any more magic. Before he was entirely lost in the powerful feelings invoked by Sharay's mere presence. He sprinted back to the caravan trailer. The pumping of his leg muscles as he ran, his forceful heartbeat, and his quick breathing, helped him to discharge his tension and clear his mind.

When he got to the trailer, he climbed in the driver's seat, looked down and swore. "Bloody hell."

Lying across the dashboard was a Tarot Trump card. A man and a woman stood naked under a rose trellis, and a vast, hooded female figure stood nearby with face obscured and hands raised above the couple in blessing. The title across the bottom of the card read LOVERS in bold black letters.

Chapter 18

"Guethyn will come around. He's got a fiery temper. Just like his grandmother." Dillon smiled at their similarity. "But he's solid as a rock, and whether he likes it or not, he's part of your destiny."

Away from Guethyn, Sharay grappled with her newfound feelings for him. They swirled inside her, fulfillment vying with bewilderment, as her earlier confidence struggled to take hold. "I do feel he's . . . a part of me. Like I've suddenly found something treasured that I'd misplaced." She lifted her hands, baffled. "This is happening so fast."

Dillon stared out to where sea met sky. "You feel a certain comfort with Guethyn? A familiarity?"

"Yes," she answered without hesitation.

He turned to face her. "The rest will fall into place naturally, Sharay. Not only because you've discovered your feelings for him, but because you've loved him before."

Sharay tried on the feeling of actually *loving* Guethyn. It came easy, softly folding itself around the harsh corners of her weary heart. In guarded response, her stomach clenched, her muscles knotted.

Yet despite her fears, her heart firmly insisted on welcoming him, a wellspring oasis in a long barren desert. "I'm not sure I could stop this anyway."

"Do you want to?"

"I . . . I don't think so." Her muscles eased.

"If you'll let them, the rites of Beltaine will guide the two of you, and help you chart your way."

Sharay picked up a handful of sand, let it sift through her fingers. Focusing on the tiny grains helped her to think clearly. "Why do you want us to celebrate Beltaine so much, Dillon?"

"Simple. It will guide you solidly back into communion with the Goddess."

"Can't I do that without the Beltaine rites?"

Dillon rubbed his beard. "Of course."

"Then why push the Beltaine celebration?"

"Because you have a lot of preparation to make up for. Years of missed training."

"Will I be able to make it up?"

"You've a strong natural ability. You're of the bloodline. But I must still teach you all I can. The Beltaine ritual is the quickest way to help you."

"I still don't see how it will help."

"Beltaine is a time in the cycle of nature when the whole of creation comes alive again. It's the early summer of lush fertility. You can smell the greenness in the air, see the flowers blossom and the fruits ripen. It's an expansive time that opens you to the love of the Goddess and to Her power." Dillon lifted his hands, as if to embrace all of nature's bounty around him. "That's why, as part of the ancient ritual, couples join in an intimate, loving, sacred ceremony. The joining of their bodies in this holy manner is offered up in honor of the Goddess. The veils are thinner and deep connections can be made with the Goddess through such joining."

"All right, I'm not saying no to the ritual. But, right now my life is so complicated . . . and now this."

Dillon rested his hands on his knees and was quiet a moment before he went on. "Sharay, I don't say these things to confuse you or scare you. It's important for you, and important for the Prophecy, that you come into your power. That you, and several more women like you around the world, embrace your destiny."

"You mean there's more like me?" Sharay said excitedly. In truth, she was vastly relieved she wasn't alone.

"Yes. There are other women with similar destinies, each within their own spiritual tradition."

"Why us?"

"Because you've all done this before. In other lifetimes, other eras of big changes in history."

"What eras? What big changes?"

"Times of great spiritual evolution. We're in the middle of one right now. This era has been predicted by many spiritual lineages. Humanity is meant to evolve spiritually and physically. With the help of the most powerful magical force. Divine Love."

"Okay. But what are we supposed to do? What am *I* supposed to do?"

"You'll come to recognize exactly what to do and when you need to do it."

"You've got to be kidding. I'm only eighteen. I've never been trained as a priestess. I don't know anything."

Dillon smiled gently. "You know more than you realize. You'll remember more once you awaken your inner power, this force of Love. The Goddess will guide you—if you let Her. You, and the others like you, were born to lead the Way of the Heart so that others can follow more easily. This is what will help fulfill the collective destiny of humanity."

Sharay sighed loudly. "What is this destiny of humanity?"

"Humanity is in the throes of enormous change. An opportunity to heal our hearts and make our bodies whole. To become the most magnificent human beings we can be. A whole new civilization awaits us. This is an evolutionary leap in consciousness."

"Why now?"

Dillon collected his thoughts. "You only need to look around to see the planet is in trouble. Because of humankind. We try to dominate others, as well as the earth and all life on our planet. We coerce and control instead of listen and cooperate. That's because for a long time we've separated from the divinity and love deep inside our bodies. We've disregarded it and ignored it, even demonized it. We've doubted the guidance of our intuition, and mistrusted anything that doesn't come from science, or our logical minds, or from those we call authorities. So, all of our power, if wielded without love, only brings on greed, hate, violence, war. Until now our very existence is jeopardized."

Dillon continued. "But you also need to know that massive turbulence precedes massive change. It's part of a long term cycle of the stars, of the planets, of life. Death and rebirth. It's a universal law."

"What do I have to do with a universal law?"

Dillon's dimples creased and he looked at Sharay with affection in his eyes. "Legend says when the cloth of the world gets torn asunder, the Weaver Goddess picks up Her loom and reweaves a beautiful new pattern. But She needs humankind to help hold the threads together. Destruction always comes before regeneration."

Sharay let out another long breath. "This is so big. Way bigger than me."

"It is. And regeneration will come from it. But humankind's transition into the regeneration, into their true destiny, can only happen through you, and those like you. You'll all play a particular role in helping the Goddess to help humanity."

"You know I trust you, Dillon. But I have no clue how to help with something as huge as this."

"I can tell you that acknowledging and communing with the Goddess is the first and most essential step."

"You mean the Beltaine ritual," Sharay said.

"Yes, the Beltaine ritual. It will help you experience the Goddess as Divine Love, the very substance of the universe. You see, Divinity expresses itself along a spectrum. On one end there's the unseen realm of the spirit, which is the realm of the Divine Masculine. On the other end is the tangible physical world, the realm of the Divine Feminine."

"But humanity has forgotten that Divinity is inherent in physical form as well as it is in spirit. For a long time now humans have believed that divinity only resides up and above, outside themselves, in the realm of the heavens. With a heavenly Father," Dillon said.

"But certainly that's not true?" Sharay said.

"It's only half of the truth. The Goddess is the other half. You only need to look to nature. Even a tree has roots that sink deep into the earth."

Sharay watched the ocean waves rolling onto the shore. "So, the Goddess is the Divine in all matter. Then, the substance of creation is Love?"

Dillon gazed at her with delight in his eyes. "Yes. And in the Beltaine ritual, you'll open to Divine Love through the sexual union of your bodies. You've done it in lifetimes before." He paused a moment. "But you must do this now with an open heart. In the midst of your grief, you must learn to keep your heart open. In the midst of your anger, you keep your heart open. In the midst of your guilt, you keep your heart open."

Dillon's eyes filled with compassion. "I know things haven't been easy since your parents died."

Sharay felt the familiar stranglehold on her heart at the mention of her parents. She sensed Dillon could see her push her grief and her guilt down and away.

Sharay lowered her eyes. "I hurt so much inside. How can I keep my heart open?"

"You allow your pain. You hold it in your heart."

"Wait a minute! Why would I want to do that?"

"When you push pain down, you abandon yourself and everyone you love. If you try to transcend your pain, if you go up and out of your body and dwell solely in your thoughts or some idealized sense of spirit, all you'll do is leave your pain behind, where it will stay neglected and then act out in all sorts of destructive manners. You can't embody love if you do either of those."

Sharay was quiet a moment before she replied. "You're asking a lot," then added with a wry smile, "Even the great Dr. Deluth couldn't fix me."

"You're not broken, Sharay. What will heal you is different from what Dr. Deluth offered. I'm not saying this will be easy on you, but know that you can't love if you close your heart. Remember this—we connect with one another and find love through our imperfect world.

That means we find it in the midst of our messy humanness, our reaching out, our suffering. Like losing your parents. Or living with Phoebe."

"I hate her."

"I understand."

"That won't change, Dillon. How can I love if that won't change?"

"That's okay. You keep your heart open anyway."

"I don't know that I can do that."

"Then it will be your undoing," Dillon said quietly.

Sharay felt her thoughts fog up with a sticky web of confusion. She sensed a dark slithering in the pit of her stomach. She shook her head to clear the sensations.

Dillon watched her with the trained eyes of a priest. "The seed of love, the Goddess, is inside every thing. *Everything*, Sharay. That seed may be hidden inside tangled knots that look twisted and ugly on the surface, but it's there locked inside."

"How do I get to it if it's locked inside me?"

"You give it love."

"Give it love?"

"That simple. You put all your anger and guilt and hate on the altar of your heart, let it sit right alongside your love, your hope, and your serenity. And you give it all to the Goddess's Love."

"Because it's about transforming it rather than transcending it?"

"Absolutely," Dillon said. "Your heart can hold both sides of any turmoil. Do you participate in the ritual, or do you not? Do you open your heart or keep it constricted? Hold both sides of your decision in your heart. Then from that place, something new and beautiful can be born."

Sharay took a deep breath. "So, what's next?"

"First, I train you so you'll have a profound encounter with the Goddess in the ritual. This happens through your body. You'll be representing the Divine Feminine incarnate."

"Okay," Sharay said, nodding slowly, trying to imagine what that would feel like.

"Then, through your sexual union in the Beltaine ritual, you'll symbolically receive the Divine Masculine."

Sharay's heart beat faster at the thought of sexual union.

Dillon continued. "This is where Guethyn comes in. He represents the Divine Masculine. You receive him in body and soul in order to create Sacred Union between the two divinities. They unite in your bodies, in your hearts. You'll be the bridges between the heavens and the earth. But none of this can happen without first experiencing the Goddess as the Love deep within you."

"Receiving the Divine Masculine," Sharay murmured, sidetracked for the moment. She picked up another handful of sand, noticed her fingers quiver. Never having been with a man before, she wasn't sure if it was excitement or anxiety causing them to tremble so.

"The Beltaine ritual will also help you balance out the intense feelings between you and Guethyn."

Sharay drew tiny spirals in the sand with her fingers and sat in silence for a long moment, waiting for her trembling to cease. When she spoke, her voice cracked with emotion.

"So much is changing, Dillon. There's so much I'm not sure I understand. One minute I'm terrified. The next, I have hope I'll be okay. When I was in the hospital, on all that medicine, I was nearly convinced I was crazy." She looked up at him, her eyes filling with tears. "If you hadn't gotten me out when you did. . . ."

Dillon wrapped his arm around her shoulders. After her sobs had lessened, he gently asked, "And what do you believe now about your visions?"

"I'm not crazy."

"No, you're not crazy. And you *will* find your way, Tahnea."

Sharay looked up at him. "How can you be so sure?"

Dillon raised one eyebrow. "Because I've seen it in you. Because that's what you were born to do."

"Dillon . . . what happens if I don't want to do this thing you say I'm born to do."

Dillon gently clasped both her hands in his large, rough ones before he spoke. "The choice is always yours. The Goddess will never force you. She only sends out the ancient calling."

He handed her his handkerchief and sat quietly beside her on the soft sand. Sharay unfolded it, wiped her eyes, and stared fixedly out to sea. She wasn't sure she'd ever measure up to all that was expected of her. As a priestess. As a prophesied one. A new world was beckoning her. One her mother had only begun to show her how to explore before she died. Her mother had taught her bits and pieces about the Goddess, things Sharay was only beginning to make sense of now.

She rubbed the nape of her neck, begged the pulse of the ocean's frothy surf to cleanse her agitation. The swooshing sound of each wave that ebbed onto shore cleansed a piece of her anguish. Its timeless murmur relaxed her tense muscles and soothed her soul, and bit by small bit removed the last of the layered veils blocking remembrance of her past lives.

The eternal waves, watery messengers of the Goddess, whispered to her, reminding her of what the Goddess had told her the previous evening, reminding her of her dream with Guethyn, reminding her of what she already knew deep down in her bones. She'd been a priestess before. Geodran and Rhianna. They were aspects of herself, fragments of her soul's life history.

The waves continued to undulate, their crashing surf informing her, prompting her in the language of misty images and cellular recollection.

"Guethyn has been with you—as the man named Theolon, long ago in Atlantis. Then, as Perigrine in Glastonbury," the waves said with surging froth.

The soles of her feet grew hot, her heart filled with emotion that spilled over in silent tears, and she simply knew. The message the waves bore was truth.

On their next swell, they told her, "You've been in service to the Goddess of the Stars and the Sea all along."

Yet even with budding confidence and reawakened intuition, there was another insistent voice that seeped through her thoughts, beating away the frothy ocean messages. "You're simply Sharay Kallah, eighteen years old, naïve to the ways of a priestess. What role could *you* have in the lineage of the Goddess during this lifetime?" the voice jeered. It felt mean, sounded just like Aunt Phoebe when she criticized her for having mystical visions.

Still, each wave flowing back out to sea persisted in reclaiming for her more of her ancient wisdom and experience, bringing it back as sea foam offering. Her body couldn't help but sigh in relief with the unwrapped memories, gift from the sea. The retrieval gave her purpose. She opened herself to the power of the Goddess' watery womb, the eternal sea. She asked the watery flood of ancient recollections to spark her inner knowing despite how they continued to be countered by the unrelenting voice that belittled them.

But the disparaging voice jeered and argued. "You have a long way to go before you're anywhere near the long-awaited priestess Rosheen and Dillon seem to think you are . . . or even the lover Guethyn might expect."

Sharay put her hands over her ears, tried to blot out the demeaning voices in her head. She wanted only the peace she felt with the ocean's gift. She fought for it. She focused on the ocean's waves, put all her attention there.

Dillon watched her intently, his fingers silently moving themselves into the mudras of strength and protection. He held his fingers in the secret hand positions for several moments, adding his strength of conviction to Sharay's budding yet tenuous confidence. The berating voice inside Sharay fell back into shadowy recess.

Sharay turned to Dillon, considered what the ocean's message had sparked within her and what she wanted to share with him. "The Goddess came to me through the ocean." She furrowed her brow. "I remembered my past lives as a priestess. I need to help Her do something now, just like you said. Damn, this all sounds so silly." She cradled her head in her hands.

Dillon waited patiently.

Sharay lifted her hands in frustration. "The Goddess tells me, Rosheen tells me, you tell me, that I know how to do . . . something. Whatever that is."

Dillon said with certainty, "I believe in you, Sharay. Have faith that you do know."

"But I really don't."

"I don't know precisely how you're meant to contribute, because this is *your* destiny." Dillon replied, his voice low and calm. "I can tell you this from our prophecies." He quoted a portion from the ancient divination of their spiritual lineage.

She will rise from where they have hidden Her.
Emerging from the infinitely within,
to guide humanity once more.
And She will call upon all of those who have helped before.
One will be silver of hair, with a star-shaped birthmark upon
the base of her neck.
The keys to liberation are locked inside this one's body,
where depth of Ocean and light of Stars will merge.

Sharay felt her whole body tingle. While something inside her responded to the words, her mind continued to argue the enormity of it all.

She turned to face Dillon. "If I do this, it will be on my own terms."

"As it should be."

"I won't be forced, you know."

"No one will force you."

"What about Rosheen?"

"She won't. She can't. It is up to you if you want to help the Goddess aid the world through this shift. But you need to know that you're enough. You're loved, just as you are, even if you decide not to help."

His answer disarmed her. The last time she'd heard she was loved was when her mother kissed her softly on the forehead and joined her father in the car to go buy her ice cream on her tenth birthday. Sharay swallowed back the lump that rose to her throat. With practiced effort, the hawthorn roots tightened around her heart, the habit of censoring her grief triumphant again. The effort of suppression felt burdensome.

Dillon spoke. "I'll show you all that your mother and Rosheen wanted you to know. I'm afraid you're in for a crash course."

"Dillon?" Sharay looked up, challenge in the set of her jaw. "Aren't the teachings usually passed on from priestess to priestess?"

"Yes."

"And isn't it important I learn from someone of my bloodline lineage?"

"The only other person of your bloodline lineage alive is Phoebe. You can not be trained by her."

"She never taught me about being a priestess, even when I begged her."

"Rosheen told me."

"So then, you, a man, a priest, are going to teach me now?"

Dillon chuckled softly. "Oh, I'll try my best. The spiritual lineage of our Goddess includes men and women. Her ways have always been made known to both. We'll do just fine, but we don't have much time. . . ." His voice trailed off.

"Not much time?"

Dillon spoke slowly. "I feel . . . something . . . pursues us."

"The hospital? The police?"

"Well, there's that, and that's serious enough. But I'm speaking of something else. I've sensed your Aunt Phoebe's meddling, Sharay."

"What is she doing? What can we do to stop her?" Sharay asked, her words tumbling over each other.

"She's using magic for her own means again. She's probing, wheedling her way in, using your fears."

Sharay felt something vile crawl feather soft across her skin. When she looked down at her arm, nothing was there. Harsh realization dawned on her. "I can't trust my own thoughts then, can I?"

"You'll have to learn discernment. Determine what's yours and what's not. What's been magnified and what's truth."

Sharay grew somber and nodded her assent. Her dislike for Aunt Phoebe simmered in her gut, fueled her resolve. "Dillon, I almost forgot. There was one time Aunt Phoebe showed me something magical."

Dillon waited.

"When she first came to live with me, she taught me a spell. A cursing spell. It didn't feel right. It felt awful. Sticky. I told her to leave me alone. I'm so sorry, Dillon. Have I ruined my training?"

"No. Your instincts served you well. I needn't warn you never to use what she taught you."

"I won't," Sharay promised. She rubbed her temples, as if to dislodge the sticky knowledge.

"The magic of your lineage is good. When it's finally safe to return to Glastonbury, Rosheen and the other priestesses will embrace you into the community that has always been your true spiritual home."

"Will it ever be safe to return?"

"We can work toward that," Dillon replied.

At the look of despair on her face, he added, "What we can do now is to help you grow into your power. Are you ready to remember what it means to be a priestess?"

Sharay nodded, though the fluttering in her stomach told her otherwise.

Dillon continued. "I'm going to remind you of the ways of the Goddess. The Way of the Heart. The power and strength of receiving the wise flow within you. I'll show you how to embrace your grief, your guilt, your anger, all of it. You do it through your open heart. Your heart is an alchemical vessel, Sharay. Your open heart can receive the transformative power of the Goddess's Love."

Sharay's mind stumbled over Dillon's words. "So, we're back to that embrace my pain thing again." Her stomach lurched.

"Yes. The Way of the Heart shows us how to *be* in our physical life, Sharay. How to accept and embrace our sometimes painful humanness in order to fully embody our divine essence. True Sacred Union."

Sharay pushed her palm forward. "Whoa. Slow down. I said I don't know about embracing my pain, Dillon."

"I'll be right here beside you, Sharay."

Sharay recalled Aunt Phoebe's derisive face, lined with frowns; with heavy blue eye make-up and mascara thickly applied. She scoffed at the image, took a deep breath and sat up straight. She would choose to ignore the contraction of her stomach in favor of Dillon's reassurances. In favor of prevailing over Aunt Phoebe. With the idea of overriding her aunt's belittlement, she finally agreed. "Let's do it then."

Chapter 19

Dillon stood, motioned for Sharay to do the same. Once on her feet, she was positioned to face the west, the open sea.

"The direction of the Sea Temple of the Goddess," Dillon told her.

He took the first two fingers of his right hand and blessed her on her forehead, drawing a symbol of two adjoining circles with a vertical line intersecting them.

Then he put her hands over her heart, told her to feel its warmth and steady beat.

"You're going to learn to build and call upon your power. First, you must connect with your heart. Simply with your intention and awareness. Use your breath to help you. Then you're to link your heart to your belly."

With her hands over her heart, Sharay brought her attention there, and breathed into it. Next, Dillon placed her hands over her belly, her left hand over her right. She then exhaled from her heart into her belly to make a connection between the two.

"Your place of power is in your belly. For you, a woman, it's deep in your womb." Dillon positioned himself next to her, his hands on his belly. He, too, faced west.

He continued. "Focus on your belly, specifically on your womb space. Take your breath right into that place in your body."

"I know how to do this," Sharay said excitedly. "Mother taught me."

"That's good you know it already. Let's take it farther then."

Sharay didn't mention to Dillon that she hadn't practiced it much over the ensuing years. That she was unable to call upon it when she first sat in Dr. Deluth's office for her psychiatric evaluation, or in all the time she was in the hospital.

"All right. I'm ready." Sharay slipped off her shoes and let her bare toes dig into the golden sand, repositioned herself with feet shoulder width apart, knees slightly bent, in what felt like a more solid stance. She noticed Dillon smile at her initiative. She closed her eyes, allowed his words to resonate within.

"Spread your hands apart, palms over your belly. Let your thumbs touch, and your index fingers touch, so that they form an upside down triangle over your womb space. Like this."

Dillon leaned over, helped her form the triangle over her womb space. She imagined the triangle as a focal point, a gateway into ancient and mysterious secrets.

Dillon returned to her side, stood still, his hands over his own power spot. "Sharay . . . your body is the bridge between mind and soul, between spirit and matter, between the stars in the heavens and the sacred earth." His voice grew deep and rich.

Dillon's voice mingled with the memory of her mother's instructions, forming one unified voice. "Your heart is the fulcrum of the bridge. Your womb, the power pivot."

"The Goddess resides deep in your body. Your body holds the keys to remember all that you need."

Tension released along Sharay's spine.

"Lamou dei tu wantna se de tu," she whispered.

She barely noticed she'd spoken the same exotic language that she'd first uttered in Dr. Deluth's office six months ago; the same language that had startled her when Dillon spoke it in the hospital dayroom.

The words bubbled up from her deep wellspring of wisdom, already translated, *I am that which is at the end of all longing. The love you desire is within.*

Dillon watched her reaction, her lack of surprise at the ancient words, her acceptance and understanding of them. He sighed, relieved.

He continued, prompting her more than instructing. "Breathe into your womb three times. On the third breath, as you exhale, envision anchoring your womb into the center of the earth. See a long cord coming from your womb and going down into the earth, deep into its center. The center of the earth is the heart of the Goddess."

Sharay could no longer tell where the instructions came from. Her mother's words long ago, Dillon's lustrous voice, or the ancient calling within her body. The breaths lulled her, and she stood transfixed within their hold.

Dillon stopped to check on Sharay's breath and her hand position. Even with her eyes closed, she felt her abdomen tingle with Dillon's silent assessment, his hands hovering slightly over her belly as she performed the breathing practice. Curiosity pulled her from her trance, and she peeked at Dillon through squinted eyelids.

Without looking up, Dillon said, "I'm feeling your vital energy." He continued to move his hands above her belly and across her back. "I'm looking for signs you're responding to the breathing exercises. Signs like flowing energy movement within and around you."

"Tell me what you see," she asked eagerly.

"I see concentrated rainbow colors around your womb and a bright straight line through the center of your body, anchored into the earth."

Sharay looked down at her belly and frowned. "I don't see anything."

"Soften your gaze. Look with your intuition."

Sharay tried harder to focus but still couldn't see any colors. "It's not working," she said. Frustration replaced her quietude.

"Keep breathing into your womb. Let your womb receive the breath."

"What do the colors mean?"

"They show your heightened energy fields."

"Oh! I feel dizzy."

"Slow your breaths."

Sharay closed her eyes again, slowed down her breaths, concentrated on feeling her womb receive her breath.

"Know that you're building a profound connection to the Goddess through the portal of your womb. That connection is where your strength lies. It is where deep wisdom resides."

"I don't feel anything yet, Dillon," Sharay whispered, disheartened.

She wondered if she'd bungled her connection after so many years of neglect. She tried even harder to do well, wanting to please him, wanting to tap into the same strength evident in him.

"Keep going, Sharay," he instructed. His deep, rumbling voice resembled the smashing of the incoming surf. "Let your breath fan the hidden star fire flames in the temple of your womb. No forcing. Just allowing."

Sharay concentrated. "The hidden star fire flames in my womb," she murmured, letting the ancient wisdom surge up. The sun shone warmly across her arms, the sea mist gathered, mingled in salty union with the fine sheen of perspiration on her forehead from her effort. After several attempts she finally felt it. "There's a warm spark in my womb space!"

Each new breath brought a more intense radiating heat that spread through her womb space and into her belly. Sharay looked down at her body. She appeared almost luminous. Sparkling rays of silver and blue emanated from her womb space and reflected off the sand beneath her and the sea in front of her. She smiled, delighted in her ability to stoke the energy of her womb temple.

"Well done," Dillon said softly, not bothering to mask his awe. His breath caught at the quality of energy Sharay manifested in her first training session. After a few moments, as the luminosity faded, he added, "It's only the first step."

Sharay grimaced.

"Practice some more and see what happens."

After several minutes of breathing in this womb way, the energy gathered in the boned cup of Sharay's pelvis. Its collected power ignited. Her body tingled with fiery flickers of heat. Pulsing vibrations grew into rocking surges. Sharay teetered to and fro and her breath came fast and deep.

"Good," Dillon said even before she could report her success. "Now you will be able to call upon your power at will. But this is incomplete in and of itself. It's time to add another piece."

Sharay pursed her lips and let out a soft whistle. "Now this is different from what I've ever felt before."

"That's because you're different, Sharay. You're building your connection to the Goddess. In that connection you're building your power. Your bodily Temple."

Dillon grew silent and breathed slowly and deeply. His eyes were focused, his body steady, with none of the wobbling Sharay felt. He glimmered, though she wasn't sure if the glow emanated from him, or the rays of the early afternoon sun. Finally he spoke.

"Breathe out. When you exhale, send your exhalation even deeper into your womb. This will increase the star fire inherent there."

Sharay couldn't imagine how anything could add to what she was already feeling. Still, she exhaled and focused her attention, for Dillon had said that where she held her attention, vital energy would follow. She measured her inhalations and her exhalations against the ebbing and flowing waves crashing before her.

After several tries with no further results, she was ready to yield to defeat. In the very moment of her yielding, her womb space opened in the receptivity of her surrender.

She heard a familiar voice, the voice of the Goddess. "The stars are in your belly, as they are in Mine."

Sharay surrendered further. The exhalations channeled the life force of her breath deeper into her womb. She felt herself drop into the inside of her body, as if she'd been sucked into an invisible vortex. She swirled round and round, deeper into the spiraling pulses that made up her watery cells, then even further in. She floated amidst the galaxies of rotating planets and starry skies that made up the atoms of her cells. The deeper she dropped, the brighter the swirling mass of atomic stars. She drifted boundlessly. Between particles of atoms and no-thingness. She dwelled in the infinitely deep of within. She felt a soft pulsation, knew it to be the energy source of her vital life force, felt its gentle rhythm rock her body.

She heard a familiar voice, the voice of the Goddess. "I am the Mother of all form."

In the next breath, energy exploded through her. Bolts of molten heat undulated up and down her spine, fed by the power built up in her womb, her living Temple. Her breath came in short bursts, her body arched; the power bowl of her pelvis filled and released more and more power in all consuming sensations of exquisite ecstasy. Sharay was held in its grip for several moments, until one last explosion left her body limp, and she gently slid onto the sand. Her fall was cushioned by the warm sand and Dillon's supportive arms. She was utterly exhausted, yet filled with more vitality than she'd ever dreamed possible.

$\mathcal{C}$hapter 20

Sharay lay back on the sand and laughed aloud. She reveled in the taste of the sea mist clinging to her lips, licked at it with her tongue, sharing her delicious secret with the eternal sea. Several moments of bliss later she opened her eyes, worked to focus them on Dillon's face a few feet away.

"Not bad for the first time." His dimples deepened.

"What *was* that?" she asked hazily.

"The liquid light of your vital life force. The liquid light of the stars. The power of Divine Love embodied in your womb."

"Does Guethyn know how to do this?"

"He was once taught," Dillon replied.

"But the two of you have no womb. How do you do this?"

"A man sends his breath to the basin of his perineum, his pelvic bowl, the same seat of the flow of life-force. Still, the woman has the special temple that a man will never know."

Sharay nodded, understanding dawning from deep in her belly.

Dillon gazed intently at Sharay. "Before you can go further, I'm afraid you'll need to tend the fire of your heart," he said evenly.

"What does that mean?"

"Your heart is wounded. Its fire burns low."

Sharay's stiffened. Her mood swiftly dampened.

"You need to be able to draw on the sacred part of your heart to fully claim your magical power."

"I don't think I want to do anything more today."

"In order to progress safely, I'm afraid you'll need to do this, Sharay. Tapping into the sacred fire of your heart harnesses the strongest magical power. But, you can't do it without facing your emotional pain. Otherwise, the power will rip you apart."

Dillon's face was serious, his eyes didn't hold their usual mischievous twinkle. "I've seen it in you," he added.

"Seen what?" The hawthorn roots around her heart stretched taut, pulled away from Dillon's magical gaze.

"Something harsh and dark around your heart."

"Leave it be. I'm okay," Sharay insisted.

Dillon spoke gently. "Take your breath there," he said, pointing his finger to the left of her sternum, to the place where her heart beat strongly.

Sharay felt pain in the spot where he pointed, a physical raw agony that ripped through her chest like a tiger's claw through its victim's flesh.

"Stop! I'm having a heart attack," she gasped.

"No, you're not. You're safe, Sharay. Breathe into your heart." He offered her his hands.

"What did you do?" she demanded, pushing his hands aside.

"I did nothing, Sharay. Caused nothing that wasn't already there."

She clutched her chest. "It hurts."

"I know, Tahnea. Give it breath and it will dissolve."

Sharay rose onto her knees, ready to bolt.

"Think of Guethyn."

The sound of his name stopped her.

"Bring a smile into your heart," Dillon instructed.

Sharay wasn't sure what Dillon meant. Yet with the thought of Guethyn, a small smile tugged on her lips. Hesitantly, she took the feelings that fueled her smile down into her chest, letting it flow like sweet golden nectar.

"Yes, that's it." Dillon raised his arms and moved his hands in spiraling gestures around her chest and sternum. "Here. I can help you begin to move the energy for your healing. But know that I can't do your healing for you. That's something you'll have to choose for yourself. Something you'll have to choose again and again."

Sharay's heart only pulled tighter in response to the incoming healing energy. She moaned. "Oh, great . . . you mean this is never-ending?"

"You'll have to practice throughout your whole life. We all do. Choosing healing, choosing love, in every moment. Now, keep breathing," Dillon said firmly. "Normally I would tell you to just softly touch the edges of your pain, as best you can. To move in slowly. But, we don't have time."

"I don't want to do this anymore."

Dillon's let his hands fall to his sides, his eyes were filled with patience. "I understand. Will you keep breathing?"

"I don't care that we don't have time."

"Sharay, the darkness pursues us. You've got to be ready to meet it."

"What darkness pursues us?" Sharay wrapped her arms around her middle and rocked back and forth.

"Something your Aunt Phoebe called up from the murky pit of her greed. A demonic entity."

"But surely it can't find us here."

When Dillon didn't reply, Sharay asked, "Can it?" She held her arms more tightly around her body, hoping to stop trembling.

"Possibly, yes . . . whatever evil she conjures can find us."

Ice water traveled along Sharay's arms. "I hate her."

"Sharay, this isn't only about your Aunt Phoebe. If it wasn't her, it would be someone else trying to stop you."

"Why?"

"Because the upcoming change for humanity is that big. Because what you are supposed to do is that important."

"But why would anyone try to stop something that's for our good?"

"Universal law in the physical realm. Glorious actions will always be met by their opposite, which will try to stop them. It's all about choice again. Practice choosing the power of love in every moment. To heal. To cultivate your power. To fulfill your destiny."

Images shot through Sharay's mind's eye in quick succession. Dug up hawthorn roots and red rose bushes along the driveway to her house in Glastonbury. Rosheen telling her that her parents had died. Aunt Phoebe and Uncle Larry moving into her manor home. Aunt Phoebe scolding her, shouting at her. Aunt Phoebe telling her that she was to blame for her parents' accident. That her visions were craziness. Long agonizing days and nights in the hospital with her arms and legs restrained.

Years of bound up grief and guilt rent her heart in two. She doubled over and screamed.

Dillon laid his hands on her shoulder, his touch gentle yet steadfast. "Don't fight your grief. Don't resist your guilt. Face it full on. Meet it in your heart. Meet it with your breath."

"Go away. I don't care about Aunt Phoebe. Or whoever she sends."

"Do you trust me?"

Sharay panted. "Yes . . . no."

"Put all your attention in your heart. Put all your feelings—your grief, your anger, your guilt—on the altar of your heart. Meet it there."

He breathed with her, his breaths slow, even, regular. Because she loved him, she tried, tried to imitate his breaths, but the thick hawthorn roots gripped her heart tighter. "I can't do this, Dillon."

The black hole inside her reached out greedily. "*I'll help,*" it seemed to call above the din of her emotions. Instinctively, Sharay's consciousness raced toward its protection, toward its numbing relief.

Dillon's voice came from far away. "Hold my hand, Sharay. Stay in your heart. You *can* do this."

Sharay huddled further behind the thick walls of the black hole.

Dillon's voice became more command than instruction. "Do not shove your pain inside."

Sharay ignored him, hid in her dark pit.

"Sharay, I know you're hurting. You've felt hurt for a long time. You've built a refuge to hide in so you wouldn't have to feel." Dillon paused. "But now your refuge is toxic."

Sharay grunted. She didn't care.

"Sharay! This is important. You're suffering more *because* you've resisted your feelings," Dillon said, emphasizing each word.

Sharay wouldn't look at him, didn't want to believe him.

Dillon pushed on. "You must feel all your feelings in order to keep your heart open. In order to heal," he said forcefully.

"No."

"Your closed heart will be your downfall," he shouted through the walls of her black pit.

Sharay didn't want to listen to Dillon any longer. She wanted relief. How dare he ask her to feel something so painful? She would die if she felt her pain any longer.

Dillon persisted. "Meet your feelings within the altar of your heart. Your heart is nested within the Goddess's heart. Her Love is the most potent transformative power. Your pain will pass if you do this." His voice boomed, but Sharay heard it as from a long distance off.

She gritted her teeth and shook her head defiantly. And she retreated into the cavernous folds of the black hole's sinuous embrace.

$\mathscr{C}$hapter 21

Guethyn parked the silver caravan in a lot alongside a few cars and two other motor coaches, signs of the modest tourist trade in the small village he'd driven to. Far from major cities, it was the same village they'd passed on their way to their coastal camp earlier that morning. There seemed to be just enough visitors for him to blend into the crowd, not too many so as to jeopardize Sharay's secluded hiding spot in the forest beside the ocean. He didn't think anyone would be able to find the well hidden lane leading to their spot anyway—he was now certain its entrance point was charmed to block its detection.

He climbed out of the caravan, threw his jacket back inside when he felt the warmth here without the direct ocean breeze. A handful of vacationers passed him in the parking lot. He overheard them saying they were stopping in town for lunch as they made their way up the rugged coast. Wanting to keep a low profile, he walked close behind them and followed them into a tiny bakery café. Perfect. What he needed was a cup of strong black tea. And time to think, away from Sharay and his grandfather.

He chose a corner table, and a young waitress promptly brought him a pot of hot water and an assortment of tea bags. She twirled a strand of her wavy blond hair and openly eyed him while he decided on a slice of currant cake to go along with his tea. Guethyn shifted uncomfortably under her direct gaze.

He was glad when a pink-cheeked toddler, two tables over, screeched her protest at being denied a second custard tart and toppled her milk glass. The waitress left grudgingly to clean up the mess. Once that was done, she hurried back with his piece of cake and waited beside his table with an encouraging smile. He thanked her and drank his tea, didn't engage her in further conversation. Frowning, she reluctantly sauntered away, giving him one last backwards glance. Guethyn stirred some sugar into his tea, and tuned out the waitress and the toddler's tantrum to attend to the jumble of his thoughts.

Okay, he reasoned with himself. First things first. He'd promised himself years ago to never again get involved in grandfather's magic.

He could still taste Sharay's lips. Moist, soft.

He shook his head. Refocused. He firmly recalled his vow to never again trust the Goddess he had been taught to revere when he was a small child.

He could still feel the eagerness of Sharay's mouth when it met his.

He drank a mouthful of tea, sat up straighter. He'd felt betrayed by the Goddess, by the magic he'd learned as a child. He'd resolutely put that life behind him. It had never given his mother any peace, and his father had still died a tragic death.

He remembered the feel of Sharay's silken, silver blond hair sliding through his fingers.

He held tightly onto his tea mug and took a steadying breath. Concentrate he told himself. As he'd grown older, he'd found another calling to take the place of the magical one he inherited from his mother and grandfather. He had studied hard at the university, plunged headfirst into the science of marine biology.

The memory of Sharay's kiss flooded his body with heat. Roused him.

He slammed his tea mug down on the table, threw his napkin onto his lap, took a huge bite of his currant cake. It was stale, but he didn't care.

No time for this nonsense, he murmured defiantly. He forced himself to continue to sort through things. He was close to getting his doctoral degree. It would be his in a few months. His life had made much more sense without the quest of the ancient Celtic Imram, without magic, without the Goddess's rituals.

His imagination flicked back to an image of Sharay.

Her eyes gazed into his. Searching. Tender. Filled with the same desire he felt.

Guethyn swallowed the rest of the dry cake in one gulp, washed it down with more tea. He'd allowed himself a few relationships over the years, testing the boundaries of his heart. No one had come close to pushing its limits or holding him in captive fascination.

Until Sharay.

She pressed him up against his resolve to reject magic. She opened his heart in a way he had dreaded and, at the same time, always hoped for. Realization came quickly and it came as a shock. He couldn't help, and couldn't stop, his feelings for her. He didn't want to. He was bound to her. There was a part of him that mysteriously knew he always had been. He rubbed his eyes with his palms, and exhaled sharply.

If Sharay came along with magic, along with the Goddess, well then so be it. Damn it.

Guethyn guzzled the last mouthful of tea in his cup, got up, and paid the bill at the cash bin.

The young waitress looked up at him demurely as he handed her exact change.

"You passing through our village? Maybe staying awhile?" she asked.

Something vaguely disturbing floated through Guethyn's mind. A sticky thread, like a fragment of a spider web. It disappeared as swiftly as it entered, but not before he sensed it peeking into his psyche, trying to probe his thoughts. He remembered, as a young student of magic, his grandfather describing such things. Grandfather had told him his was a strong and well-trained mind, not easy to manipulate. He glanced at the waitress. She was definitely focused on him, but her interest wasn't on magically probing his thoughts.

Guethyn shook his head. "Um. Yes. No," he answered, distracted by the experience.

"Come back and see us. We have great lunch specials."

She was prettier than most. She didn't hold a candle to Sharay. He sighed again, ran a hand through his long hair. He needed to call Rosheen, then he'd head back to the shore. Back to Sharay.

The waitress extended her hand, persistent in her efforts. "Well, if you drive back through again, my name is Angela."

Guethyn barely noticed the gesture. Without returning the handshake, he left the café and walked across the dirt parking lot to the silver caravan. The ship of their Imram. His and Sharay's. He shook his head and rolled his eyes. So much for best laid plans and solid resolve. His dissertation would have to wait. He would need to get involved in the magical arts once more.

After he climbed into the front seat, he pulled out his cell phone. It was the rental one Rosheen had given him, one of the pair she'd gotten so they could communicate without worry of being traced by police surveillance. He closed the door and window so no one could hear his conversation, and was relieved when he saw the signal was strong enough to make the call. Checking the piece of paper Rosheen had put in the glove box, he punched in the code for the prepaid phone card and called her.

Rosheen's voice was guarded when she answered. "Hello. Dillon, is that you?"

"It's Guethyn," he said.

"Oh, Goddess, Guethyn. I've been worried. Where are you?"

"Along the coast of Wales. We're hidden in a secluded spot Dillon knew of."

"Good. The police came back early this morning," Rosheen reported in a rush.

Worry crept along the skin of Guethyn's back. "And?"

"They know you were at the hospital. You didn't sign in, but the ward clerk, Connie I think they said her name was, remembered you."

"Damn," Guethyn muttered.

"Sharay and Dillon are now officially listed as missing patients. Escapees."

"Have they made a connection among the three of us?"

"They can't prove it, but they're suspicious you and Dillon are with Sharay."

"Damn," he repeated. "Did they see my van?"

"Your van won't give you away. I drove it over to Catherine's right after you left. It's safely stowed in her garage."

"Well, at least they won't be able to use that to follow our trail."

"Guethyn . . . there's something else," Rosheen hesitated. "You and Dillon are suspected as accomplices in Larry Wentworth's murder."

"Oh, great," Guethyn said, sarcasm icing his words. He tapped his fingers against the dashboard, picked up the 'Lovers' Tarot card, laid it down again.

"I'm sure I've convinced them when I told them I haven't seen either of you. They've no evidence you've been here, and they've no clue where you've gone. They're baffled."

"I'll make sure we keep it that way."

"Good. I'll do what I can from this end. The Claddaugh rings should protect you from snooping eyes. Particularly Phoebe's."

"Claddaugh rings? What rings?" Guethyn replied.

"The protection amulets. Didn't Dillon give you the ring I imbued?"

"No."

He could hear her mutter under her breath.

"Does Sharay have one?" he asked.

"Yes. I gave it to her myself."

"Good. Because I sensed something, someone, trying to probe my thoughts. Just a few moments ago."

He heard her sharp intake of breath. "Let me talk to Dillon."

"He's back by the camp site with Sharay. I came to the village to pick up some supplies and call you."

"You *must* get your amulet from Dillon the moment you return." Rosheen paused. "Guethyn?"

"I'm still here."

"Yes, well . . . are you okay?" Rosheen asked.

"Of course not. This is a serious mess."

"You just sound . . . I don't know. Like something else is bothering you."

"I won't let anything happen to Sharay, if that's what you mean," Guethyn said, with far more passion than he'd intended.

"I see."

"You've asked me to protect her. I will."

"I have total faith in you, Guethyn."

Guethyn vacillated, sure Rosheen somehow knew about him and Sharay. Unsure why he wanted to confide in her. It annoyed him.

Rosheen continued. "Guethyn, there's something you need to know. I'm not sure how to tell you. It's about you and Sharay."

"Straight up would be best," Guethyn replied.

"All right then." She cleared her throat. "There was once a man who never left her side. It makes sense he'd return in this lifetime with her. *You'd* return, I mean."

Guethyn would have dismissed Rosheen's comments as gibberish a few hours ago. But now he understood exactly. "I don't intend to leave her now that I've found her again. She's in danger. I'll be here to help."

"Then you do care for her?"

"Yes." The word rolled off his tongue, as easily as the next beat of his heart.

"Then Beltaine will be a lot easier."

"What? You're pushing for that, too?"

"Wait, before you get riled. Sharay needs to tap into the mysteries of the Goddess if she's to become all she's intended to become. Beltane's the perfect ritual to help her with that. It was my idea. Dillon and I thought. . . ."

"You *thought?*" Guethyn said, feeling his temper rise. "What about Sharay's feelings? Or my feelings? I don't appreciate being used."

"Guethyn, if you only understood what's at stake here."

"I don't care. You can't use people for your magical purposes, Rosheen."

"We'd never ask you if we didn't think it was for a greater good."

"To hell with that. Sharay and I will do what suits us."

"The Beltaine ritual's in Sharay's best interest. It truly is. Do it for Sharay."

"I'll think about it," he said reluctantly, the spark of rebellion still stirring in his chest.

"Sharay has a special destiny, Guethyn, whether you want that to be true or not."

Guethyn thought he heard the sound of a thousand bells surrounding him on all sides. Startled, he looked around for the source. It stopped as abruptly as it had started. He noticed the blond waitress peeking at him around the lacy curtain inside the bakery cafe. It made him uncomfortable. He hadn't intended to be noticed at all, much less watched, even if by a flirtatious waitress.

"Rosheen, I've got to go. If you're so concerned about Beltaine then come here. With us. Dillon said he wanted you here for the ceremony for himself anyway."

Guethyn snapped the cover of his cell phone shut. He started the engine and quickly pulled out of the parking lot, deliberately heading in the opposite direction from the way he'd come.

Rosheen cried out. "What? What did you say? Dillon wants me there? Guethyn, answer me!" All she heard was a dial tone. She let the phone drop from her ear, her hand suddenly limp. She stared at the mouthpiece, her lips parted.

Dillon wanted her.

Chapter 22

Inspector Henley relied on gut instinct. It had gotten him out of danger more times than he could count. It was nothing he could ever explain, but more often than not, his gut instincts were spot on.

"She's lying," he mumbled, scribbling notes on a pad of paper while he sat in the passenger seat of the police car. He raked through his thick gray hair with his free hand.

"Who's lying?" Everett, his new recruit, asked.

Henley lifted his pencil, pointed it at the large manor home in front of them. The site of the murder of Larry Wentworth. "Mrs. Wentworth. Everything points to that kid Sharay, but something isn't right. Something in Phoebe Wentworth's voice. In her eyes. . . ."

Henley viewed the manor home with speculation. A forensic officer stepped onto the front porch. Henley knew the man carried a plastic bag of fingerprinted scissors, the murder weapon, tucked into his leather briefcase. Phoebe Wentworth, red eyed from crying, closed the door behind the officer. The lights were still on all through the house. The investigative team had been there most of the night.

"Everything seems in order, sir. It all clearly points to that girl. She escaped the loony bin. Evidently she'd always said she'd kill them," Everett said.

"I know what Mrs. Wentworth and that doctor said." It irritated Henley when nobody else could sense when one plus one didn't equal two.

Everett sat silent for a moment. "Is that why you wanted us to return here? To make sure we didn't miss anything."

"Yes, lad." Henley grew pre-occupied with the bad feeling brewing in his gut.

"It looks like we didn't miss anything, sir."

"Appearances can be deceiving."

"No disrespect sir, but can you tell me why you're not calling this a cut and dried case?"

Henley recognized Everett was only trying to learn from him, this being the lad's first year out in the field.

"It's that Phoebe Wentworth . . . ah, forget it," Henley said with a wave of his hand. He couldn't explain his sense of foreboding to his young trainee.

"Drive us back to Little St. Michael's Retreat House," Henley ordered.

"Again? We just left there a few hours ago."

Henley shot him an angry look. Everett was proving to be as obtuse as all the other rookie partners he'd been paired with.

Everett swallowed hard. "Yes, sir," he said, and he started up the car's engine.

Henley felt a twinge of guilt and dutifully took up his role as senior detective again. "Okay, lad. Say Sharay committed the murder. You need to ask yourself, where would she run afterward?"

Everett glanced at his older partner, not sure if Henley would bark at him again. He said tentatively, "I'm not sure what she might think, or what her plans might be. Sharay is crazy, after all."

"What are they teaching you at forensic school nowadays?" Henley snapped. "You've got to think ahead, think like Sharay would. Ask yourself the right questions. Who are the two accomplices? Why would they want to help her kill Larry Wentworth?"

"We find that out once we capture and question them," Everett stammered.

"After we visit the Retreat House."

"Detective Henley?" Everett said timidly.

"What?"

"Do you have any ideas? I mean, answers to those questions?"

Henley looked out the window. "No."

Henley picked up his radio mike. Despite his foreboding, he still had to follow protocol. At least until he could find some tangible reason not to.

He radioed the police station, ordered an all-points bulletin for Sharay and her accomplices to be sent to all police headquarters, and to be broadcast on the television news and radio stations across the whole southern half of the country.

"Angela?" Ivan called loudly, his voice impatient.

"Hmm . . . what?" Angela tucked a wayward strand of her blond hair more securely into her barrette, and continued to stare out the window as the silver caravan pulled onto the main road.

"Stop dawdling. Your order is ready. Bring it to our customers." Ivan, the café owner and baker, was also Angela's father.

"Oh, bloody hell, I think he saw me." Angela hurriedly closed the stained lace curtain and jumped back from the window.

Beatrice, Angela's mother, adjusted her apron around her thickened midline and clucked her tongue. "Oh, my flower, don't waste your time. You heard the lad say it yourself. He's only passing through." She deftly stacked Angela's order, a plate of two scones and two pork pies, in her hands and delivered them to Angela's customers.

"I don't care, mum," Angela said. "He was really cute. Don't get many like him. He may come back through, you never know."

Ivan strolled out of the kitchen into the front of the café and leaned against the glass counter that displayed an assortment of his bakery specialties. Currant scones, custard tarts, and pork pies were the most popular. He had just put another batch of pork pies into the large oven, and the aroma of freshly baked pastry wafted through the kitchen door before it shut behind him. Ivan stared at the small television set beside the cash register, absorbed in a daytime talk show, his favorite past-time when business was slow.

Beatrice pulled a bottle of brown sauce out of her apron pocket, set it on the customer's table, and walked back over to the window where Angela stood. She put her arm around her daughter's shoulder.

"Flower, you're never going to get a man by chasing him. Come on, sit down and have a cup of tea."

"He ignored you anyway, Angie," Ivan muttered, eyes still focused on the TV.

Angela pouted. "Maybe he just didn't hear me when I introduced myself."

Beatrice and Ivan exchanged glances.

Angela put her hand on her hip. "Well, maybe!"

Ivan shook his head, and continued to gaze at the screen. He switched the dial to another station, one of the two he was able to tune into this far out in the country.

"Oh, you're both right," Angela sighed. "Actually, he was downright rude. He heard me introduce myself all right and he didn't bother to answer."

"There you go, Angela. I'd rather see you all spit fire mad than walked over like a door mat," Beatrice said.

Angela took the cup of Earl Grey tea her mother poured for her and sipped it. "Men are insensitive. All of them. Just plain insensitive." She looked over at her father. "Sorry, daddy," she added.

"Well, what do you know about that, eh?" Ivan rubbed his unshaven face with hands dusty with baking flour. He removed his dingy white baker's cap, pushed back his unkempt hair, and squinted at the TV.

"Angela, isn't that the pretty boy you're mooning over?" he asked, pointing a thick finger at the TV set.

Angela set down her cup and leaned over the counter to see, Beatrice right beside her.

Beatrice answered first. "Well, my goodness. It sure is. Couldn't miss those blue eyes," she exclaimed.

Angela stared long and hard. Yes, it was the same face.

"Police looking for that one. Want him for murder. Him and two others," Ivan said, smirking. "You sure can pick 'em, Angela."

Angela grimaced at her father.

"Ivan," Beatrice said. "Call the police. Tell them the lad was here."

"Wait," Angela said, walking over to the cash register with the phone beside it, the exact spot where the lad had rudely ignored her eager introduction just a few moments earlier. A vague sensation stirred in her mind, sticky like the threads of a spider web. She shook her head, put her hand to her forehead. Something angry uncoiled inside her. She picked up the receiver with determination. "Let *me* do it."

Chapter 23

Phoebe didn't know how long she'd been leaning against the front door. She'd watched the last police car, the gray sedan carrying the aloof Detective Henley with his disconcerting gaze, drive down the long driveway, gravel crunching loudly beneath its tires; past the hedge of blossoming hawthorn bushes and red roses, and out onto the country lane that led into the town of Glastonbury. After all the commotion of forensic teams and detectives, she reveled in the quiet.

She wiped the sheen of perspiration off her forehead with the handkerchief she had earlier cried into when giving the police officers her alibi. She had always been a good liar, finding it easy to credibly alter the truth. She'd told the police how Sharay had banged loudly on the front door late the prior evening. How, when the door wasn't promptly answered, Sharay had broken the side library window to get into the house. How, angry and out of control, Sharay had screamed she would finish what she'd promised. Phoebe had managed to interject hysterical sobs at this point in the telling, clutching the detective's arm for support. Detective Henley had given her arm over to his young assistant Everett.

After an appropriate amount of tears, Phoebe relayed how Sharay had lunged at her with the scissors that were lying on the desk. And how her dear, poor husband had jumped in between to intervene, only to find the sharp scissors fatally speared deep into his own chest. She told them Sharay ran from the house screaming her promise to return and bring her two friends from the hospital to help finish the job she'd set out to accomplish.

Phoebe felt confident and clever. She figured her incriminating accusations would bring about murder charges. Then Sharay would truly be out of the way for good.

"I'll get what should have been mine all along," she murmured. She played with her diamond wedding ring.

She blew out a sigh. "Now I can get down to the final touches. Magic out in the open in my own home."

She turned to look in the mirror hanging on the wall by the front door, fluffed her hair, pressed her cool palms against her tired eyes. No need to hide the next phase of her plans or to keep her thoughts to herself. Larry was no longer able to impede her. She gazed down at her left hand. With one swift movement, she maneuvered her wedding ring off her finger and put it on the foyer table alongside her wedding photo from twenty years ago. To her surprise, her heart clutched.

Her cast off diamond ring threw rainbow hues onto the glass covering the picture of Larry and her. She barely recognized herself back then. Her long blond hair was styled to allow thick ringlets to frame her face, and light pink lipstick outlined her practiced smile as she stood stiffly in a white brocade dress. She remembered how her heart had raced, boldly hoping the child growing in her womb on that day would bring her rightful status in the priestess community. She had purposefully conceived the child with Larry, used him, daring to believe the community's prophesied daughter would be born to her and not Blanche.

Larry had been kind to her, and passionate. But her pregnancy had betrayed her, as had her fate. Her tiny infant, a boy, was born four months early. With perfect little fingers and toes and a shock of black hair, he had gazed up at her before he closed his eyes in eternal sleep—dashing her dreams for the high priesthood and the respect of the elders. Phoebe lost interest in Larry after that.

One year later, Blanche birthed Sharay, with her silver blond hair and star-shaped birthmark.

Ah, yes, Larry. Taunting images of silver scissors and his blood trickling down her arm invaded her thoughts. Phoebe's hands began to tremble. She walked over to the library, now cordoned off with yellow police tape. She felt chilled, and vigorously rubbed her upper arms.

"Don't be sappy now," she chided herself.

She clicked off the overhead light, and the library darkened, the heavy velvet curtains blocking out the morning sun. For a moment she thought she heard voices whispering, calling her name on lengthy sighs. Voices issuing from the shadows curling out of the corners of the room, arising from under the desk where Larry had taken his last breath.

Phoebe shuddered, turned, and resolutely closed the door behind her.

The sun was high above the wooded shoreline and shone brightly on Sharay. But she couldn't feel its warmth. Dillon's voice came from far away, muffled in comparison to the stark relief of her black hole.

"Sharay!" he called again.

The black hole murmured reassuringly in Sharay's ear. *Ignore him. I'm here now.*

Sharay relaxed, safe once more inside the dark cavity, the armored barricade of her childhood making. She wouldn't venture outside of its protection again. Not for Dillon. Not for anyone.

That's right. Safe with me, the blackness purred.

Curled on her hands and knees on the sandy beach, Sharay crouched within the hole that lived inside herself.

Dillon towered above her. "Sharay. Look at me," he said thunderously.

Sharay blocked him out. Soon even his voice would fade.

Dillon fell silent and watched her, compassion flooding his heart, his kindness softening the rigid walls of the cavernous black pit. Sharay vehemently turned her head, averted his gaze. She wouldn't allow his compassion to weaken her refuge. She wouldn't allow her love for him to coax her out.

She sat back on her heels. "Go away," she half growled.

"No," he said simply.

She scuttled backwards, her hands and feet clawing at the sand to push away from him.

Dillon did not chase her, much as he wanted to take on this fight for her, to demolish her black shadowy wasteland forever. His knowledge of magical law forbade him from intervening with her free will. She had to ask for his aid before he could give it. And while he could then assist her once she asked, Sharay would still need to be the one to heal herself. On her own—but not alone.

While he had always known it to be his destiny to help Sharay, what he hadn't foreseen was how his own heart would open to her. He feared if he had to wait much longer he would do anything to help her. Anything.

Dillon paced in the sand. He must hold back, must be patient. Must allow Sharay the opportunity to step through this portal of initiation. It must be her choice to free herself from the black hole that was siphoning her soul.

It pained him to know she had to break her own heart open in order to liberate herself. That she must descend into her pain, into those withered, parched places in order to strengthen. Only then could she heal and truly open to love. Only then could she fully claim the greatness he saw in her, become what the Prophecy spoke of.

If she were unable to face her unmet grief, her suppressed rage, her tenacious guilt, then the shadowy darkness would win. Sharay, and the Prophecy, would be lost forever. Her destiny, the world's destiny, hung in the balance.

Sharay watched him through narrowed eyelids.

Dillon knelt beside Sharay, waiting for her to give him the permission he needed to help further. But he knew he couldn't wait much longer or the hole would forever lay claim to her.

With a keen sixth sense, he suddenly recognized something else laying hold of Sharay's soul besides her black hole.

"What's this?" he murmured.

It wasn't the Thorazine—the medicine was out of her system by now. The raised hairs on his arms and the pressure at the back of his head told him something sinister was at play. He prodded Sharay's mind with his inner senses, found a distinctive sticky threadlike substance. He discerned what it was.

Phoebe's perverse meddling.

He now understood. Phoebe's twisted dark arts had keyed into Sharay's emotions and into the black hole, playing upon both, manipulating them for years, using them to try to drive Sharay insane. Using them even now to try to locate her. This knowledge changed everything. Sharay's emotional healing was still hers to do, would always be. His responsibility now was to counter Phoebe's magical entanglement.

With practiced discipline, he grew still. He called forth his priestly powers, readying himself. Waited for precisely the right moment to act, to lay siege to Phoebe's curse and give Sharay the chance she deserved. To heal, without the corrupt blanket of dark magic impeding her.

Sharay flung her anger against the black pit. "I can still feel Dillon. Where's my protection?" Her words ricocheted off its slick walls and struck her, bullet sharp, in the middle of her chest. She fell back with the force of the rebound.

I will deliver your protection, came the sinewy answer of the black hole.

"You hurt me," she accused, startled. "I said you hurt me," she yelled, her anger rising.

The haze in Sharay's mind intensified, and long black fingers stretched out from the hole, knotting the hawthorn roots about her heart. Her chest ached. She felt the black hole expand, engorged on her rage. Its bloated walls fortified themselves with her censored grief. With the hawthorn roots knotted securely, the hole reached greedily for Sharay's womb. Its voice was sugar, its touch burned cold. Sharay hesitated, feeling a disturbing sense of impending loss.

"Wait. Stop!" Sharay tried to pull away. Never before had her dark refuge wounded her like this.

The black pit pinned her down. Its tendrils crept toward her womb space. She felt it desperate for all of her.

"No!" she cried.

Now, Dillon thought, and seized the crack in Sharay's angry resolve. "Come back, Sharay," he shouted, his voice raised loud above the roar of the ocean and the guttural mutterings of the cavernous black pit.

Too late, the black pit said in icy declaration.

From the Inner Realms of magic, Dillon felt Phoebe's psychic energy dart in, spying, intruding, trying to get a handle on Sharay's location.

Dillon stood tall. Time to act.

"Sharay! It's Phoebe's magic. I'm going to remove it," he said.

He leaned over her to zero in on Phoebe's foul infiltration. Sharay didn't answer, didn't understand. Her womb throbbed, fiery heat spiraled throughout her belly. Almost fully ensconced in the black recess, she scuttled backwards again, this time her hands and feet not gripping sand, but the tarry mud floor of the black pit within her. It would not relinquish its iron grip. Her long buried rage unearthed itself from its tarry grave. Black fingers rushed to shove it back down, immobilizing Sharay in a frozen stranglehold. It no longer cajoled Sharay into numbness, it forced her.

Somewhere inside her, yet sounding far away, her golden lion totem roared. Sharay raised vacant eyes, could barely see Dillon through the haze. She whispered to him, her energy so low he had to kneel beside her once more to hear her.

"Help," she said hoarsely, and weakly slumped back on the sand.

Dillon's hands moved swiftly above Sharay's body, creating swirling patterns of spirals and circles before he stood again. Abruptly, his one hand pointed down to the earth, the other aimed towards her, with ring and little finger curled into his palm, index and middle finger aimed directly at her heart.

"Please, help me, Dillon," Sharay groaned.

"By order of fire and air, give her fresh breath," he bellowed.

A gust of sun streaked wind rushed into the black hole. Sharay's lungs hungrily sucked in its vital life force.

"By order of water and earth, give her rebirth!" Dillon commanded.

Droplets of ethereal water showered the hole, seeped into its walls, softening them. Sharay's womb pulsated, her spine tingled and undulated, her head felt dizzy. The black hole revved up its stronghold. It clutched her greedily within itself. Black walls clamped down in a vice like grip.

"Elements come to her aid," Dillon intoned.

The elements of air, fire, water, and earth united. On the beach, funnels of sand rose and fell around Sharay. But within the Inner Realms of magic, howling wind tore at the walls of the hole. Waves of seawater added to the pounding force. Blazing cauldrons of fire combusted beneath the black tarry pit and the weight of mountain granite bore down on its roof. The black hole thrashed. Its walls buckled. Sharay covered her head with her hands, but she remained untouched, unharmed by the magical assault on the black cavern. She watched it crumble around her. Felt the sudden rush of the feelings it had long buried. Blinding rage, immobilizing fear, wrenching grief, putrefying guilt.

The black hole contorted, and in frenzied effort to save itself, spewed her out in one violent contraction. Sharay sprawled face first on the soft sand.

She gritted her teeth, spewed her anger. "You lied to me. You told me I could trust no one but you," she said to the hole.

The black hole churned out a feeble reply. *"You created me."*

"You betrayed me," Sharay said. "I don't want you any longer."

"You want me. You need me. You're safe only with me."

"No. You tricked me," Sharay hissed.

Deflated of power, the hole shrank, grew smaller and smaller. Beneath the hole Sharay caught a fleeting glimpse of a pulsing, luminous, golden heart, but a web like film veiled her view. She brushed at the film with her hands, but couldn't get rid of the sticky coating to see clearly. The film stuck to her hands. She couldn't get it off. Panicked, she rolled over in the sand and thrashed.

Dillon knew it wasn't over, that there was one more thing he must do. The four elements, having done their part to free Sharay, withdrew, leaving Dillon with the final purging. With fierce determination, he moved his hands above Sharay's chest, pulling, pulling.

From the Inner Realms, with his hands and breath, he suctioned out the toxic links Phoebe had magically forged with the black hole.

"By order of Sharay's free will, by the power of Divine Love, you will leave this girl," Dillon commanded loudly. His breath grew labored but his magic held strong.

Sharay felt the sticky film begin to dissolve. Heat spread around her core where there had been icy cold.

With hands still working to cleanse Sharay in the Inner Realms, Dillon extracted the remaining pieces of Phoebe's meddling magic—invisible formless sticky threads. He clutched them fiercely within his fists, flung them out to sea where they were engulfed and drowned in the salty water, to be cleansed and purified in the watery womb of the Goddess.

Sharay sank back into the sand, unable to move. Her eyes reflected her gratitude.

Dillon sat down a few feet away, his exertion apparent in his breathing, which came in quick, rattling gasps.

He reached out one hand and directed two fingers toward her chest. "I've done what I can . . . the rest is up to you." he said between rasping breaths.

Sharay couldn't speak, was overwhelmed by the rising intensity of the emotions the hole had buffered for so long.

"Now, for your own good, do as I say. Give it all to the Goddess, Sharay . . . all of it . . . your grief . . . your rage . . . your guilt."

Sharay felt a strong energy surge move through Dillon's arms and flow into her. She sank into another reality, the realm of heart and soul.

The sound of a thousand bells rang clear. Blue and silver mist surrounded her, and she recognized the swirling opalescence that heralded the presence of the Goddess. Sharay couldn't see Her, but knew Her by the fiery heat she felt in her womb, the golden warmth that permeated her heart. When the Goddess came to her, the outside world dissolved.

Dillon eased his arm back onto his lap and his breathing slowed to normal. He closed his eyes and concentrated.

A melodious voice, both tender and resolute, spoke to Sharay. "Are you willing to be vulnerable?"

Sharay hesitated, tears of fear welling up.

"Are you willing to be vulnerable? To feel your pain?"

"Why do I have to do more?" Sharay protested.

Surrender and resistance fought in her chest. The spot in her stomach where the black hole had resided burned. But she knew she now had no choice but to trust and surrender. "Yes," she finally conceded.

"Then go to where your black hole once resided inside you. Go deep into that place in your body."

Sharay cringed. Still, she chose to step into the initiation. She moved her awareness into her upper abdomen, the place her black hole had lived in her body. With her awareness, she descended through that spot and far beneath her abdomen, to her very cells and below, to a place deep enough that even her aunt's twisted magic could not reach.

In the next instant, Sharay envisioned her fragile beating heart cupped in her hands. It flailed wildly, clinging to agonizing images of all precious things lost. Mother and father. Her childhood. Priestess training. Sharay sobbed. Unable and unwilling to hold onto her saddened heart any longer, she flung it into the lap of the Goddess.

Everything inside her grew quiet. Empty. Still. Without the black hole, she became her grief, bleeding wound. She felt her rage, rigid armor. She gingerly touched her guilt, tenacious glue. Her feelings broke her heart wide open. Emotions and heart existed together. But she did not suffer with the feelings. And she was no longer tormented.

The Goddess picked up Sharay's heart and reshaped it, with holy breath and wordless song, with primordial seawater and vital lifeblood. She spread silver and blue ointment around the heart and bathed it in Her compassionate tears. When She returned it to Sharay's chest, it beat slowly, peacefully, in perfect rhythm with the ocean waves. It was open. And it tenderly held her pain.

Within the realm of inner vision, Sharay heard the Goddess bid her to sit back, to nestle into Her enfolding arms. And inside that warm embrace, alongside her anguish, Sharay discovered peace. There, she encountered the exquisite Divine Love of the Goddess, a satiating golden nectar.

It filled the parched cracks within her heart, offered her a wellspring that would never run dry if Sharay remembered to drink from it.

"Can it be like this always?" Sharay asked. She thought she heard the Goddess sigh tenderly.

"You must remember to open to Me. Over and over again."

"Remember to open," Sharay told herself.

She knew she must now welcome her grief and rage and guilt; that they would be held in the alchemy of Divine Love. She noticed that the fibrous hawthorn roots, while loosened, were still wrapped around her heart, and she wondered why.

Within the blanket of Her love, the Goddess heard Sharay's silent question, and responded. "I have eased the strain. Now you must go deeper yet to heal."

Sharay leaned back, her heart and her body nested in the embrace of the Goddess.

The image of her parents slowly formed in her mind's eye, distinct and life-like.

Her mother's delicate hand reached out and tucked a lock of Sharay's silver-blond hair behind her ear.

Her father picked her up and twirled her round as if she were five years old again.

Sharay paused. Competing with her joy was even deeper grief and rage, long masked. She turned to her parents. "You promised you'd never lose me. You left me," she said bitterly. "With Aunt Phoebe."

She couldn't bear the look of agony on her mother's face.

Her father replied, tone soft, words firm. "We've come to help you find the truth."

"The truth is you left me."

"No. Those are the facts. The truth is something different. Your feelings will lead you toward the truth."

"My feelings left me lonely and abused."

Her father's brown eyes grew gentle. "The black hole is gone. You must now meet your deepest grief and anger. Therein lies the hidden trail to the Truth."

She recalled Dillon's instructions. Meet your pain. Give it breath. Meet it in your heart. Your open heart.

She had nothing left to lose. She grabbed the shirttails of courage and hung on, lay her heart open yet again, and once more nestled herself in the Great Heart of the Goddess. She peered beneath the lava flow of her anger, the torrent of her grief, breathed deeply into her newly formed heart. It took an eternity of incremental moments to meet what had been neglected within her for so long.

Breathe in. *Stomach churning.*
Breathe out. *Muscles clamping.*
Breathe in. *Painful purging.*
Breathe out. *Wildfire raging.*
Breathe in. *All consuming.*
Breathe out. *Rat-a-tat-tat, kill the anger.*
Breathe in. *Hand-cuffed fist clench.*
Breathe out. *Fiery anvil.*
Breathe in. *Storm cloud sorrow.*
Breathe out. *Wild eyed screeching.*
Breathe in. *Choking, gasping.*
Breathe out. *Look it in the eye.*
Breathe in. *Give it AIR.*
Breathe out. *Stomach cooling.*
Breathe in. *Chest imploding.*
Breathe out. *Tears unfrozen.*
Breathe in. *Melting, sobbing.*
Breathe out. *Spinal throbbing.*
Breathe in. *Rose strewn heart altar.*
Breathe out. *Goddess arms enfolding.*
Breathe in. *Peaceful floating.*
Breathe out. *Nothing.*
Breathe in. *No thing.*
Breathe out. *Rock Bottom.*
Breathe in. *Bliss. Silence.*

Beneath the shadow of her rage and grief, where her black hole had once been, there was—stillness.

Sharay peered under the eternal stillness and discovered something else yet. A hidden jewel. A deep pulsation. It began to throb and it coursed throughout her being. Tiny throbbing waterways, leading to greater rivers and oceans of spiraling pulsation. It emanated golden luminosity. Sharay felt its heat in her heart and in the core of all her cells, pulsing from the inside out.

She knew it to be Divine Love. The Goddess that resided inside every created thing. It had been there all along, waiting for her.

Her parents wrapped their arms around her.

"Your mother and I did what our destiny required. Trust that there is a bigger purpose here."

Breathe out.

Her mother's compassion etched her words. "It broke our heart, but we had to follow the path carved out for us."

"As you must do, Sharay," her father added.

"No love is ever forgotten," they told her in unison as their images slowly dissolved.

Their warmth remained within her, softening the ropes around her heart.

Breathe in love transforming. Breathe out.

The Goddess spoke. Her voice echoed in the distance, the sound of a thousand silver bells permeated Her words. "Lamou dei tu wantna desire se de tu."

"I am that which is at the end of all longing. The love you desire is within."

Chapter 24

Slowly, the blue and silver mist faded. The Goddess's wellspring oasis remained within Sharay. She curled up on her side, and burrowed into the softness of the warm sand. Dillon covered her with his jacket. The sun was low in the sky and the air slightly chilled before Sharay spoke.

"She put a balm on my heart, Dillon. She told me I'd have to do the rest," she said, her voice low with the effort of talk.

"She'll never take away your free will, Sharay. The choice is always yours. Over and over you'll need to recommit to Her. To a path of being true to yourself, true to Her. A path where love is always available."

Sharay could barely move her arms and legs. She was sore with the purging, exhausted with the labor of her newly birthed heart. She wished, with what she knew was naiveté, that her heart's rebirth would be the end of pain in her life.

"You've passed through an important portal, Sharay. Tomorrow I can teach you the path to the Void," Dillon said.

"There's so much to learn."

"Aye. Now that you've experienced the Way of the Heart, you must follow it through to its end. It's a path of alchemy. Where the union of the two, feminine and masculine energies, produces something far greater."

"Dillon, you're speaking in riddles again," Sharay murmured sleepily.

"The Way of the Heart transforms and heals. And it also has a mystical side, a magical side that I will teach you. Tomorrow."

"I saw something around my black hole. Something sticky and web like. Phoebe used magic on me, didn't she?"

"Yes," Dillon replied. "It's good you can recognize it now. Remember what her magical intrusion feels like. Phoebe used your raw emotions and twisted them for her own use. She fortified your black hole for that same end."

"I still hate her for that, Dillon."

"I know. But, remember this—it was you that created the black hole in the first place. She only magnified what was already there. And made it harder to find the love buried inside your wounds."

"Dillon, I'm so tired."

"I know, my dear. I'm sorry it had to be done this way."

Sharay managed a faint smile. "You mean Cliff Notes version? Fast and furious?"

Dillon's dimples deepened. "Hmm. Yes, I mean forcefully. Between Phoebe's invasive magic and our time urgency, I'm afraid it was our only option. Normally we'd ease you into the Way of the Heart more gently. Help awaken your powers more subtly."

"Powers?"

Dillon reassured her. "That will be for the morning, Sharay."

Sharay fell into exhausted sleep before she could respond.

Dillon sighed heavily. "And I'm afraid it's still not over yet, my dear Tahnea."

He drank in precious sea mist air, willing it to fill every crevice of his lungs and flow into his heart, his arms, his legs. He stretched out his hand, curled and uncurled it, shook his arms to release their knotted tension and allow the vital air to revive him.

"That's better," he murmured, able to breathe freely again.

He ignored the ache that ran down his left arm, bent over Sharay, and checked her pulse. Weak and thready. She'd probably feel ill once she woke up. But she'd passed the first initiation of her destiny. She'd opened her heart, embraced her long buried feelings. It was a good start. A crucial foundation. He turned to look for the basket he'd brought to the beach, with the soft blanket and medicinal herbs tucked inside. Once she'd woken, he'd fix her a special tonic to ease the strain on her body. He caught sight of the basket further down the beach, behind the stand of birch trees before the sandy shoreline, and went to retrieve it.

Guethyn found her on the beach just as the sun was kissing the sky goodnight. The time of dusk, of deep magic, spread its twilight blue haze over the ocean, casting the forest behind him in a net of shadow and muted light. Sharay's silver-blond hair covered her face. She lay wrapped in Dillon's plaid jacket.

He leaned over her. "Hello," he whispered, thinking her asleep after their exhaustive escape only a day ago.

She didn't respond.

Guethyn knelt closer beside her. She was pale. He picked up her hand, cool and limp, held it in his.

He shook her shoulder gently. "Sharay?"

Still no answer. He prodded her more forcefully. "Sharay! Are you okay?" he repeated, his voice now filling with alarm.

Burrowed deep inside rejuvenating sleep, Sharay could hear him, feel him, but she couldn't rouse herself to answer. With great effort she tried to open her eyes but was unable. She tried to move her mouth but no sound came out. She tried to lift her hand, but her muscles only twitched uncontrollably, prompting a curse from Guethyn.

Guethyn's jaw clenched. Her breathing was shallow. Guethyn rubbed her hands between his own.

Sharay wanted to tell him she would be all right, that she needed time to come back from her healing. She wished she could tell him she was better than all right. She was ablaze with raw power. Drunk on divine love.

Guethyn's movements became frantic. He put his arms under her back and around her, and lifted her. Sharay's head lay against his chest, then lolled to the side and her arms swung lifelessly. She was rag doll limp and it terrified him. Something was very wrong.

"No," he shouted.

He willed the force of his own pounding heart to pump vitality into hers. Ancient urge to protect her, to love her, flooded his being, reminded him of the many times he had come to her aid in lifetimes past.

He heard the sound of breaking twigs, and a grunt. Dillon emerged from the shadowed tree line, the sun now well below the horizon.

Guethyn carried Sharay to where Dillon stood, holding a large wicker basket in his hand.

He held Sharay's body out toward Dillon. "Bring her back," he demanded.

Before Dillon could answer, Guethyn raised his voice. "I said, heal her, grandfather."

He placed Sharay at Dillon's feet.

"She'll be all right. Truly," Dillon replied gently. Guethyn barely noticed the exhaustion lining his grandfather's words, just as it lined his face, setting the crevices of his wrinkled skin deeper.

"What did you do to her? More magic?" Guethyn said, his temper rising.

Dillon leaned over and put his hand on the crown of Sharay's head in silent assessment. "I said she's all right." His own exhaustion made his head swim.

Guethyn swiped impatiently at his tears, surprised how easily they had come, how deep his worry. "She doesn't look all right to me."

Dillon's gaze turned stern, his voice deep. "I said she's fine. Better than she was. You can carry her to the motor coach." Basket in hand, he slowly walked back into the woods, heading in the direction of the campsite.

Guethyn brushed a strand of hair from Sharay's face, leaned over and kissed her on the mouth. "Mi cariad chi," he said softly

Dillon stopped, nodded his head when he heard Guethyn's words. Guethyn had declared his love, spoken it in his native Welsh.

"That may be the very thing that saves her in the end," Dillon murmured softly.

Guethyn didn't follow Dillon to the trailer. He picked Sharay up, wrapped her in the blanket, and headed back towards the beach.

Phoebe pulled the attic window curtains closed. She knelt, bent over the squat candle facing the direction North and lit it, the last of four that encircled her on the attic floor of the manor home in Glastonbury. Wooden trunks of her sister's clothing and mementos, boxes of old dishes and used children's toys were piled neatly against the attic walls. She'd remove these remnants of Blanche's life now that Larry was gone, and Sharay soon to be out of the way. But for now she had work to do.

Phoebe surveyed her magical circle, made sure she had all she needed. The symbolic implements used for ceremonial magic were neatly laid out in their proper position. Her mother, the High Priestess Dana, along with the elder priestesses, had taught her the practice of magic well. The dark arts she had learned on her own.

The silver bowl of water placed in the direction West shimmered with the reflection of the flickering candlewicks. West, the element of Water. Heavy incense burned in a small coal brazier in the direction South, its smoke rushing to escape out the drafty stained glass window behind it. South, the element of Fire. A small knife, unsheathed, sat in the direction East. East, the element of Air. The North held a hand mirror with a heavy black onyx handle. North, the element of Earth.

Phoebe struck another match and lit the candle in the center, felt the rush of concentrated power from her well cast circle. The four elements of air, fire, water and earth merged with her focus and intention. The combined energies permeated the air. She felt tiny electrical charges along her skin and a mild pressure in her head. She lifted her chin and breathed in, claimed the raised energy for her own use rather than the traditional balance and protection it was meant to provide. She sat back on her heels and grunted. Protection could come later. There were more important things to accomplish now.

She released her ponytail from its tie, and her dyed blond hair cascaded around her shoulders. The gesture allowed the power within her to spread, to feel no bounds. She set the bowl of water next to the central candle and leaned over it, her hands tingling in eager anticipation. She would scry—gaze into the water and seek a vision. Enter a trance state where she could connect to Sharay.

Phoebe smiled wryly. When she was a young girl of nine, she'd begged Rosheen, then almost twenty-five and a consecrated priestess, to teach her this art of scrying.

It was a means to predict the future, or search out information in the present. Rosheen had trained her in the technique, mentoring her outside of class time. Phoebe tossed aside the rules surrounding its proper use.

Scrying had come in handy in the last few years, keeping her linked to Sharay with viscous psychic tendrils that left a trail she could traverse time and again to work her magic. Enabling her to enter the inner landscape of Sharay's mind and play upon her fears. Magnify them and drive the girl crazy. Until recently. Recently, she'd been unable to maintain a psychic connection to her niece, been unable to sustain the sticky, web-like tie. Phoebe dipped one of Sharay's silver-blond strands of hair, one she'd been saving for a long time, into the water, and swirled it around thrice, moon-wise.

"Tell me where you've gone to, Sharay," she commanded, her voice a mere whisper.

The bowl of water offered nothing. No image, no words.

Phoebe frowned, tried again. "Where are you hiding, Sharay?" she repeated more loudly.

The waters turned murky. Phoebe recognized the energy pattern of Sharay's repressed grief, guilt, and rage, those spinning vortexes of gray and red. She followed their energy trail, psychically hunting for Sharay through the images of the girl's black hole. She'd discovered the black hole her niece had created within herself a few years ago, when she first began to scry to keep tabs on her niece. She'd learned to enhance the shadowy pit to manipulate Sharay. It had been a very useful bit of magical manipulation.

The waters in the bowl changed. The attic room filled with the sound of moaning. The vortexes of gray and red were weak and no longer spun. Phoebe saw a shriveled tarry pit. Mere remnants of the once powerful black hole.

"What's happened?" Phoebe's eyebrows lifted. "Who did this?"

Phoebe fervently hoped it wasn't Sharay's doing. The girl's powers couldn't have grown that strong so soon. She peered closer into the surface of the water. Sensed the magical workings of the old bardic priest, Dillon.

Phoebe's eyes narrowed. "You're very clever, Dillon." She paused, alternate plans forming in her mind in quick succession.

She chanted. "Come to me by strength of bloodline, Sharay. Show me where you've strayed."

Still no clue appeared.

Phoebe grew impatient. "I need to connect with you," she muttered angrily.

She stared into the water again. She reasoned Sharay couldn't have fully erased her fears and pain in one fell swoop, no matter how strong she'd grown or how powerful Dillon's assistance was in severing her hold on Sharay's black hole. It simply wasn't the nature of fear to totally disappear. Especially fear that had been magically magnified.

Phoebe shook her head. "Crave the damn hole, Sharay!"

Her impatience caused the watery images to go blank. Phoebe sighed heavily, refocused, and waited.

After a few minutes, the water rippled. Phoebe bent closer, puzzled by the images that filled the bowl. A baker's oven and a counter filled with pastries appeared. There was a young man Phoebe had never seen, with vivid blue eyes and long tawny hair. She cast an energetic thread to link with the man, tried to probe his thoughts. They were filled with Sharay but his mind was not easy for Phoebe to enter further.

"And who are you?" she whispered to the image. "Ah," she exclaimed shortly. "You must be the young man the police spoke of. Guethyn, is it? The one that helped Sharay escape from the hospital."

The water swirled again, the image changed. A teenaged girl with a ruffled white waitress apron sat between a cash register and the same counter of pastries she'd seen in the image with Guethyn. She was pouting, and emanated strong emotions of rejection and humiliation, emotions easy to spot. Phoebe didn't recognize the girl, but knew from years of experience that she was never shown anything that wasn't useful to her. Somehow the girl was connected with Guethyn. She cast her net. This young woman's mind was easy to enter, her negative emotions simple to latch onto. To twist and manipulate.

Phoebe whispered a simple spell to the image of the girl in the rippling water, a straightforward curse designed to play on her emotions.

"Hear me now and hear me clear, as you ponder someone near. You deserve better than to be scorned and ignored. This young man deserves your wrath."

She watched the girl lift her head, eyes first empty, then slowly filled with anger. The girl put her hand on her hip and walked over to a phone next to the cash register. Grey clouds of resentment formed around the girl's body as she dialed. Phoebe wasn't sure what was happening, but she trusted in the vengeance spell she had just projected into the girl's mind.

But she still hadn't found Sharay.

She shook her head. "Not good enough." she murmured.

It was time for her to work the larger spell. The one of great power. The one she'd used with Blanche and Jarred. The same one she'd used to frighten Rosheen in her bedroom a fortnight ago. Phoebe set the bowl of water back in the direction West, no longer needing it. She paused a moment and steadied herself, knowing she must be careful with this stronger conjuring spell. For whatever she conjured and sent out, magical law said would come back at her three-fold. But she had a way around that, something she'd discovered shortly before Blanche's death.

Phoebe had crossed the line into black magic long before her sister's fatal car crash, by rebelliously treading into the realms of self-serving magic and conjured psychic entities. Desperate to usurp Blanche's place and reclaim what she felt should have been hers all along, she'd turned to the dark arts to aid her. Therein, she'd stumbled upon a forbidden magical loophole in the three-fold law by uncovering an arcane secret of protection. She reasoned she was one of the ancient lineage after all, and didn't that entitle her to utilize any and all available powers? She never spoke of her findings to the other priestesses.

Armed with the dark secret of protection and sheer determination, she'd strengthened her magical abilities enough to suppress the law of three-fold return. As a result, she had successfully commanded the psychic entity she'd conjured twice before, with no resultant harm to herself. Once sent to her sister. Once sent to Rosheen. She felt confident she could do the same again. Perhaps even better this time, for her need was greater.

Phoebe put more resinous incense on the coal brazier and inhaled the sweet scent that swirled around her. She sat back on the floor and closed her eyes, let the smoke assist her transport to otherworldly realms. She called up the images and memories that would help form the entity she would re-create to serve her wishes.

She saw herself as a child of twelve. Her younger sister Blanche was seven and still made a habit of clinging to her hand, large blue eyes holding immeasurable trust and love. Rosheen was scolding Phoebe for something, as usual. It seemed Rosheen always tried to tighten the reins, telling her she was willful, suspecting her of meddling in dangerous magical areas beyond her means. Phoebe resented the interference. Yes, Rosheen was her elder—twenty-eight and a consecrated priestess—but she was not of the bloodline of Geodran as Phoebe was.

Rosheen discovered Phoebe had cast a spell to change the poor grades on her public school report card. She'd told Phoebe's mother, the High Priestess Dana, about Phoebe's using magic for her own personal gain. Dana, in frustration with her daughter's continual disobedience, had grounded Phoebe as consequence for her most recent transgression, forbidding her to attend that evening's priestess event.

The night's event was the second and last time Dillon had come to visit the priestess community. Phoebe remembered how she'd snuck around the side of Little St. Michael's Lodge and peered at the gathering from a distance, behind the cover of hawthorn bushes. Her stomach clenched hard with the memory. She called up her fury and her wrath, her pride and her jealousy. They boiled inside her gut. She put her hand to her stomach and took a breath, steadying the curdling boil. She mustn't let the dark energy inside her dissipate, but she mustn't let it eat her alive either. The candlewicks around her flickered, and the air grew icy cold.

Phoebe brought up another image, one of Dillon, Rosheen, and her mother Dana, taking an inordinate interest in Blanche's abilities and training from that evening forward. She hadn't known then that her mother Dana was very ill and had initiated the discussions of who would succeed her. All she remembered was their favoring Blanche over her, Phoebe, the first born and rightful successor. They told Phoebe she was talented, and would always be loved and cherished. But, despite the help and guidance offered her, her rash behavior over the years caused them concern. Most importantly, the priestess elders' mystical visions, along with Dillon's input, had told them in no uncertain terms that it would be Blanche, not Phoebe, who would win claim to the title of High Priestess successor. And it was Blanche, not Phoebe, who would birth the special prophesied child. Phoebe's heart broke yet again with the memory. Sadness and jealousy churned violently inside her, ready for her use.

The last two images pulled from her memory completed the ingredients for the conjuring recipe. Blanche and Jarred on their wedding day. Smiling, happy. Only in her twenties, Blanche had it all. Everything Phoebe had ever wanted. Their insolence soured within her. She wrapped her arms around her waist, holding it all in, congealing her hatred. Jealousy burned her soul.

The image of Blanche and Jarred was quickly followed by the one of Sharay's birth. Births in the priestess community were attended only by other priestesses. The ever-trusting Blanche had especially wanted her big sister Phoebe present for the delivery, asking her to coach her with her breathing, asking her to be involved and be her support. Blanche had been silly to hope it could somehow make up for Phoebe's miscarriage the year before, but Phoebe allowed Blanche to believe she was eager to help. When Blanche's coveted baby girl crowned through the birth canal, her silver-blond hair and star shaped birthmark were clearly evident beneath the fluids of birth. Taunting Phoebe. Reminding her of her own blood stained baby boy, born too early. She'd lost her ability to conceive after that premature birth. Lost her baby. Lost everything.

At the moment of Sharay's delivery, Phoebe had her cursing spell ready. She spoke it softly as Rosheen and the other priestesses sang

Sharay her welcome song into the world. While they cooed in awe at the prophesied one, Phoebe cut the umbilical cord, and unobtrusively snipped a curl of the baby's hair, too. She used it to set a curse for a life filled with pain and grief, one that would keep the girl from fulfilling the Prophecy.

That stolen lock of baby hair was the same she used tonight to scry. The honor place of having the first born child should have been hers, but all that was left to her was the remembrance of the tiny, still bundle of her infant son in his casket. Phoebe fanned her grief and her rage to boiling. Ready was the clay for her conjuring.

She glanced at her burning candles to make sure they would last the duration of her spell. The waxen pillars held a steady flame. Reaching inside a small cloth bag retrieved from her pocket, she pulled out a secret packet of incense. Her own special blend. She had carefully selected and mixed together its resins and herbs, making sure yarrow and oil of clary sage were included in the mix. They would strengthen the intention of her spell along with her mind's ability to travel between the everyday world and the otherworldly dimensions in order to carry it out.

Phoebe poured the incense into her brazier with hands trembling from her frenzied emotions. Lighting the magical blend, she inhaled its smoke, almost gulping it in. She garnered the energy raised within her cast circle to add to the power growing within her. Her body felt weightless as she entered into deeper trance. She opened her mind to her inner vision.

The incense was working, enhancing her consciousness to travel amongst otherworldly realms in search of the perfect one for conjuring her malignant entity. She found the place she wanted, the one shrouded in shadows and fog and filled with the sound of raspy whispers. The smell of decay and feeling of suffocation told her it was the dimension she had visited before.

With magic acting as the bridge between this world and the other, Phoebe began the task of building her creature—a Tracker. With intention, tenacity, and breath, she constructed it using the clay of her poisoned emotions, fiercely swirling gray and red energies, to create an effigy of hate. Its form was amorphous at first. Phoebe pursed her lips and blew into it. It moved. She breathed into it a second time, infusing it with will. Her will. Created to obey her. Its form grew more distinct. Its features remained vaporous.

Birthed from her self-righteousness, she fed it with her wrath, nursed it with her cunning. It suckled on her ambition. She molded its wraithlike appearance until it finally swelled large as a grown man. Half beast in structure. Demon in soul.

By adding a drop of her blood and a bead of spittle to her incense, she connected the demon to the everyday world, giving it the ability to emerge out of its shadowed dwelling when needed. No one but those of her priestess lineage would be able to see it.

The candle flames leapt high, their tallow almost gone. Sitting back, Phoebe smiled with the Tracker's completion. Testing its obedience, she summoned it, with three arcane words spoken aloud. The air moved. Something flickered in and out. The Tracker materialized in front of her. Into her magical circle. Into this world.

Phoebe linked her mind with her creation. She grasped Sharay's lock of baby hair in her hand as she held an image of her niece in her thoughts. To embed her command into her creation she pointed at its chest with index and middle finger joined. "Go. Track Sharay."

Phoebe watched it stretch its ghostly neck and sniff the air. A deadly hunter.

The Tracker was not fashioned to speak. It moaned and turned red eyes on her. Phoebe shivered and stared back. She had a moment's hesitation.

"Yes. Find Sharay. Steal her power, suck it out of her, and bring it to me. Destroy those she loves."

The Tracker howled, its vaporous form rose up in mist, and it left the attic in a dark fog that slipped out a drafty crack in the window.

Phoebe crumbled to the floor and lay still. The candles flickered out, one by one, around her. All light gone.

The darkness startled her awake. Her mind lifted from trance and she remembered herself again. Memories of Sharay suddenly arose. Sharay as a tow-headed toddler, ambling up to her with smiles and coos. Sharay playing with the doll Phoebe gave her at her second birthday party. Those were the times before Phoebe had grown too angry and proud to remain a part of her priestess community. She drew in a jagged breath and wiped away one tear, vestige of lost family love, before she succumbed to the inevitable sleep of exhaustion that helped her to forget.

On the coast of Wales, in a remote section of wooded shore, Guethyn shivered, and mumbled in his sleep. Lying on a blanket in the sand, he rolled over and placed his arm tightly around Sharay, hugged her closer to him. Sharay slept the deep sleep of recovery.

Less than a quarter mile away, in his makeshift bed inside the caravan, Dillon tossed and turned uneasily. In weary sleep, he sought the ring, the amulet Rosheen imbued for him, felt it snug against his finger. It burned hot. His arm twitched convulsively as he roamed amid restorative slumber turned nightmare.

Chapter 25

The midnight black, star-dappled sky blanketed Sharay in velvet embrace. Unable to sleep any longer, she opened her eyes and drank in the rich darkness of the night. Guethyn's arm lay heavy over her shoulder, his body pressed warm against hers, his breath blew softly across her cheek as he rhythmically exhaled in deep slumber. She didn't remember how he came to be there but was glad for the comfort of him. She lifted her head, searched for Dillon, but he was nowhere to be seen.

She felt nauseated and dizzy and lay her head back down. Bits of memory floated back to her like so many fragile seashells along the shore. Black hole shriveling. Heart rebirthing. Was it only a few hours ago she willingly opened her heart? Felt the golden nectar of transformative love? She put her hand over her belly, intrigued with the power that brewed there. She felt the sudden urge to be on her own. Sitting up gradually, she silently unfolded herself from Guethyn's hold and the tangle of blanket that covered them both.

"Ooh," she said softly. Her muscles ached.

Guethyn mumbled incoherently. Sharay stilled her movements,

afraid she'd woken him. After a moment, she could hear his rhythmic breathing again, and she slowly rose to her feet, fought her dizziness, and gingerly made her way closer to the breaking waves of the sea. They sang to her, called to her in pounding sea foam demand. Sharay listened for the sound of the surf and used the silvery glow of the moon and the stars to guide her way. She took small unsteady steps and soon reached the small cave she and Guethyn had discovered earlier.

Its gray stone entranceway rose up dark and silent in the moon's glow. It opened out in the beguiling shape of a woman's vagina, like the almond shaped outline formed when two circles intersect. This time she didn't want to be inside the cave. She wanted to be closer to the water.

Feeling her way around the cave's exterior, she headed for the end that directly faced the sea, her palm against the outside walls to lend her support. The stone was moist, and mottled with clumps of light green lichen and streaks of white crystal that glittered in the moonlight.

When she finally reached the seaside entrance, she grabbed hold of the tall boulder directly in front of it and slid to the ground, tired and weak. The boulder was lingam shaped, nature's phallus to pair with the cave's round opening. Facing the sea, Sharay leaned back, felt the boulder cool and slippery against her denim jacket. It was still low tide, and the cave and its seaside entryway would be empty of the ocean water for hours.

Sharay felt unmistakably at home.

Dillon's instructions rose in her mind.

Breathe into your womb space. Fan the fire of your strength there. Exhale into your womb space. Deepen the connection.

She could almost hear his rich, lilting accent interweave with the ebb and flow of the sea. She felt a tug of affection for him before her intuition caught hold of her attention once more. She raised her arms above her head and inhaled deeply, prepared for whatever her intuition had in store. She felt nervous, even fragile, but willing and humbled by the difference the last two days had made in her life.

The horizon shimmered, and the moon, close to full phase, hung low, cutting a moonbeam corridor across the ocean surface that ended right at Sharay's feet. Beckoning her with the gift of its illuminated trail. A glowing silver passageway into the mystical Inner Realms.

Chanting a prayer that arose naturally, she lifted her face to the moon.

Moon's ray
drapes across my body
liquid silk caress
of the Goddess's watchful eye.
Waken my yoni
to memory
of worshipping thee.

Sharay creased her eyebrows together for a moment. She wondered who she would be, what power she would hold, had her mother, or Rosheen, or even Dillon, been there to teach her all along. Chiding herself for letting her mind wander, she again focused inward.

She began the holy breathing exercises, acutely aware of their ancient power flowing through her, rejuvenating her. She was treading a path many had tread before, including herself in other lifetimes. She drew on that to fuel her remembrance of how to sharpen her focus. She linked her breath with the moon above.

Breathe moon into womb.
Power of the tides.
Breath stirs the embers.
Embers fan star fire flame,
deep within the watery depths
of womb space.

Her womb space grew hot in resonant response to the moon and the sea.

Moon into my womb.
Exhale into womb,
deepening the connection.

Sharay lowered her arms. She heard the chiming of a thousand silver bells, song of the stars. She saw the familiar mist rise around her in blue and silver wisps. She welcomed the Goddess's presence.

The Goddess furthered Sharay's intuitive garnering of her womb meditation, teaching her how to deepen it.

"First inhale into your sacred heart," the Goddess told her. "Exhale from your heart down to your womb. Connecting them."

Sharay followed the instructions, inhaling and exhaling. It set up a connection between her heart and womb that she experienced as a vibrating magnetic flow.

"Now breathe into your womb. Breathe My moonlight into your womb as you inhale. Do this thrice."

Sharay breathed slowly into her womb; one, two. . . .

"On this third breath, breathe into your womb then send the exhalation into the center of the earth. Into My heart and womb."

Sharay felt her womb embers blaze up in fiery response to sending her exhalation into the earth's center.

She did the sequence of three breaths over and over. Breathe moonlight into her womb Temple. Third breath from her womb's core to earth's core. Her hands fisted in the sand, binding her with the earth, grounding her in its solid presence. Her legs seemed to become like tree roots, burrowing miles into the underworld beneath her. Her mouth parted and she raised her voice in pure melodic tone. Her voice exalted the starry sky and the molten earthen core.

The Goddess sang Her reply in whispers carried on shining silver mist. "I am the Divinity deep in your cells. I am the Divinity deep within the earth. I am the Divinity within all matter. I am the substance of Love inside all the forms in My creation."

Sharay opened to the Goddess's love embodied in her. She held firm to her rooted union with the earth. With her womb connected to the earth's core, her exhaustion left her. Her nausea and dizziness, gone. She was rejuvenated.

The moon's unblinking eye hovered in the west, watching her, bathing her in rivulets of silver. It would soon kiss the sun good morning before it retired. Dillon had told her that dawn and dusk, the time when the sun and moon exchanged places in the heavens, was a potent time for magic. The tingling throughout her body, and the fiery heat in her womb space, confirmed it.

She didn't flinch when Guethyn came to stand beside her, and put his hand on her shoulder.

"You're feeling better."

"Yes." More than she had words for. Home.

She turned to him, lifted her arms and drew him down to her. No longer anxious about loving him, not afraid to be with him. She didn't want to wait until Beltaine, and the look in his eyes told her he didn't want to wait either.

Chapter 26

Dillon woke with a start, eyes wide open. Alarm flooded his body. He shoved his bed clothes aside. With a sixth sense finely honed through long years of practice, he sensed it coming. Something far more menacing than he'd anticipated. And it was coming for her. His charge. Sharay.

He knew it would stop at nothing to get to her. Not himself, not Guethyn. Guethyn! Dillon's hand flew to his shirt pocket. The Claddagh amulet ring meant for his grandson's protection was still there. He chastised himself for forgetting to give it to the lad in the rush of escape. He had to get it to him right away.

Dillon rolled over to his side, used his elbow to raise himself. Guethyn could certainly protect Sharay from physical danger. But it was up to Dillon to crush the psychic power aimed to destroy Sharay's destiny. He prayed to the Goddess that Rosheen sensed it too, that she'd be working alongside him in the magical realms to divert the destructive force of what was coming their way. He was certain Phoebe had sent it.

He sat up and groaned, hand to his chest, willing the ache behind his sternum into submission. No time to call Rosheen. He had to act.

He would construct a magical fortress so thick and high that nothing could penetrate it. He would summon the powers available at the full moon of Beltaine to magnify his protection. As had already been planned, Rosheen would add her magic to his during the Beltaine ritual from her altar far away in Glastonbury. Sharay *must* consent to take part in the holy ritual. It was crucial for her and Guethyn to join in sacred union, to birth their deeper connection to the Goddess and to Divine Love through that union.

He trusted Guethyn to watch over Sharay's physical safety as he set to work on her spiritual protection.

Sunlight sparkled on the ocean surface and brightened the interior of the cave. Inside its moist stone walls, Sharay stretched, sublimely contented. She was a woman, fully initiated, aroused and fulfilled. She knew what it was like to be loved.

Sharay laced her arm underneath Guethyn's and curled it around his waist. She tucked her leg between his, drinking in the smell of his skin mingled with the salt air inside the cave. They had moved into the seclusion of the cave in the semi-dark cover of pre-dawn. First consummating their passion slowly and tenderly, they had gently explored the depth of their rediscovered love for each other. Sharay's memory had traced back to the times she'd made love with him before. As her partner Theolon in Atlantis. As her lover Perigrine in Glastonbury.

The second time they made love, their desire flared uncontained. Guethyn had picked her up and held her against the smooth cave wall. Sharay wrapped her legs around his torso and surrendered to her body's instincts. Her memories added to her ardor, directing her passion as she gave herself to Guethyn over and over. They finally rested when the first shaft of sunray pierced their hideaway.

She felt him stir beside her. He yawned and smiled.

"Do you remember the time we raced our horses across the Somerset plains in summer, only to find the winter marsh had not dried up?" she asked him, outlining his mouth with her fingertip.

Guethyn wrinkled his brow in concentration, his eyes staring into nothing and everything. His memories were unmistakable, clear as if they happened in this lifetime. Which of course they had not. But the recollections had grown in clarity, had grown more familiar. As had the renewal of his ancient bond with Sharay. Guethyn plucked the memory from his soul and chuckled.

"Of course. That's when we conceived our firstborn."

He could see their baby boy birthed, with his mother's silver blond hair and his own brilliant blue eyes. The coloring of the Atlantean star-race, the blood that flowed through their veins in that time long ago.

Guethyn lifted his hand and smoothed Sharay's silver blond hair from her cheek and kissed her ear. Her head nestled on his shoulder. He loved the smell of her hair, the salty taste of her skin.

"And do you remember . . ."

"Enough memories," he said, and his mouth covered hers once more.

Detective Henley knocked on the Glastonbury manor door for the third time. Bloody hell, Phoebe Wentworth was taking her time answering.

He hadn't brought his assistant Everett with him. He wanted to sort out a few details on his own before he picked his partner up for their day's work. He still couldn't put his finger on what tugged at his gut, but he meant to find out. Ask Phoebe Wentworth a few more questions, see how she responded.

The front door opened slowly, and Phoebe appeared, rubbing her eyes, smoothing her hair. "Goodness, it's early Detective. What brings you here at seven in the morning to wake me up?"

Detective Henley averted his eyes from her silk robe, her cleavage, the way the material hugged her every curve. She might have said she just woke up, but Henley hadn't seen a woman yet who looked that good straight out of bed. She even smelled good. And for as much crying as she'd done yesterday, why weren't her eyes red? She didn't look much like the grieving widow. That was the problem. What she said just didn't match what he sensed underneath her words. Henley wasn't going to fall for her tawdry act this morning.

"Just a few more questions. Won't take much time."

"All right," she replied, opening the door for him to enter.

Henley accepted a seat on the couch, declined the cup of tea she offered. He averted his eyes once more when she bent over to pat the seat beside her on the settee for him to sit. He chose the chair across the room.

He pulled out his small pad of paper and pen from his coat pocket and began, his approach his usual straightforward one.

"We got the forensics report back. The scissors, the murder weapon, has only yours and Mr. Wentworth's prints on them."

Not missing a beat, Phoebe answered him. "Why, of course, detective Henley. I told your men yesterday. Sharay wore those silly lace gloves the kids are wearing nowadays."

"I see." Henley watched her closely now. "And tell me again. What did you do as Sharay was stabbing your husband?"

Phoebe's eyes narrowed almost imperceptibly. She sniffled and reached for a tissue from a box on the coffee table. "You say that so . . . coldly. How many times do I need to relive this?" Phoebe cried, dabbing around her nose.

Henley looked her straight in the eye. "Just once more."

"I told you. Sharay meant those scissors for me. Larry intervened to protect me. It all happened so quickly. I was so scared." Her chin trembled and large tears appeared in her eyes.

"Yes. I'm sorry. Were you standing behind the desk in the library or in front of it when all of this happened?"

"Why, in front I believe."

"You believe?"

"I told you, it was all so quick."

Henley paused, compared his notes to the other night. Yes. She'd given the same story. It made perfect sense, all blame pointing to Phoebe's niece Sharay.

"Mrs. Wentworth, as you know we put out an APB. Televised Sharay's picture, along with the two men accompanying her. They're called . . . let me see. . . ." He checked his pad, took his time. "Ah, yes. Thomas and Guethyn." He looked up.

Phoebe had moved to the edge of the settee. She played with her tissue. "Yes, I saw their pictures on the television."

"Well, we've received a call. A tip." Henley leaned forward. "The young man, Guethyn, was seen in a pastry shop in a small town in Wales. The local police are investigating."

Phoebe's eyes opened wide, dark and almost hungry looking. She said nothing, waited for him to continue. That's just what Henley was looking for. If she'd exclaimed, shown signs of hope, even a desire for revenge, he'd have believed her story. Hope or revenge was what most people felt with the possibility of catching the criminal who'd murdered a loved one. But something else gazed at him behind her eyes, something that confirmed his gut was right. She was hiding something. He just didn't know how to prove it.

Sharay hummed as she dressed. Guethyn hadn't moved, was still huddled beneath the blanket. The morning light filtered dimly through the two openings in the cave. Outside Guethyn's embrace Sharay suddenly felt shy.

"You're staring," she chided him.

"You're beautiful," he replied softly.

She wished he'd joke with her, make light of it. Somehow his sincerity left her feeling vulnerable. She tried to button her cardigan, but her trembling fingers left her fumbling.

"Let me help," he offered, sitting up.

"Oh, no you don't," she said, turning away from him. "My sweater is just as likely to come off as stay on with your help."

By the Goddess, she really wanted him to touch her again, but she knew Dillon would soon make his way back to the beach. She didn't want him to find her thus. She wanted to tell him first, hoping it wouldn't ruin the plans he'd tried so hard to persuade her to participate in on Beltaine. She hoped she hadn't ruined the magic by making love with Guethyn before the Beltaine ritual. But she swiftly scoffed at her foolish thought. What could be more magical than the intimacies she'd just experienced with a man she'd loved for ages? Guethyn had taught her how to love deeply again in this life. He'd awakened the dormant blaze of her sensual rhythms. And she wanted more. More of his loving. If Beltaine offered only a tenth of the magic she'd experienced already, she would be happy.

She wondered if Guethyn was still naked under the blanket, and secretly hoped he hadn't clothed himself yet. Just as he'd said he thought her body beautiful, she found him so, too. She'd been intrigued by the ripples along his muscles, the strength of his hands that could turn tender in an instant, the way perspiration had formed a sheen across his back while they'd moved in and around each other. She wanted one more peek at him. She glanced behind her, took in a quick breath. He was standing naked, the blanket and all his clothes in a pile at his feet. He smiled at her.

Dillon would have to wait.

Chapter 27

A blustery wind swept through the trees and rattled the caravan's windows. Inside, the caravan echoed with the words of Dillon's final incantations. He leaned over the pull-down table, snuffed out his candle, and sat back in the cushioned bench, pleased with his efforts. He had drawn an impenetrable magical wall around Sharay—around Guethyn and himself as well—and a veil of protection over their Imram quest. Even without Rosheen's presence, he had still felt her invisible support from across the miles. It had raised the candle flame higher, tightened the circle of purification and balance, and buoyed his energy to do what needed to be done. Hers was a potent magnification to his protection spell.

Dillon rubbed his chest with his palm, wriggled his aching left arm. It was less sore, yet it still troubled him with occasional twinges that left him breathless. No time for that now. He wanted to get back to the beach. He had to give Guethyn his amulet and continue teaching Sharay. Standing, he groaned with weariness and an unaccustomed ache in his bones.

"Silly," he chided himself. "You're too young to feel this old."

Dillon grabbed his jacket, exited the caravan, and headed through the woods toward the beach. The wind was calmer now, and the day's light shone bright. Today was Beltaine.

Laughing, Sharay and Guethyn clambered out of the cave just as high tide began to swell inside. They held hands and scrambled onto the sandy shore. Sharay shielded her eyes with her other hand against the sudden glare of a sun prancing solo in a cloudless sky. Guethyn whirled her around and kissed her on the mouth.

"So. You'll participate in the Beltaine ritual," Dillon's commanding voice said from farther down the beach.

Sharay pulled away from Guethyn, ran to Dillon and knelt in front of him. "Dillon, we haven't ruined the ritual have we?" she asked, lifting her gaze and searching his face for approval.

Dillon's eyes twinkled. "Well, we'll see what we can do to salvage it."

He rubbed his hand over his beard and wrinkled his brow, looking as if he was in serious contemplation. He knew it mattered not one bit to the Beltaine ritual if one was virgin to the arts of lovemaking. What mattered at Beltaine was the intent for two lovers to join on all levels—physical, emotional, mental, and spiritual. To receive communion with the Goddess, and from there to aim for the deepest sacred union possible.

Guethyn dropped down onto the sand next to Sharay, shook his head, and tried to suppress a grin. He'd experienced that look on his grandfather's face often in the past. When he was a child, even through his teenage years, his grandfather would tease and riddle, stretch out Guethyn's earnest questions until Guethyn would be forced to come to his own conclusion, find his own inner wisdom. Well, today, Guethyn didn't want to share Sharay for however long that process would take.

"Grandfather, tell us what you want," Guethyn pleaded, his smile finally escaping.

Dillon turned serious. His eyes no longer twinkled and his dimples didn't crease. What did he want? He wanted to hide Sharay and Guethyn from pain and from attack. He wanted them to love each other deeply and live an uncomplicated life. But that wasn't their fate, and it wasn't for him to decide. He was here solely to make sure he'd arm them with the greatest defense through the deepest experience of the Goddess. Only then would Sharay have the chance to fulfill her destiny.

He replied, calmly, "I will teach Sharay all that will prepare her for the Beltaine ritual. If you've decided to stay for Beltaine, I'll teach you too, Guethyn." He looked over at his grandson.

Sharay turned her attention to Guethyn. "Please, will you?"

"It will help Sharay?" he asked his grandfather, already knowing what the answer would be.

Dillon nodded. Guethyn agreed.

First, Dillon reached in his pocket and handed Guethyn the amulet ring Rosheen had imbued. It didn't take much explaining to convince him to wear it. That taken care of, Dillon opened to his powers and began to teach them, there on the beach in the warmth of the sun on the morning of Beltaine. He would give them everything he had, for he knew time was short.

First, he taught them how to enter into the Void; that space of existence where there is no time, no place, no movement, only stillness; the space of both no-thingness and the potential for all creation. He showed them how to still themselves and from that stillness to reach into the realm of inner being-ness.

"Within the Void all is possible," he instructed. "Within the Void is the seed of stillness, balance, peace. And most importantly, the soul of the Goddess, She who births all potential into physical manifestation."

Guethyn leaned back on his elbows, eyes closed in contemplation. Sharay sat cross-legged beside Dillon, back straight, hands in her lap. Letting her womb guide her, she dropped her awareness into the pulse of the stillness of the Void Dillon spoke of.

The waves crashing to shore behind her felt like a mere droplet in this newfound space of eternal infinity.

Dillon monitored the pair as they moved into the stillness of the Void then back out into the world of duality and matter. He made them perfect their transitions until they could flow back and forth with ease. He didn't stop until he sensed they were well taught and well practiced. This much they needed to master. This much was the foundation in all they would do magically.

"The Void is the center of every thing and the place of no thing. In it you will find the matrix of the worlds within worlds. You will find the radiant Light of Infinite Love. And that is your biggest and best protection, for therein protection is irrelevant."

He looked into their eyes for their understanding and saw their burgeoning comprehension of the mystery he wished to impart. "We'll spend the morning working with the seven directions and how to call them in to form a magical circle," Dillon said.

Guethyn turned on his side and leaned on his elbow. He had learned to call in the directions long ago, and the recollection resurfaced easily, as did the rush of excitement he'd first known studying magic as a boy. He reminded himself that he was doing this for Sharay.

Dillon continued. "In the beginning, you will need to call in the directions in their proper order—East, South, West, North, Above, Below, and Within."

Sharay, still sitting cross-legged beside Dillon, stole a sideways glance at Guethyn. The soft wind blew his hair away from his face, his jaw was relaxed, and the muscles in his forearm flexed and released with each handful of sand he picked up and let sift through his fingers. She watched with ardent interest the movements of his fingers.

He looked up, caught her staring, and a slow, secret grin, meant just for her, tugged at the corner of his mouth. Sharay swallowed thickly, wondered how long the morning's lessons would take.

Dillon coughed loudly and continued. "We'll work with the essence of the power of each direction. With the elemental energies and the Archangels associated with them."

Dillon's voice grew compelling. "The circle is formed for balance and protection. It holds our intention and concentrates it."

Guethyn added, from memory of his childhood teaching. "It's like a cup of tea. The tea cup holds the boiled water that turns the tea bag into a drink."

Sharay squinted her eyes. "What?"

Dillon smiled. "A good allegory, yes. Our circle is an alchemical vessel, a tea cup if you will, within which transformation can occur.

Magic and conscious intent are the boiled water. The brewed tea, our desired result. The keys to this are focus and attention." He looked at Sharay, emphasizing the last word.

She felt herself blush.

Dillon set his intention to be the energetic container for Sharay and Guethyn. His focus formed an alchemical vessel within which the two could progress in their training. He was the vessel that would hold strong against any dark meddling from Phoebe. He reached out with his senses, testing the boundaries of his protective vessel. He could feel something vague prowl the perimeter. It tried, but it couldn't get in, couldn't reach them. They were safe. Sharay was safe. He would make sure things stayed that way.

Dillon stood. "Let's meet the directions."

He appeared calm, his gestures steady as usual. But there was no twinkle in his eye, no dimple in his cheek. Sharay sensed a barely perceptible urgency in his voice when he spoke, a laser sharp determination that almost frightened her in its intensity. It drove her to pay full attention. Whatever motivated Dillon's urgency was surely because of her predicament. She owed it to him to try her best.

Guethyn stood and closed his eyes. Sharay followed suit.

Dillon took in a slow, controlled breath. "East," he called out, stretching out the vowels and the length of the word in melodic intonation.

Sharay became acutely aware of the visible and invisible powers that occupied the direction East. In the inner visionary realms, she smelled the moist newness of springtime grasses, felt yellow daffodils thrust upwards through their earthen beds as they stretched toward the morning sunlight. She stretched her body like the growing daffodil, her torso lengthened and arms raised high. After a few moments, she felt herself switch from budding flower to hollow bamboo reed, with fresh air rushing through from end to end. The air grew in force, from gentle wind to blustery gust, whistling throughout her hollow reed form, blowing her this way and that.

Dillon called out another compelling invocation. "South."

The wind died down, and Sharay felt another shift. A different energy signature arose. In her mind's eye, she saw dry desert plains and volcanic mountains with smoke and lava spewing high into the cloudless sky. Arid heat and blinding brightness surrounded her. Her skin flushed warm with the fire of the South, and the flames of her heart fire blazed.

Next, Dillon invoked, "West."

The power of the ocean rose up in Sharay's mind, its pounding surf vivid beside her on the beach. Cleansing, rolling waves. A liquid cool caress flowed through her fluid body, her blood and lymph. Water of her body flowed in rhythm with the tides of the eternal sea.

"North," Dillon intoned.

In the Inner Realms, a star lit night and the opening to a mountain cave beckoned her. Rich, germinating, fecund darkness. Her feet sank into the earth, her legs burrowing like the roots of an old tree. Vibrancy sourced from the depths of her fertile womb. A low-pitched humming pulsated against the halls of her womb temple and synchronized with the heartbeat of the earth.

The chambers of Sharay's psyche glowed with the candle flames of awakening and remembrance. Ancient familiarity rose in her belly, and tears welled beneath her closed eyelids. She was relearning something she had done many times before.

Sharay sensed Dillon pause to appraise her progress. She shifted her awareness to watch him, stole a glance through half closed eyelids while he assessed her with his inner senses. He was tracking her through the Inner Realms. His assessment felt gentle, and reminded her of the times her mother used to look in on her when she thought she was asleep.

Sharay waited for further directions.

"Now you'll put into practice what you've just learned." He gestured in a spherical motion with his hands, indicating for them to form a small circle on the beach. Each was to stand in a particular direction.

Sharay stood in the West, her back to the sea. West was the direction of the yielding element of water, of the ebb and flow of the life cycles and of the ocean. The direction of the Inner Realm Temple of the Stars and the Sea. The direction that carried the potent force of Divine Love. Sharay dropped her awareness into her body and focused on the quiet stillness of the Void within. A bubble of warm energy accumulated in her heart, the source of her true protection. Heat flamed in her womb, the place of her true strength. Between heart and womb there ran a vibrating connection.

Sharay's blood thrummed to the cadence of the ocean tides. She moved in subtle undulating spirals, her body's fluidity resonating with the watery sway of the sea. Power rose from liquid's rhythm and, in a sudden outburst, radiated from her womb into the center of the circle. A blazing energy surge.

"Ah, yes," Dillon whispered.

Guethyn watched Sharay, his mouth parted in admiration. Standing in the direction East, his back to the stout trees in the forest behind him, he held the polarity of the direction opposite to Sharay's. He closed his eyes. After a few moments of silence, he wrinkled his brow and opened his eyes again. Something had shifted. There was a pressure in his head, a buzzing sensation throughout his spine. Sharay raised her eyes and locked gazes with him. His body shook with their connection. A current arose between them, flowing through Sharay in the West and to him in the East. The current, a stream of movement like cool flowing water, grew in strength. The energy passed back and forth between them, swelling from rivulet to raging river. Every time it passed through the center of the circle, the river of energy dipped deep into the earth, then rose up again to meet the other side. It formed a magical pattern of power.

Dillon watched the current and was pleased. "Sharay, you are mediating a direction traditionally representing feminine energies. The West. Guethyn, you are mediating a direction representing masculine energies in the East. Much the same as North and South hold a polarity with each other. All seven directions meet in the center of the circle."

"Yes, the center." Guethyn nodded his head enthusiastically. That's where he'd felt the energy most forcefully.

Dillon continued. "The center is the place of balance, where all energies, masculine and feminine, flow together in perfect unity."

With Sharay standing across from him, Guethyn's experience was more alive, more potent than he remembered from doing this alone. Their polarities had united to form something stronger.

Dillon confirmed it. "It is magnetic feminine energy converging with electric male energy."

Dillon closed his eyes, reached into the Inner Realms with his magical senses to assess Sharay and Guethyn's progress. They were mediating their directions well. Within the alchemical vessel he had created, and the memory of their lifetimes behind them, Dillon was more than satisfied with what they were accomplishing. He couldn't help but smile. Having Guethyn participate added exponentially to Sharay's learning.

He allowed his attention to move to the direction he stood in. The direction of the South, the place from where his personal magical abilities arose most strongly.

As a magical priest representing the direction South, with its element of fire, he held foremost the Power of Light. This power offered the keys to illumination, to the fiery sun within. Dillon fanned the familiar power surge within his body.

He sensed Rosheen participating in the Inner Realms of visionary magic, linking into their circle from far away in Glastonbury. His dear Rosheen. Ever vigilant, holding true to the vision of Sharay's prophecy, helping in any way she could. He felt her mediate the direction North, the polar opposite to his. The place of the element of earth; the cycle of death and rebirth. From the many small deaths and letting go inherent in everyday living, to the ending of physical form and its conversion back into its elemental parts and essential essence. The direction North, with its laws governing physical matter and the transformational liberation from those laws, where mind can influence matter, where beautiful gems can be retrieved from the most painful of experiences. North, the direction where destruction precedes the cycle of regeneration. The power of Dillon and Rosheen, holding their own opposite polarities within the circle, added another layer of potency for Sharay and Guethyn's learning, for their remembering magic.

Dillon's rich voice rang out above the pound of the surf, invoking the heavenly realms above. "I call upon the Archangels. The heavenly guardians. Raphael. Michael. Gabriel. Uriel."

Each Archangelic name was articulated slowly with musical intonation. Sharay memorized Dillon's pronunciation. With each name he spoke aloud, she felt the circle amplify in power. Raphael of the direction East. Healer of God. Followed by Michael of the South.

Protector of Faith. Gabriel from the West. Hope and strength of God. And Uriel in the North. Fiery Light of God.

The Archangels appeared as vast brilliant whirling vortexes of color and crystalline sound. They filled the circumference of the circle to its infinite height and depths. Sharay couldn't move, couldn't speak. Her mind emptied of thought. All that was left was color and sound and joy.

The wind gusted, blew against her skin, and she remembered she was standing on a beach in Wales. She glanced over at Guethyn. His eyes were closed, tears silently coursing down his cheeks.

While she could still feel the presence of the Archangels, she no longer saw them in her inner vision. Something else, something bright and gleaming, emerged in each direction. Peering closer, she turned to each direction so she could see more clearly.

Where each Archangel had stood, there was now a shimmering image of an object—the sacred prototype for that direction's magical implement. Sharay recognized the four implements from lifetimes past. The archetypal objects, when consecrated by a priestess in the physical world, acted as tools to enhance the great work of magic.

In the East was a gleaming *Sword* of justice, fist sized emeralds and rubies in its hilt. It rose up on its own, tip pointed to the sky.

In the South was the powerful *Rod* of integrity, strength and courage, crafted from the sturdy branches of the sacred oak tree. It stood tall and majestic with a green glow around it.

In the West was a *Cup* of brilliant blue glass with a silver embossed base. It held the refreshing waters of soul purification and everlasting life.

In the north was a polished black *Stone*, the ancient Philosopher's Stone that represented the divinity inherent inside all physical matter. On one level, it was the mysterious creation of gold from base metals. On a deeper level, it was the alchemy that created life immortal.

The four objects gleamed with an otherworldly brilliance. They carried the promise of powerful magic. Sharay's soul sang its jubilant remembrance for the gifts each implement offered. She recalled how she had used the implements in lives past. Priests and priestesses still used them, gathering their own personal implements from the mundane world, imbuing them with the sacred powers from the archetypes. To see them in their pure, unadulterated form made her body tremble in awe, and her heart ache with their beauty.

Dillon waited while Sharay recognized the implements. Once he was sure she did, he sang out again. This time evoking the directions of above and below.

"I call the direction Above. The moon, sun, and stars, and infinite heavens. The realm of the Heavenly Father. The Sacred Masculine of the transcendent spirit."

"And I call in His polarity, the Earthly Mother in the direction of Below. The realm of the Sacred Feminine, the Deep Mother. The womb and heart of the Goddess in the center of the body of the earth. She who is the life-force within all physical beings."

Above and below culminated like a flash of lightning in the seventh and final direction. The direction Within. The Center.

"I call in the direction Within. The golden sun of sacred union."

With eyes closed, her body still swaying, Sharay was transported into her sacred heart, a place where she sensed her solid physical body and her radiant invisible energy simultaneously. A place of union. Interwoven with the brilliant filament threads of Divine Love and the glowing matrix of Divine Light.

The central direction blazed before her in the Inner Realms of magic. It was a candle flame, a bonfire, a column of pure gold, a stream of silver starlight. She felt its streaming luminosity link up with her inner heart flame.

Softly, so as not to interrupt the peace emerging within her, Dillon whispered, "This golden center flows out to the seven directions. And all directions flow back into it to form perfect balance. This is all you need to work with magic. All the rest originates from this."

Sharay stepped into the center. As did Guethyn. As did Dillon. And to Sharay's surprise, so did the ethereal form of Rosheen.

And from within this center, Dillon gave the blessed instructions for the Beltaine ritual.

Chapter 28

Phoebe nursed a growing sense of unease, despite the fact she had successfully sent her conjured Tracker to scout for Sharay the night before. Cup of strong tea in hand, she wandered listlessly around the house, avoiding the library. She fluffed pillows on the settee here, straightened pictures on the wall there. The eggs she'd made herself hours ago sat cold and neglected on the dining room table. She had little appetite.

She leaned her elbows on the kitchen counter and sighed. She had to do something. Had to give an outlet to the whispering shadows that slinked through her mind. Waiting was driving her mad. It was Beltaine, and if she knew Dillon at all, he would be taking this opportunity to use the holy day for Sharay's benefit. Phoebe set her teacup down with a clink. She would scry once more for Sharay.

Scrambling up the narrow attic stairs, Phoebe flung the door open and slammed it shut behind her. Soon, squat candles were lit in all four directions. Their flames silhouetted her body, crouched in the center. She lit a central taper last, and quieted her mind before pouring consecrated water from its storage pitcher into her metal scrying bowl.

Setting the bowl in front of her, she leaned over and gazed intently at the shimmering surface. The central candle flickered low.

The water rippled then stilled, revealing swiftly moving clouds racing over a moonlit seaside landscape.

"What seashore is this?" Phoebe asked of the scrying water.

The water rippled again, and she peered closer. Frothy ocean waves, moonlit sky, but no trace of Sharay. Phoebe frowned. Deep down in her bones, she could sense her niece was by that seashore. Their bloodline connected them in ways scrying could not.

A brilliant lightning flash sparked across the surface of the water, and Phoebe jumped back. The bright zigzag flare confirmed her worst fears and she scowled. Sharay was growing in power. Phoebe refocused, and bent over the bowl once more, clutching its rim. She tried to trace the powerful lightning flash trail back to its source. Back to Sharay. She could only trace it so far before she slammed up against something impenetrable. The force of it knocked the wind out of her, hurled her backwards, and left her lying flat. She frantically sucked in precious air.

Like a hound on the scent of a fox, she smelled Dillon's magic. Layered over Rosheen's. They had stopped her probing as solidly as a brick wall keeps out wind and rain.

Phoebe howled her frustration. She lurched forward, grabbed the scrying bowl and flung it away from her. It clanged sharply against the wall, its water emptying onto the floor in little rivulets.

Breathing hard, she swept her hair away from her face, and worked to steady herself. She had to find Sharay before the girl grew fully grew into her power.

Phoebe closed her eyes and began to chant a strengthening spell, one she'd prepared earlier that morning to bolster the power of her Tracker. She called the incantation out loudly, determination edging her words. After a few moments of effort, she felt weak and was covered with perspiration, but she had successfully sent the spell on its way.

Now she would just have to wait for the Tracker to find Sharay and strip her of her powers. Then she would claim the girl's powers and send her back to the psychiatric hospital. Or better yet, to prison as a condemned murderer.

Detective Henley tapped the tip of his pencil on his desk. It took only a few staccato raps for him to make his decision. He would personally follow up on the telephone lead.

Since the police department had released their all-points bulletin and aired the story on television, they had gotten over twenty-five calls. Most of them were crank, or of no consequence. But the one from the coast of Wales had caught his attention. Of course he'd already phoned the local police there, asking for their assistance. But he wanted to speak with the girl who called in the sighting himself, the one from the pastry shop. Something about her story set off alarms in his gut.

He flung his pencil down.

"Come on, we're going," he said to Everett with a curt nod of his head.

Not waiting for a response, he grabbed his keys off his desk and walked out to the parking lot. The air was still warm, the sun not far from setting. Opening his car door, he slid along the seat and started the engine, then leaned over to unlock the passenger door for Everett. A bloody nuisance to have to drag his over-eager, naïve rookie with him everywhere. It slowed him down. Still, if they shared the driving, they should be able to reach the coast by midnight.

The sunset reigned purple and magenta, herald to the forthcoming rising full moon. Dillon had insisted that Sharay and Guethyn spend time apart to prepare for their Beltaine eve. Sharay sat at the mouth of the cave she and Guethyn had first made love in the night before. She leaned against the lingam stone, the sea churning several yards in the distance.

"Watch for the Seven Sisters," Dillon had instructed her.

She looked up at the sky, still too early to identify the cluster of seven stars, the Pleiades. They would dance across the nighttime sky, hovering just above the western horizon, later in the evening. Dillon had told her the star formation first became visible in the night sky in

November, and would eventually dip out of sight in May. But on May 1st, Beltaine, their powerful presence was still in attendance and would watch over her ritual as it had done for lifetimes of Beltaine lovers. She liked the idea that their starry ancient guardianship connected her to all Beltaine rituals.

She sat in silence, tried to meditate, but found herself going over Dillon's directions again in her mind so she wouldn't forget any detail. She rolled the vial of rose oil he'd given her in her palm. She could smell the light amber colored oil, sweet and light, even with the cap closed.

"Rose oil holds the highest vibration of all the essential oils. Its vibration enhances the energy of love," Dillon had told her.

She laid the rose oil beside her in the sand, and picked up the vial of resinous frankincense oil he had left for her.

"This oil will assist in transporting you into the inner worlds, the Inner Realm. It offers protection during ritual," Dillon had said.

The third bottle contained myrrh, another resinous essential oil. "For magnifying your awareness. And connecting with your deep emotions," Dillon had explained.

The three oils were traditionally essential in augmenting the ritual of Sacred Union and were to be used to anoint herself at the appointed time. The fourth and last vial, the oil of spikenard, was to be used to anoint Guethyn. He would do the same to her in return. Spikenard was a special oil that would mark their sacred marriage, along with the union of the individual inner masculine and feminine aspects within themselves. She opened the cap and sniffed its pungent aroma. The scent brought her deep into her body, into her pelvis and her womb space. She capped it again, holding back its power until Guethyn arrived later in the evening.

She put the vials in her shirt pocket, quieted the fluttering in her stomach, and refocused on meditating. Her mind soon returned to Dillon's reassurances, clung to them. He said he had prepared her as best he could in the time they had. Soon she would experience the deepest meaning of union—in joining with Guethyn, in communion with the Goddess, and in the merging of Divine Feminine and Divine Masculine within her. She sensed the magnitude of the ritual and for a moment her breath caught.

"You can do this," she whispered to herself. "Dillon believes in you. Rosheen believes in you." And with sudden warmth she added, "Mother believed in you."

Dillon had earlier left her with some last thoughts, before the sun began to settle on its ocean horizon bed.

"Remember, Sharay, there's Divinity in your body, the spark of Divine Love. It's called the Goddess. Her Love comes *through* your body and expresses out into the world. Your body is not some lifeless shell that gets animated with life force, like a computer powered by electricity. It's the other way around. Her Love flows, and forms the shape of your body, powered from the inside out. The most direct way to find Divinity is through your body. Not somewhere outside of you."

He had held both her hands and looked her in the eyes. "*That* is what you're celebrating this evening. It's about learning to consciously embody the Love of the Goddess."

"Embodied Love," Sharay repeated to herself.

The sun sunk below the sea. It was time. Stretching her tight muscles, she stood, and walked into the small cave behind her. She felt safe here. Not only did it hold the fresh memory of loving Guethyn, but she knew that Dillon, back at the caravan, would be working through the night to provide her with magical protection. Rosheen would do the same back in Glastonbury.

Dillon didn't need to tell her that such extreme caution was not normally necessary. Her Second Sight told her something dark had sniffed at the corners of her awareness since early that morning. For a fleeting moment she felt a chill trace along her spine, having nothing to do with the sea air at twilight. The shadow of a large—creature?—darted around the outside edges of her inner vision. It's fleeting presence felt so real that she shuddered and turned around, peering behind her. Nothing frightening was there. She wasn't sure what it was she sensed, but she knew it was something she didn't want to meet. She centered herself, and let the magical gridiron of Dillon's protection reassure her.

In the thick of the forest, Guethyn readied himself amidst a grove of birch trees. He had chosen the spot not only for the ring shaped thicket, place of nature's ancient earth magic, but for the color of the birch bark. The silver hue reminded him of Sharay's white-blond hair.

He sat cross-legged, spine erect, in the center of the grove. He was able to quiet his mind easily enough. What he was having trouble with was stilling his heart beat and the ache in his body that wanted only to touch Sharay in the yielding places that had brought her moaning with pleasure the night before. While pleasure was part of Beltaine's gift from the Goddess, he knew this ritual meant more. Through the portal of pleasure, it would also be Sharay's initiation into her true power.

His grandfather had given him a set of invocations and prayers as part of his preparation, and Guethyn set to work. First, he pulled off all of his clothes and dropped them in a pile beside him. He closed his eyes and shifted his attention to the verdant ground he sat upon, to the trees that surrounded him in leafy canopy.

He'd spent many years exploring the woods of his grandfather's home in Northern Wales where he'd played amidst the huge oaks, learning how to forage for berries and mushrooms, how to make himself a bed of soft moss and leaves inside the cradling arms of the oak roots. Grandfather had made sure also to teach him about the invisible beings and the secret language of the forest realm.

"The forests of Wales are the poetry of the Goddess," grandfather had said. "This landscape shaped our people and our culture, uninterrupted by invaders, for centuries."

Guethyn's body and blood carried this Welsh heritage and effortlessly thrummed in tune to the ageless pulse of the forest. It was as much a part of his being as his ancestors were.

Freshly blossomed blue bells spread their sweet scented carpet to blanket the ground around him, fanned out in a king's mantle of brilliant blue and purple. He opened his hand to touch the delicate flowers and his fingers extended further, seemingly merging with the gnarled roots of the ancient oak tree in the midst of the birch grove. Lichen and moss inched their way up the tree's trunk, and he felt their feather-soft greenery tickle as if it grew along his own torso. He lifted his arms like the tree's branches, where red kite and cuckoo balanced delicately, quieting their birdsong in anticipation of their native son's invocation.

He began his chant, first in English, then unknowingly switching to the guttural lilt of Welsh. His deep voice rang out throughout the grove, and the earth answered his calling. The birch trees held their breath, their leaves unmoving, providing a deep primordial stillness through which the chants reverberated.

While Guethyn merged with the forest, Sharay spread her blanket on the sandy floor of the cave. She pulled off her blue jeans and t-shirt, undergarments, socks and shoes, and set them aside. There was to be no clothing and no fire to warm her until she had cleansed and purified both herself and the ritual space inside the cave. Her skin formed immediate goosebumps, and her nipples hardened against the early twilight chill.

Setting the oil vials on a small rocky ledge, she opened the box of matches Dillon had left alongside a large white candle. Striking a match, she lit the candle. It was to symbolize the central pillar of light she had learned about earlier in the day. The flame would hold the power of perfect harmony, of the golden streaming flow between formlessness and form. As she touched the match to the candlewick, a sense of familiarity arose. She aligned with all priestesses of all ages who had ever lit a central candle and merged their inner fire with the outer flame.

She sat in silence within the cave until the moon lifted a rounded corner of her luminous face where sea met sky. Sharay held her bottle of rose oil up to the muted light of twilight.

"I anoint my heart with this oil that resonates with the One Great Heart," she whispered, putting a drop on her finger and drawing two interlocking circles on her chest, with a vertical line penetrating them down the middle. The Vesica Pisces, sigil of her ancient priestess lineage. Immediately, the rose oil warmed her chest. Her heart sped up before it slowed to a steady rhythm as the oil penetrated her skin.

While she'd been taught exactly where to put the oils, including a drop on each of the seven energy centers of her body, she found she did not need to remember the detailed directions. After some initial uncertainty, her hands and fingers began to move with surety and skill, her actions guided by the cellular memories of Beltaine rituals performed in other lifetimes.

She anointed the crown of her head with a dab of the rose oil, following that with a drop on her forehead, and before anointing her throat chakra, she added a drop on her lips.

"With this oil, I sing the song of Divine Love." She emulated the melodic intonations she'd heard from Dillon earlier in the day.

The heady scent of rose perfumed not only her body but also the space around her. She placed a drop on her throat, one on her mid-abdomen over her solar plexus, another on her lower belly. She rubbed some around the outside of her vagina, threshold to the Temple of her Womb. The base of her spine was next, then the nape of her neck, the portal of her Spirit Self. Through that gateway of her neck she felt a sudden rush of wind, a whispered 'whoosh' of indwelling Spirit rising to awareness. The rose oil anointing was completed on the palms of her hands and the soles of her feet.

Inhaling slowly, she let the oil seep into her body. She put a very thin layer of the musky frankincense oil over the same spots as the rose, paying particular attention to the portal of her Spirit Self for blessed protection. While her fingers were still on the nape of her neck, she traced the indentation of the six-pointed star, her birthmark, with the oil.

"Oil of sovereignty, purify me. Protect me on my journey into the Inner Realms tonight."

A drop of precious myrrh was added to her belly, her heart, and the center of her forehead. "Oil of awareness, keep me focused. Keep me connected to my deepest feelings."

She felt the oils cover her in a mantle of harmony and magic.

Atop a natural rock formation inside the cave sat an abalone shell filled with saltwater, which had earlier been consecrated by Dillon. Standing, she picked up the shell and raised it above her, her head tilted back. "By the power of this water, I cleanse myself."

She dribbled some of the water over her head and face, allowing the rivulets to stream down the whole of her body, cleansing her physically and psychically. Shivering against the evaporating water, she dipped her fingers in the abalone shell once more and turned slowly in a clockwise motion, flicking droplets of consecrated water around the cave to purify the space for the upcoming ritual. She set the abalone shell back on its rocky shelf, and grasped the central candle to hold high above her head.

"By the power of the brilliant flame, I purify myself."

She set the candle down in the sand and walked around it thrice, allowing its light to infuse both her energy field and the cave's interior. The heat of purified power begin to course through her body, warming her, causing her breath to become deep, and her mind to enter trance. Leaving the candle burning, she left the cave to sit on the beach, awaiting the moon's full rising. Now that the initial purification and cleansing was complete, she was allowed a coverlet, and she wrapped a light woolen blanket about her while she prayed with words and song to honor the Goddess, to honor the Beltaine ritual.

"I offer my love to you, dear Goddess. I offer my body's pleasure as a gift and a portal," she sang high and clear.

The sand beneath her cushioned her, still holding the warmth of the day. The ocean sang with her, ebbed and flowed as her body instinctively rocked in a subtle circular movement. The sky, its last hint of magenta sliding under the blanket of the horizon, became the muted royal blue of twilight turned evening. Above her, the black robed stars emerged, among them the Pleiades. Their seven sparkling eyes watched her, accompanied her through her prayers.

Her body was awash with anticipation of loving Guethyn again. Another part of her felt quiet and still. She waited for the moon to travel high overhead, and sang to its rising with wordless toning. The stars and the sea, the sand and the trees, joined in her song. The wind picked up and rustled through tree leaves, as if to awaken all the forest life to the moon's arrival. The sea surf crashed to sandy shore in time with the earth's heartbeat. Sharay's heart hummed in resonance. Finally, the moon responded to her song, emerging in its full glory above the cover of the sea.

Sharay stood, dropped her coverlet, and bathed herself in silver moon gaze. She didn't feel the chill, felt nothing but adulation for heaven's silver threshold. The moon sent her a pathway, a shimmering passage across the ocean surface to lay prostrate at her feet. Sharay drank in the moon, followed its passage deep into her primal self, the still place of the Void.

From there she connected her heart to her womb, then breathed moonlight into womb, just as the Goddess had taught her. Hands on her belly, she received the power of the Divine Feminine through the moon's rounded eye, and let it light the embers of her womb place. She followed the sequence of sacred breathing.

Heart to womb

moon into womb

womb to earth's core

She became sheer magnetic energy of moon and sea. Her soul danced in her cells, and in her ecstasy she raised her arms high.

Upon the summons of rustling leaves and moon's rise, Guethyn had walked to the woodland's edge. There he'd waited for this signal of Sharay's upraised arms to join her. But he found he could barely step out from behind the trees. She was too beautiful, too magnificent to approach, let alone touch. Her face was upturned, her smile ecstatic. Her skin shone with the brilliance of the Goddess. For him, she was already the Goddess incarnate.

He lost sensation of his own body, felt his spirit fly to meet hers. Shaking his head no, he swiftly reined it back. Dillon had firmly told him this ritual was intended to meet the imminent divinity within their physical bodies, not the spirit of transcendence outside of their bodies. They were meant to commune with the Goddess who resided inside them, within all creation, within all matter. And Dillon was emphatic they would only meet Her through their bodies and through their loving. Guethyn was meant to touch Sharay. He pulled his spirit back into his trembling body and he walked toward her, breath quickened, heart pounding as forcefully as the surf.

Sharay felt his approach. Neither of them spoke. When at last he stood beside her, she turned and gazed at him. She put her hands on his chest, felt the nearness of him, the heat of his skin. His heart raced beneath her palm. His muscles quivered. His shaft raised and reached between her legs.

Chapter 29

On the shoreline beneath the full moon, in the presence of stars and sea, Sharay began the Beltaine prayers.

"I am Priestess Queen and I come to you, Guethyn. I embody the Goddess of the Land and as such, I am called Sovereignty. I come to you, and in our joining, in the mixing of our fluids, we create the magic that ensures the fruitfulness of the land."

Sharay paused, added the words that were not normally a part of the Beltaine ritual, the words that Dillon had instructed her to add. "We join to assure the good not only for this land we stand upon, but also for the whole of the earth and the beings that live on it."

Guethyn's voice was a throaty whisper that grew in volume as he spoke his part. "I come to you as King, as embodiment of the God. As you are the land, body of the earth Mother, I am your protector. The future good of all peoples depends on our Sacred Marriage. In our joining, my seed impregnates the earth so that she may bear her bounty and provide goodness for all peoples."

Sharay felt herself connected to the land beneath her. Her head swam with the energies they were calling forth. She spoke her next lines with focus and clarity.

"I wed you as Goddess Sovereignty. I wed you as Priestess Queen. As Sharay. As your beloved." She couldn't stop her tears.

Guethyn gripped her shoulders firmly yet gently. "I wed you as God protector. As Sacred King. As Guethyn. You are my beloved."

It was a moment before Sharay found her voice again. She spoke softly yet with a growing authority she hadn't known she possessed. "In Her honor we come together." She felt she would drown in the brilliant blue of Guethyn's eyes.

"In Her honor we will join together," Guethyn answered.

"In Her honor, we offer our union."

"Pure of purpose, our heart is our guide," Guethyn replied.

"Our goal to merge our hearts and bodies, spirit and soul."

"And therein to merge with the One Great Heart of the Goddess. To call down her consort, the Divine God. And to create the Sacred Union," Guethyn said, his voice growing husky.

Still facing him, Sharay grasped his hand, felt it hot and trembling in her own.

Guethyn took in a sharp breath. He did not tremble from the cold. Sharay was glorious in her nakedness, her body both muscled and curved, soft and strong. Her nipples stood erect, her belly gently rounded. Her hair lifted with the breeze, a white-blond halo that framed her full lips and eyes smoky with desire. She was radiant. He stood in awe as the woman he loved embodied the Goddess.

Eyes shining, he could not help himself from whispering words that were not part of the ritual. "I adore you."

His adoration sent Sharay spinning further into ecstasy. She spiraled deeper into her heart, felt it open wider than she'd ever felt. She discovered a depth of love she'd never felt before, in this lifetime, in any other lifetime where she had loved him. Warmth gathered in her chest and expanded, radiating out toward Guethyn. Now in trance, she saw him clothed in gold light. His chest was infused with it, opened wide by it. He radiated pure golden brilliance in contrast to the silver moon energy emanating from within herself. Her heart received his heart. She lost sense of herself in the merging of their two hearts as one. Found herself again when he touched her. Flesh meeting in a timeless caress.

"Let us proceed with the Sacred Marriage," they said in unison.

The words had been spoken. The High Magic set into motion. Sharay reeled with the enormity of what she was about to take on. Participating in the ancient Beltaine. And so much more. She was stepping into the Prophecy. The thought of it took her breath. She held tight onto Guethyn to steady herself. There would be no turning back from this point onward. She calmed her breathing, and reaffirmed her choice to go forward.

Holding his hand, she led Guethyn inside their specially prepared cave. The candle in the center of the sandy floor flickered, sending soft shadows across the rocky walls. The moon sent a silver beam through the sea facing cave opening, a gift to illuminate their bodies.

Sharay turned to face Guethyn and her heart suddenly ached. Seven years of emotional drought, barren of love and affection, had made it dry. Passionate, consuming love with Guethyn had revived it. She felt softened, moistened. Drenched in his tender love, doused with his ardent affection. The remaining hawthorn roots around her heart snapped free. Her chest and stomach shuddered with the release and she felt a free flow of energy move through her.

Guethyn wiped the tears streaming down her cheeks with his fingers tips and leaned his forehead against hers. "I love you," he whispered.

She hugged him fiercely, and as she did, she felt the bodies of every woman who turned to face her lover in a Beltaine ritual since the beginning of time. She raised her head and looked into his eyes, into his soul, and knew without being told that he had become every Priest King who had ever joined with a Priestess Queen. They were more than priest and priestess or Lord and Lady. They were God and Goddess embodied.

The collective voices of every woman's experience spoke to Sharay, quietly adding their instruction to Dillon's, and to her own innate knowing. "It has begun," they said.

Guethyn caressed her cheek, lifted her chin and opened his mouth to hers, searching for her tongue. His warmth, his touch, his loving devotion, roused a need deeper than the first time they had lain together. Moments of delicate, slow exploration—mouth, neck, chest, breast—left her yearning. She felt his need match hers.

The voices of the ancestors continued, whispering collectively in her ear. "Ground yourself once more," they said.

Sent with her awareness and will, Sharay felt her energy connecting into the core of the earth, the heart of the Goddess. With her inner senses, she felt Guethyn grounding in the same manner. The surge of the Goddess's Love traveled from the earth's core and into her. Pulsing, throbbing, vibrating. Nourishing her.

"Send your breath to your pelvis. Make your breath quick and short," the ancestors instructed.

She sent her breath to her pelvis, quick and short, as directed, and heard Guethyn's breathing match hers.

Guethyn held her close and slowly knelt, laid her on the blanket she had spread out on the sand earlier that evening. His eyes never left hers as he straddled her body. His hands were urgent yet gentle. Sharay had to focus to keep from getting lost in his caresses. He parted her legs and slowly roused her to exquisite readiness with his fingers. She moaned with pleasure when he entered her.

Quick, concentrated panting intensified the exquisite sensation in her pelvis. Her womb quivered with power, her vagina pulsed in anticipation.

"You are nearly ready," the ancestors sighed.

"Can you . . . hear . . . them?" she asked Guethyn.

He stopped his gentle thrusting to look down at her. "Men's voices. Priests. The voices of the many," he replied breathlessly.

Sharay heard the women ancestors whisper their next instructions to her, guessed that Guethyn heard the same directives through his chorus of priestly ancestors. "Your sensations are the energy that forms an alchemical vessel."

The words grew louder in Sharay's ears. "Your arousal is held in this alchemical vessel. Your sexual energy is pure life energy. It is the starlight energy you are sourced from."

Sharay ran her tongue along Guethyn's chest, tasted the salty wetness. Their thighs slid seamlessly against each other with the same salty moisture, mixed with the dew of her arousal.

The priestess ancestors spoke again, more slowly now. "Put your attention on this alchemical vessel you're creating together. Remember your intent to join as one. To use that as a pathway to the Goddess. And from there to Sacred Union."

Their voices grew in pitch. Guethyn's thrusts grew more forceful. The sensations in Sharay's pelvis quickened, and became potential explosion.

"Hold on until you can hold on no longer. And then hold on some more," said the lineage of women, the lineage of priestesses, in commanding tones.

Sharay let wave after wave of sensation build and collect in her pelvis. She focused on her breathing. Soon she and Guethyn breathed as one.

Their gazes locked. Within moments Sharay felt the undeniable need to surrender to the ecstasy. Her vagina opened wide, her wetness moistened the folds that led to the lush portal of her Womb Temple.

The voices swelled in intensity. "Now is the time of joining. Dedicated to the Goddess."

Sharay molded to Guethyn's body, and moaned in release. She pulled him to her, her body demanding his in climax. Again and again she received him. Their bodies intertwined and met with a force that matched the pounding surf beyond their cave. Her body arched in ecstasy and the next instructions came quickly.

She whispered them aloud, her voice throaty, following the journey laid out before them.

"On your exhalation, send your arousal up your spine." Her voice grew strident with the demands of her body. "Do not let the energy dissipate."

Guethyn, deep and full inside her, breathed with her in synchronistic union. Their hips pulsated with the rhythm of the tides, strong waves that crested higher and higher.

The energy of her climax coiled at the base of her spine, snake like. The undulations captured and amplified her orgasm. Agonizingly pleasurable. Her orgasm became an erotic current of two energy strands, one red and one white. Contained, and not dissipated. Her back arched and bowed rhythmically as wave after wave of explosive climax filled her.

Guethyn leaned nearer to kiss her, and she lost herself in his touch, in the depth of love in his blue eyes, nearly forgetting her instructions.

She used her passion to fuel her will. She saw with her inner sight that Guethyn was molding his orgasm as she was. His two strands of red and white energy paced exactly with hers.

"Red for the magnetic of feminine energy. Your blood. The blood of the earth," the ancestral voices whispered to Sharay. "White for the electric male energy current within you, the impregnating seed. You contain both this masculine and feminine energy current."

Sharay panted and softly moaned. The red and white energy strands wove in and around each other, crossing over themselves like a figure eight as they reached the first of her seven chakra energy centers.

In an explosion of red liquid light, the dual current twined across her base chakra, the energy vortex at the tip of her spine. The chakra felt solidly grounded. It sounded like hundreds of beating drums in Sharay's ears. The next orgasmic pulsation, accompanied by her will and intention, pushed the energy current farther along her spine.

The current crossed her second chakra, the energy center in her low belly. It gathered up her sexual arousal and her fecund creativity in a cloud of fiery orange.

She clung fiercely to Guethyn atop her, and held him close as he experienced the undulating current weave up his spine simultaneously with hers. Each chakra crossing was nourished by the pulsations of the Goddess's heartbeat in the center of the earth where they had grounded themselves.

The threads of the current moved up, wove over her solar plexus in the center of her abdomen, passing through its yellow rays, dazzling as the noonday sun.

The undulation rose farther upward and across her heart chakra, green whirlpool of love and joy. Sharay heard each singular beat of her heart, felt each strand of her heart muscle in harmonious syncopation with the others. With Guethyn's.

"There is a tone that emanates from your heart center. Find that tone. Sing it aloud," the priestess voices of instruction told her.

Sharay let the tone emerge from her heart and she sighed out, "*Ah*." The tone energized her heart. She took Guethyn's hand and placed it on the center of her chest, then put her hand on his chest, strengthening their heart bond.

When the exotic current reached her throat, she was instructed to find the tone that resonated within her throat chakra. She parted her lips and sang the tone of, "*Eeh*." The song emerged as turquoise blue sound waves and helped move the energy further up her spine.

The undulating energy current reached the chakra in the middle of her forehead in an explosion of midnight blue, majestic as the late night sky.

Guethyn gazed down at her with unconcealed adoration and she returned his gaze with love. And then the current of energy strands entered the center of her head, readying for the final pinnacle of release.

The voices of the ancestors spoke one last time. "Meet the Beloved in each other."

The red and white energy strands condensed in the center of her brain. With inner vision she saw therein a radiant cup, royal blue rimmed in gold. The cup tipped slightly and two drops of liquid flowed, distilled from the alchemy of their focused love-making.

One red and one white
feminine and masculine
blood and semen
body and spirit
Red Well and White Well of Glastonbury.

As the red and white liquid dripped out of the cup, it merged to become one drop of liquid gold. A burst of magnificent luminosity that filled Sharay's body with liquid heat. Nectar of the Goddess.

She saw it fill Guethyn, too. He held her close, lending the strength of his presence, for what came next he instinctively knew was Sharay's to do on her own.

Sharay felt one end of the stream of liquid gold nectar trickle down through her to the ocean floor and onwards into the core of the earth, while the other end of the liquid gold stretched up to the heavens. Her body became the pivot point that anchored the connection between below and above. She dare not move lest she break the link. With eyes now closed, Guethyn also ceased movement, and continued to silently offer his energetic support.

Sharay called the Void forth from inside her, its utter stillness solidifying her anchoring pivot. She, a mortal human, uniting heaven and earth in her body. She was both as vast as the infinite universe, and as small as the cells in her human body. She could barely breathe and she was breath itself.

From this stillness, a sacred presence emerged. The Goddess showed Herself in blue and silver misty wisps and the song of a thousand stars. She was the creatrix of the First Breath, and it was She who had uttered the first holy sounds of creation.

"I rejoice in how you have reached communion with Me," the Goddess said.

Sharay sighed with joy. She and Guethyn had accomplished the Beltaine ritual's purpose.

"Where are you?" Sharay asked.

"I call to you from the watery elements of your depths. From the twirling atoms of your cells. I come from the fiery center of the earth. From the infinite expanse of the cosmos. My voice echoes throughout the infinitely deep to the infinitely vast."

Sharay heard Guethyn gasp. She reached for his hand, felt it tremble as hers did.

"I am Sister to the Stars. Mother of the Moons. And My name is Love."

Tears streamed down Sharay's cheeks. She felt Guethyn's wet cheek against hers.

The Goddess whispered. "You are so precious to Me."

Sharay couldn't see Her but she felt herself relax into a cocooned embrace of brilliant golden luminosity and abiding peace, with Guethyn beside her. The exquisite Love of the Goddess enveloped her in sweet warmth, surrounded her in spirals of blue and silver, permeated her cells in a crystalline chorus of star song.

"You have touched upon the Divinity within your body. You will find it is I who reside there."

Sharay, still holding the balance of the strand of golden light between heaven and earth, suddenly felt the yearning of the Goddess's absolute love for humankind. The ultimate yearning for the loved and the beloved to unite. And she surrendered to this understanding.

Guethyn sank into the silent embrace, knowing that while he was a crucial link, it was Sharay who was the Prophesied one.

Sharay spoke. "What would you have me do?"

"Be devoted to Love."

"And more than that?"

"There is no more."

Sharay longed to see Her face, but the Goddess's form remained hidden amidst the watery blue sea and the silver light of the stars. There was only the warmth of Her invisible arms wrapped around them, and the music of the stars.

"What of the Prophecy? What am I to do?" Sharay asked.

"Know that My Love is the ultimate power."

The pounding waves outside the cave grew gentle and the wind stilled. Guethyn remained silent, cocooned in that love. Sharay felt her hold on the golden liquid strand release. She suddenly felt the Divine Masculine descend into her prepared body, into the depths of the Divine Feminine within her.

She felt her body expand simultaneously out into cosmic vastness, and deep into her bodily depths. She was hot and cold and fluid and solid all at once. She spiraled through galaxies within galaxies, worlds within worlds of the fiery star power that glowed in the eternal heavens above, in the earth below, and in the infinite depths of her cells. Swirling, flame-tipped fragments of liquid starlight showered her, water and fire, sparking her to new awareness. Of Love. Of the infinite Divinity in her body. The star fire center of each of her cells reflected the golden brilliance of awakened Love before softly fading back into physical form. The love of the Goddess filled her with peace. Body had married spirit. Sacred Union.

Only when Guethyn softly called her name, lovingly stroked her thighs, suckled her breasts, did she awaken to the sunlight of the morning after Beltaine.

Chapter 30

Ivan was sleeping soundly in the apartment above his bakery when the pounding on the café door downstairs startled him awake. He blinked hard and peered at his alarm clock on his bedside stand. It was 1:30 in the morning. His wife stirred beside him. She was awake with the next insistent knock.

"Who could that be?" Beatrice murmured, waiting for him to get up and answer.

Ivan pulled his robe over his pajamas and stepped into his slippers.

"I've no idea," he answered, tying the belt around his robe.

He rubbed his eyes and yawned. In only four hours his alarm would go off to wake him for his early morning pastry duty, and someone had cut into his sleep.

As Ivan fumbled with the bedroom door handle, he heard footsteps thumping down the apartment stairs.

"Angela, wait for your father!" Beatrice called out.

The knocking at the café door stopped and their daughter's voice could be heard downstairs.

"Yes, detective. My name is Angela. I saw the lad in my dad's pastry shop the day before yesterday . . ." her voice eager.

Beatrice sat up. "Ivan, get downstairs, for the love of God."

Ivan shot her a worried look and headed downstairs.

Dillon had seen it. Murky and black, skirting the perimeters of his inner vision. Skulking, hiding, peering out at him with fathomless eyes. He smelled Phoebe's twisted magic, nearly gagged on the stench of her black art. She had conjured something vile, a Tracker demon programmed to hunt its prey. Sharay.

Dillon had brought all his focus to protecting this important night for Sharay and Guethyn. If the pair succeeded in the Beltaine Rites, the fulfillment of the Prophecy could begin. He had called out to Rosheen on the Inner Realms of magic, requiring her help. She had been sitting in the center of her own cast circle in the inner sanctum of Little St. Michael's upper room, eagerly awaiting his request.

"Do you need me to come to you?" she had asked telepathically. Her ethereal form hovered in Dillon's clairvoyant vision.

"I need your help right now, right where you are. I can't wait for you to drive all the way here," he told her in psychic response.

Rosheen lit her candles and called forth the protective helpers from the Inner Realms of magic. Dillon did the same.

They worked with meticulous attention to detail. Through ancient chants and invocations they had called upon the benevolent assistance of the unseen helpers, guardians, and ancestors. With prayer and magic they had built a fortress of will, a moat of shielding that cloaked the young couple in invisibility to the Tracker. It was well into the night before they'd built a defense so strong that the stink of Phoebe's Tracker could no longer be smelled, its red eyes blinded in its search for Sharay. With the strength of tempered steel, the magical shielding would last throughout the evening's Beltaine sacrament. In the morning they would begin again to fortify it.

With the night's task completed, Dillon bid Rosheen goodnight and sank into fitful sleep. Not telling her, he intentionally ventured into an inter-dimensional realm where the Tracker might stalk only him and no one else. Offering himself as bait, he kept the Tracker busy chasing him, deflecting its attention from Sharay for added safety. By morning's light, he was exhausted. Phoebe had created a strong entity. He'd used up a great deal of energy and magic keeping it at bay.

Yawning, he sat up from his fold-down bed, and pulled on his pants and shirt. He craved a breath of fresh air. With the battery operated radio and the makings for strong tea tucked under his arm, he stepped outside the caravan. Early morning dew embellished the loamy smell of the forest campsite that bordered the ocean.

He flipped on the radio and lit the small propane camping stove to put water on to boil. The end of Mozart's "Requiem" trumpeted through the encampment. Dillon let his tea bag steep longer than usual, hoping the extra caffeine would give him a needed energy boost. After he added a splash of milk, he sat on a log to listen to the news at the top of the hour.

"... and now for local news. Police are searching for a young female wanted for the murder of one Larry Wentworth of Somerset County, England," came the female voice speaking in the guttural Welsh.

There it was. Sooner than he'd expected.

"The main suspect, Sharay Kallah, escaped from an English psychiatric hospital in Bath. She is eighteen, five foot eight, about nine stone in weight, and has white-blond hair. She's accompanied by a young man in his twenties, one Guethyn Sulwyn, and another patient, an older man with a gray beard called Thomas Emrick."

Dillon grunted. The hunter on their trail this time was the police, not the conjured Tracker of the dark night.

"Consider them extremely dangerous. Her young male accomplice was last seen off the coast of Wales. . . ."

Dillon jumped up, spilling his tea. "Holy Mother of us all," he spat and quickly flipped off the radio. They had to leave. Now.

Sharay stretched languidly. Her body felt moist, supple. Loved. She turned to face Guethyn, ran her finger along his lips. He smelled of musk and sweet sex. A pocket of warmth settled in her chest. She was deliriously happy, and somehow also achingly sad. She'd known grief since childhood. Love seemed to be a double-edged sword.

Too easy to lose. She prayed silently she would never know the painful edge of that sword again.

Guethyn woke slowly, Sharay's touch soft on his lips. He gently wound his hand through her silky hair and drew her head closer. Her thigh was between his, and his need for her grew again. He was lost once more in her hair, her mouth, her breasts.

"Guethyn?" she whispered.

He stopped his exploration and lifted her chin to look into her eyes.

She said the words gently, carefully. "I love you."

Last night Guethyn had seen galaxies of stars, and the fiery center of the earth. As priestly King, he had joined with Sharay, priestess Queen. He had embodied the Divine Masculine, the God. And he had communed with the Goddess. Yet it was Sharay's tender words this morning that made his eyes tear.

Once he could speak without his voice catching he told her. "I will never leave you, Sharay. I've waited lifetimes to be with you again. We're in this together now. Whatever happens."

She let her body answer where her words could not, surrendering to his love.

Afterwards, they bathed in the cove, one moment sober with what they had accomplished on Beltaine, the next moment, playfully reveling in their reunion.

Sharay put her head under the chilly waves, dove down, and swam under Guethyn's legs as he tread water. He dove down after her and lifted her up and out of the water. She wound herself around him, laced her arms about his neck and her legs around his waist.

"Mercy, woman," he cried, wanting her yet again.

She laughed, then went still, her gaze focused on the shore.

"It's Dillon," she said. "Something's wrong."

Sharay's story continues in Book Two, *Carry on the Flame: Ultimate Magic*

Hunted by the police, stalked by the demonic Tracker, and separated from Guethyn's protection, Sharay resumes her Imram quest in the spellbinding conclusion of *Carry on the Flame.*

Carry on the Flame:
Ultimate Magic

Preview Chapter I

Once he'd caught Sharay's attention, the wizard Dillon sat down on a low-lying boulder on the secluded beach in Wales, elbows on his knees. He waited for her and his grandson Guethyn to towel dry and dress.

"They're close to finding us," he told them.

"Who?" Sharay asked.

"The police." The craggy wrinkles that etched Dillon's face were shadowed with concern.

Guethyn's arm tightened around Sharay's shoulder. "I thought we'd covered our tracks pretty well."

"It seems Phoebe has been trailing us magically. I'm certain she has something to do with it," Dillon replied.

"But I don't feel her awful magic around me . . ." Sharay's voice trailed off. She looked hard at Dillon, noted the dark circles under his eyes, the unusual pale hue of his skin.

"Oh, Dillon," she reached for his hand. "You've been working hard to protect us."

"That's what I'm here to do. As is Rosheen," he replied, covering her hand in his.

"Rosheen, too." Sharay repeated. "Sending her magic from Glaston bury. The two of you have been fighting my demons all night. I can't bear the thought of you being worn out because of me."

Pulling her hand away, she touched the protective amulet ring on her finger, then looked at Dillon and Guethyn's fingers to make sure they wore theirs.

Guethyn followed her gaze. "Aye. My ring is here. I haven't taken it off since grandfather gave it to me," he reassured her.

"I'm going to finish my Imram on my own. Keep you two away from the danger I've put you in. After all, it's my quest, and my problem," Sharay said, her voice tight.

"Nonsense." Dillon stood. "Rosheen and I have always known what's ours to do, and it's a journey you're meant to share with Guethyn."

He reached inside his shirt pocket, pulled out a card. The Tarot Lovers card.

"Oh! I thought I'd lost this," Sharay said.

She held out her hand, eager for the return of Dillon's mysterious and precious gift. She studied the couple standing under the rose trellis, the Goddess' hand poised over their heads, granting blessings and boons. She held the card up for Guethyn to see.

Guethyn nodded. "I've seen this. Found it on the dashboard of our caravan."

"Your grandfather gave it to me the first time I met him in the psychiatric hospital." Sharay looked up at Dillon.

Dillon winked. Sharay had forgotten to take the Tarot card with her when Dillon, posing as a patient, and Guethyn helped her escape the mental institution where her Aunt Phoebe had her unjustly committed.

She put the card safely in her jacket's upper pocket. Next to her heart.

Dillon stood and rubbed his hands together. "All right. Time to move on. Now that the police suspect we're here, they're our main concern. Phoebe has convinced them Sharay killed her Uncle Larry."

Sharay scowled. "Aunt Phoebe's a nasty liar."

"But the police believe her ruse. And now they know we're here on this beach? How?" Guethyn asked.

"I can't be sure just how much they know, but the local news reported our caravan was sighted in town." Dillon said as he turned, heading for the woods.

"I was certain you charmed the entrance trail into the woods, hiding it from view," Guethyn said.

"I did. You're very good at spotting magic," Dillon said over his shoulder, with a hasty grin for his grandson.

"If it's charmed, then shouldn't we just stay here?" Guethyn asked. "Where we're safe."

Dillon kept walking. "There are other entrances to the woods and the beach. Farther along the coast. The police will eventually find them. They'll be combing the area. It's best we leave while we can. No sense being trapped here."

Guethyn couldn't argue with Dillon's last point. He and Sharay followed single-file behind Dillon along the narrow dirt trail that led back to the camp site.

"I should never have gone into town. It's my fault for exposing us," Guethyn said.

Dillon called back to them, in a voice breathless from walking. "Stop blaming yourselves. The both of you. Your Imram is a powerful quest. Imrams always attract the guardians at the gateways."

"Guardians at the gateways?" Sharay asked.

Dillon took in a couple deep breaths to keep up the pace. "Yes. Every action based in bright magic—like the Sacred Marriage you two represented in the Beltaine Ritual last night, or your prophesied destiny, Sharay—every action like that will attract its direct opposite. If you're indeed ready and capable to continue on your Imram, you'll pass the guardians at the threshold and carry on."

The hairs rose on Sharay's arms and she shuddered. She feared she was hurtling toward some unnamable threat. Toward something horrible she was sure would snap those she loved in its jaws along the way. She lifted her hand and rubbed the star-shaped birthmark at the nape of her neck, a habit intended to calm her. The Lovers Tarot card was warm against her chest.

"Why?" she demanded. "Why do there have to be guardians?"

Dillon paused for only the briefest of steps. "The cosmos simply works that way. Remember, I told you about it? It's the law of opposites."

Sharay frowned.

"If the guardians are fierce, you can be sure you're doing something right," Dillon said.

He resumed his trek and didn't speak again until they arrived at their campsite. Guethyn climbed inside the caravan, looked for the key and the maps, and checked the gas tank. Dillon and Sharay gathered the camping stove, coffee pot, and lawn chairs. Sharay stopped when she found five white candles, all burnt nearly down to the nub, atop a boulder. One candle for each of the four directions, and the fifth for the center of a magical circle. Evidence of Dillon's hard work last evening protecting her and Guethyn during their Beltaine Ritual. She glanced over at him.

Dillon looked up. His eyes revealed a connection with her as ancient as Guethyn's. In ages past, he was mentor and protector, just as he was now. Her gratitude and affection swelled, formed a lump in her throat that peaked in silent tears. She couldn't bear to see his labored breathing and his slowed movements.

She stuffed what she had gathered into the back of the caravan and walked over to him. Tenderly, she laid a hand on his cheek. His eyes twinkled, just for her, reflecting his devotion. He reached into his coat pocket, and this time brought out the roll of money the High Priestess Rosheen had given him the night they fled Glastonbury after Sharay's escape from her psychiatric hospital confinement.

"So, we leave in haste again." Dillon stuffed the wad of money into her hand, then closed her palm over it.

"You keep it safe for us." His eyes never left hers.

"But why give it to me?" Something in the giving clenched at her gut.

Dillon held his hand up. "No arguments. I have plenty to take care of without being the banker, too."

Sharay stuffed the money into the side pocket of her blue jeans, and patted down the bulge.

"You two about ready?" Guethyn called from the side window as he started the ignition and revved the motor into wakefulness.

Sharay sought the reassuring twinkle in Dillon's eye but it had already faded.

"Yes, we're coming, Guethyn," she answered.

www.ingramcontent.com/pod-product-compliance
Lightning Source LLC
Chambersburg PA
CBHW031942110726
47902CB00001B/270